ONESHOTAWAY

ONESHOTAWAY
A WRESTLING STORY

T. GLEN COUGHLIN

An Imprint of HarperCollins*Publishers*

HarperTeen is an imprint of HarperCollins Publishers.

One Shot Away: A Wrestling Story
Copyright © 2012 by T. Glen Coughlin
www.epicreads.com

Library of Congress Cataloging-in-Publication Data
Coughlin, T. Glen.
    One shot away : a wrestling story / by T. Glen Coughlin. — 1st ed.
        p.   cm.
    Audience: 13 up.
    Summary: "Three high school seniors face mounting pressures, at home and
school, as they start their last season on the varsity wrestling team"— Provided by
publisher.
    ISBN 978-0-06-208323-4 (hardback)
    [1. Wrestling—Fiction. 2. High schools—Fiction. 3. Schools—Fiction.]
I. Title.
PZ7.C83045One   2012   2012019091
[Fic]—dc23   CIP
                                                                            AC

Typography by Michelle Gengaro-Kokmen
12 13 14 15 16   LP/RRDH   10 9 8 7 6 5 4 3 2 1
❖
First Edition

For my son, Tom, my wrestler and inspiration,
for my daughter, Jacqueline, who shared my passion,
and for those who give it their all

PART ONE

Trevor

TREVOR CROW RUNS UNDER LOW CLOUDS ON A RAIN-SLICKED road past houses already strung and lit for Christmas. He cuts through the iron Civil War cannons next to the VFW Hall, past a slab of limestone that marks Molly Pitcher's grave, past the shoe repairman's window with its giant-sized boot, past the travel agency store window with posters of families at the beach. He stops at the police station, gasping for breath.

He clicks off the stopwatch at thirty-two minutes. He has completed four 8-minute miles around his neighborhood. His dad would be pleased. If only Trevor had listened to him last year, maybe he would have made the varsity squad.

He peers down the long driveway between the police station and the post office at a sign that says IMPOUND LOT. His father's truck is being stored there. Their landlord, Harry London, plans to sell it for partial payment for three months' back rent. Trevor told his mother he wanted it. But she said she couldn't look at it.

Trevor jogs up the driveway. A cyclone fence surrounds the impound area. He rattles the fence and waits for a guard dog to leap from the darkness. Nothing. The gates are secured with a bulky lock and a battered chain. He crosses to the corner of the fence and hoists himself over. He scurries onto the top of a van that looks like it has had a run-in with a tree, then hops to the ground.

His dad's truck is jammed against the back fence. He tugs the passenger door. The cold metal creaks open. He slips in on the stiff seats, trying not to look at the windshield, at the spot where his father was watching the road when the truck in front of him hit a pothole, launching a two-inch copper pipe, twelve feet long. He imagines the vibrating pipe, working free, then blasting off like a wayward missile, smashing through the windshield.

His dad's chest took the full impact, cracking ribs, crushing his heart, which couldn't pump, or do anything except leak all over his blue flannel work shirt that he liked to wear on Fridays because it put him in a good mood. A birthday gift from Trevor, a thirty-dollar shirt on sale at Macy's.

In the truck's dim interior, Trevor touches the tan bench seat that is dark with stains. It's dried, caked blood. His father's blood! Panic swells in his chest. Then terror overtakes him like a wave knocking him down at the beach. He covers his face. His cheeks are wet and he is coughing. He tries not to look at the windshield. His mother was right. They shouldn't sit behind this steering wheel where his father's blood spilled.

He hurries from the truck.

In the yard, he lifts a cement block and heaves it onto the windshield. It fractures the glass into tiny cubes and rests there like a giant, legless, gray spider in a web. He finds a fence post and beats the truck, beats it until there isn't a smooth side. The sound reverberates off the police station. London won't make a profit from this sale.

A dog barks in the distance. Lights snap on in the station. Two men walk to a rear-door landing. Trevor beats the truck again and again. No one cares about the wrecks in this lot, or the blood on the seats, or that his family's name was misspelled in the newspaper, "Joseph Craw Dies in a Freak Turnpike Mishap," or the fact his father died for no reason except that some lazy jerkoff forgot to properly secure his plumbing supplies.

The men jog toward the lot. "Hey, you, just stay where you are," one yells.

Trevor drops the post. He scales the fence on the other side of the yard. He scrambles over, head first, then swings his legs to the ground at the last second.

Trevor slips into his house, closes the door, and touches his father's bare coat hook. The feeling of emptiness rocks him. His world is permanently tilted. Nothing is the same without his father. He wipes his forehead on his sleeve.

He's coated with sweat.

"Trevor, is that you?"

His serious expression and intense black eyes reflect in the hall mirror. His cheeks are hollow. His hair is thick and past his shoulders. His complexion is marked with acne. He looks like his father, like an Indian. He doesn't look like other kids in Molly Pitcher. He's been called a half-breed, Tonto, Chief Sitting Bullshit, Indian Boy, Injun Joe, Geroni-ho-mo. His father told him to be proud. "You are a member of an elite breed. You can trace your blood directly back to the tribe," he said. But Trevor doesn't feel proud. At school, he walks, hood up, eyes to the ground, hiding himself, hiding the color of his skin and, most of all, his nose, wide and flared, like an outgrowth of his skull, more than a nose. Last season, Diggy Masters, a guy who rides Trevor endlessly, joked that if Trevor ran into a wall with a boner, he'd break his nose first. Trevor just stared at him. No comeback, nothing.

"Trevor, don't be rude, we have company."

He hangs up his hoodie.

Harry London is in Trevor's dad's chair at the kitchen table. No one has sat there since the accident. Why is London here? Could the police have already called his mother? Could London and his mother know about the truck?

"How you doing, Trevor?" Harry London shifts his weight forward. His chair creaks. He's big and bulky as a bear. His black mustache hides most of his smile. Trevor's sure London has his eye on his mother. She's Italian, strong and square-shouldered, with large, dark eyes. She doesn't have to put on fancy clothes or use expensive creams. Tonight, she's wearing sneakers and a blue house-dress with the hem falling down in the back. The collar is visibly frayed, but it doesn't matter.

Trevor ignores London and looks at his mother for some explanation.

"You didn't get hurt, did you?" She always asks this.

"I was jogging." He keeps his hands in his sweatpants pockets and watches their faces.

"You look upset about something," says his mother. "You did get hurt, didn't you?"

"No, I'm fine, just tired." They don't know anything. He releases a breath.

"Trevor's been working extra hard. He's trying to make the varsity wrestling team," she says. "He has to beat the top wrestler."

"He's not the top wrestler, we're just in the same weight class," explains Trevor.

"As long as you don't get hurt," she says.

She's not the greatest listener. His father was the listener. Camille's the doer, always hustling. She's sold Mary Kay Cosmetics, Tupperware, opened a kiosk at the mall pushing men's ties and costume jewelry, and distributed food samples at an outlet store.

Camille nudges Trevor over and opens the oven door.

She pokes muffins with a toothpick. "Wrestling is so brutal. It was my husband's idea. Joe wrestled in high school. I can't watch it."

"It wasn't all his idea," says Trevor. "And he didn't wrestle for his high school. He wrestled for the reservation. They had their own team."

"I said he wrestled *in* high school, not *for* the high school. But my point was, your father did it and loved it and now he has you doing it." She closes the oven and drops the toothpick into the garbage. "I think it's dangerous, all that physical contact."

"No, Mom, it's not dangerous. Skydiving and bungee jumping are dangerous. Wrestling is a sport."

London is listening and nodding as if he understands everything; it's pissing Trevor off.

"I've made your mother a proposition." London keeps his eyes on her. "I'm buying a motel. I want her to work for me. You both could live there."

"Live there?" asks Trevor.

"It's a business venture, a risk, and I need someone dependable."

"Where are you going to live?"

"Oh, I'll keep my house. I'd just work there."

Trevor turns to his mother.

"We were only talking about it." She brushes stray hairs from her face like she always does when she's put on the spot. "It's totally up in the air," she says.

"I'm not moving," says Trevor.

"Harry, let me talk to him," says Camille in a hushed voice.

"I'm right here," says Trevor. "I'm not ten years old."

"Hey." London smiles. "I'm excited about maybe making a little money, that's all."

Trevor holds an impatient stare at his mother. His father is buried in the cold ground and here's Harry London sitting comfortably in his chair. It doesn't seem possible.

Jimmy

IF ANYTHING HAPPENS, IF ANYONE PULLS UP ON US, TAKE OFF running. You run and you run until you can't run no more. You got that?" Jimmy's father swings his blond hair off his forehead. His mouth is tight over his squared-off jaw.

"What about you?" asks Jimmy.

His laugh breaks into a pack-a-day hack. "I'll have the load in the back, I wouldn't get far. I'll talk my way out, somehow."

What could his father say at one in the morning with his truck stacked full of fresh lumber?

They hit a watery pothole, sending the truck lurching forward. Jimmy's knees bang on the dash. At six-foot-one, he is lanky and lean, with broad shoulders.

Pops accelerates. "You know where you are, right?"

Jimmy stares at the dark stretches of rolling hills. His narrow face, gold crew cut, and blue eyes reflect back at him in the glass. "At the old horse farms?"

"So, if you have to run, you take Iron Ore Road. Stay

low. If a car comes by, duck behind a tree. I'll meet you at the church on Molly Pitcher Road."

"Which one, the one we don't go to, or the one we never went to?"

"Just be on your toes." Pops enters a driveway, passes a gate, and stops the truck.

A stooped-over man shuffles toward them carrying a flashlight.

"What about this guy?" asks Jimmy.

"He's okay."

"Define okay."

"He's okay," snaps Pops.

The man flashes the light in the truck's passenger window. Jimmy shields his eyes with his hand. Embroidered above the man's breast pocket are the words "Ever Vigilant Guard Patrol."

Pops gets out and crosses in front of the truck's headlights. Jimmy cranks down his window. Past a rectangular work trailer and mounds of sand and gravel, a white sign reads HORSEMAN'S ESTATES. COUNTRY LIVING IN A SUBURBAN SETTING. OPENING SOON.

Jimmy's palms are sweating, yet he's ice-cold. He just wants it to be over. He doesn't want to be here, and Pops knows this. It's Jimmy's senior-year season. The only one that really counts. He's ranked the best 160-pounder in the county. The favorite to win the New Jersey States. But he hasn't won anything yet.

"It's stacked a half mile on the right," says the guard. "Take the exit after the dirt road, that'll lead you right back to town."

Pops removes a wad of bills from his shirt pocket and hands it to the guard.

Jimmy's risking it all because his uncle Johnny is stinking drunk. Jimmy is the "stand-in" and it makes him hate his father, because maybe the truth is, Pops is a selfish prick who doesn't really care about him. Pops could be destroying his senior-year season, a wrestling scholarship, his way out of Molly Pitcher, New Jersey. Jimmy also hates himself for climbing into the truck tonight. But Pops, he's so good at getting over on everyone.

Pops gets back in and drives with the lights off. "Tonight's my only chance at the load," he says. "Tomorrow morning, the carpenters will be pulling the pile apart."

"And what do they do when it's not there," scoffs Jimmy.

"I'm just saying it's tonight or never. You can't leave lumber sitting for too long. It warps."

"Yeah, right, and this is just an educational father and son outing."

"Whoa, what's with the attitude?" Pops drives slowly around new cement curbs. "Everything's going fine. I'm more scared when I look in the mirror." He tries to laugh but coughs again. He's a smoker, something else Jimmy would never do.

At a curve in the road, a doe leaps and bolts into the

darkness, its white tail flashing side to side in the moonlight.

"You're a good son. I'm proud of you. I think of you first, even before your mother and brother. Did you know that?"

"If you're so proud of me, then what am I doing in this truck?"

"It's one small favor, and do you think I'm doing this for me? I told you, I got bills."

Jimmy's heard this before. With Pops, it's always, "all I need is this one small favor." Tonight, at Jimmy's bedside, Pops said it was "this one small favor" or foreclosure on the house. "You want us living in a homeless shelter?" he asked. "You want that on you?"

Pops must know that everything Jimmy's worked for is on the line. Pops is practically the leader of the "Varsity Dads," a clique of fathers who sit shoulder to shoulder at the wrestling matches and keep the Minute Men Wrestling website updated and the *Asbury Park Press* informed of wins and losses.

Up until tonight, Pops kept Jimmy away from his "side business." Jimmy glances over at his father and doesn't see the handsome face that cheers him at his wrestling matches. This man scares him with his hair hanging over his forehead and his hands tense on the steering wheel.

The road becomes bumpier. Pops's cigarette bounces in his lips. He backs the truck to a dark pile, then shuts off the engine.

The November night is chilly and damp. Jimmy steps across the soft, raw earth, gouged from toppled trees and machines. The smell of the old horse farm fills his nostrils. Stars splash the sky. Jimmy chooses a bright one and wishes, "Get us home safe."

Pops slits a tarp with a razor knife. The ties snap like stretched rubber bands. "You see, this isn't going to be difficult."

"Pops, that's not the point. I shouldn't be here. Period."

"You think you're too good for it?"

"I know I'm too good for it."

"You're going to learn family comes first. I'm going to be paying the mortgage this month, and your mother, you, and your brother are going to have a roof over your heads."

They lift the boards four at a time and slide them into the truck bed. Mostly two-by-sixes, over sixteen feet long, heavy and awkward. Dew seeps through Jimmy's Nikes. The work numbs him to what he's doing. He tells himself that soon he'll be back in bed, warm, protected.

Pops turns left after the nursery on Wright Street. Ahead, a police car is parked on the side of the road. The officer has the interior dome light on and is reading something. Jimmy's stomach levitates into his throat. "Pops, that's a cop."

"Relax."

"What if he stops us?"

"He won't."

"But what if he does? Do I jump and run?"

"No, act normal. I'll talk us out of this. Just remember, we're going to a job site. We've got to be there at dawn." When they pass the police car, its headlights snap on and it pulls onto the road. "We're doing a job in Bergen County," says Pops, making it up, "building a deck, and we left early because the truck is loaded and we've got a long, slow ride. You got that?" The police car's headlights reflect in the rearview mirror. "You got that?"

"Got what?" Jimmy wants to run. He would feel better running than sitting in the truck waiting to get arrested.

"The story!"

"I'm going to be sick." His voice is high and cracks. He feels panic from his balls all the way to his throat.

"Get a hold of yourself." Pops's eyes dart from the rearview mirror to the road. The police car speeds up. It's directly behind them. The emergency lights flash on.

"He's pulling us over!" Jimmy unlocks his door.

"Just calm down."

"Should I run?"

"I'll handle it." Pops pulls the truck over in front of an abandoned vegetable stand stacked with wooden boxes. Gravel crunches under the tires. "Jimmy, keep your mouth shut, you understand?" He stamps his cigarette in the overflowing ashtray. "Sit back and listen. You might learn something."

The policeman stands to the rear of the truck cab, shining his flashlight into the driver-side window. "License and registration."

"What's the matter, officer?" Pops fumbles through his wallet. Jimmy grips the door handle; one flick and he's sprinting.

"You've got no warning flag on the back of that lumber. It's sticking ten feet off the truck."

"Jesus, my son forgot the flag. Didn't I tell you about the flag?"

Jimmy wants to yell *You're blaming me?* Jimmy looks across his father, trying to locate the policeman's face. All he sees is his flashlight's beam shining into the truck.

"You haven't been drinking tonight?" asks the officer. "Have you?"

"Of course not. We're on our way to a job."

"Why don't you step out of the truck?"

Pops opens the door. "I haven't had a drink since last Sunday's Jets game."

What a liar! He was drinking at dinner and after dinner.

Pops laughs, coughs. "Right, Jimmy? That's my son in there." The flashlight shines on Jimmy's face. "We're heading to a job site in Bergen County. I'm real sorry about the flag. I can tie on something."

The policeman holds his flashlight on Pops's driver's license. "Your son, is he the wrestler Jim O'Shea?"

"He sure is."

"I've seen him wrestle," says the policeman. "We get to work those events." He hands Pops his license. "How's the team going to do this year?" calls the policeman into the truck, his voice easy, like a regular guy.

"We have a meeting tomorrow." Jimmy's voice is choked and dry. "I just want to get home."

"He means Monday," says Pops.

"Well, hang something on that load and good luck." The officer walks back to his car.

After tying a handkerchief on the longest board protruding from the truck, Pops gets back into the cab. "What the heck, a meeting tomorrow? I just told him we were going to a job. You could have blown it."

Jimmy stares daggers at him. "Don't ever ask me to help you again. You just put my season on the line. Do you realize that?"

Diggy

DIGGY MASTERS FINISHED DINNER AN HOUR AGO AND IS STILL starving. He rises from the couch and peeks out the window. Randy Masters stands on the deck with a cigar between his fingers watching the dark golf course that extends from their backyard. His tan-colored drink in a fat glass drips on the rail.

Diggy scans the kitchen. Apple pie on top of the refrigerator at twelve o'clock. He retrieves it, opens the box, and plows his fingers into the cut side, into the gooey apples, and scoops the filling into his mouth. He shovels another handful and swallows it, then checks on Randy, who is still gazing at the golf course as if something besides someone whacking a golf ball is going to happen.

Diggy and his brother, Nick, call their father Randy. When he put them in wrestling, he told them to call him "Coach Randy" instead of "Dad." Their mother thought it was ridiculous. "I'm the coach of Team Masters," he said. After they moved to the Hills, he built a wrestling room in their basement. He put together a library of wrestling and coaching books. Diggy was in the sixth grade. Nick was two grades ahead. So they called him Coach Randy. They forgot that it was a goof. He became their coach. Now his brother doesn't wrestle anymore and they call him just plain Randy.

Everything that means anything in the Masters' family is somehow linked to wrestling. Example: Diggy's real name is Devon. Nick's first year on varsity, the team picked a Kid Rock song as their team's anthem. A dumb song, which was sacked by the team the next season, but that year, Nick and every wrestler chanted the lyrics like shorted-out robots: "Bawitdaba da bang a dang diggy diggy diggy said the boogy said up jump the boogy." Diggy was in seventh grade, already wrestling on the high school freshmen team. Not because he showed great talent, but because Randy convinced Coach Greco it would be better to keep his sons together. So Nick and Diggy wrestled in the same gym. Diggy on freshmen. Nick on varsity. Devon morphed to Diggy and it stuck like a wet paper towel on a locker room ceiling.

Diggy slips into the bathroom to wash his hands and figures he might as well puke. A lot of wrestlers do this during season. He turns on the sink water for background noise, then kneels in front of the toilet and shoves two fingers into his throat. He gags, waits, then sticks them in farther. His eyes water. Nothing. He washes his face and gives the toilet another look. Maybe he can sneak up on it. He tries again, this time more quickly. He gags. Bingo. The pie and some of his dinner blow into the water.

"Diggy!"

It's Randy.

"Diggy!"

He returns to the kitchen. The pie is on the island.

"What's this?" asks Randy.

"That?"

"Yeah, this."

"Pie." He's stalling, trying to figure a way out.

"I know it's a pie. Why does it look like someone just stuck their fingers in it?"

Diggy shakes his head and does his best "beats the hell out of me" look.

"Come on, let's go," says Randy.

"Now?"

"Yes, right now."

Diggy follows him down the basement stairs. Randy turns on the light. The floor is wall-to-wall wrestling mats, with a separate room for weights. A balance scale is at the foot of the stairs. Not a twenty-five-dollar department store scale, a real black-and-white doctor's office scale with sliding weights. Randy sets the larger weight at 150, then slides the other weight to two pounds. One-fifty-two, that's Diggy's wrestling weight. He wrestled 152 last season, his junior year, and had a winning varsity record. Last winter, it felt good to be Diggy Masters.

He slips off his sneakers and steps on the scale.

"Take off your shirt."

Diggy pulls it over his head. He's standing in basketball shorts and socks. His body is smooth, not ripped, but not fat. His belly is almost flat, but there's no six-pack or any signs of muscle. Randy moves the weight along the balance bar: 153, 154, 155, 156, 157, 158, 159, 160, 161.

"What the . . . ?" Randy's mouth hangs open. At 162, the scale balances. "You're ten over."

"I got time." Diggy is supposed to be weighing himself every day. One-sixty-two is actually a surprise. Not a good surprise, but not a nightmare either. "I can cut."

"You can cut? That's it? That's all you're going to say?"

What is he supposed to say? *Randy, I just puked. Randy, I have a fat ass just like you.* "I won't eat for a few days. I've done it before."

"You just ate half an apple pie."

"Not half."

"Go do some sit-ups!"

"I just ate, you said so yourself."

"Now. Greco is going to be weighing you. What's he going to think?"

"Randy, I'll cut, don't worry."

Randy grabs the back of Diggy's neck and digs his fingers into his flesh. "Get going." He tries to lead him toward the weight room.

"Get off me."

Randy releases him. "Diggy, you should want this more than me. Your entire high school career is going to be summed up in the next twelve weeks. You made a name for yourself last season. You proved to everyone you were a Masters. If you don't make weight, what's going to happen?"

This season is Randy's wet dream. He wants Diggy to win the districts. Diggy wants to win as much as Randy, but he's hungry all the time. And worse, he knows all about starvation and hunger pains that keep you awake, that rip his gut like a banzai sword. He once sat in a sauna until he was so dehydrated he couldn't blink, couldn't spit, couldn't speak. Then he went two days on sliced carrots, which may not sound impressive, but a carrot is ninety percent water. It was terrible. He had orange diarrhea for days.

"Let's get serious," says Randy. "You want your name on the Wall?" The Wall is the Wall of Champions in their high school. Diggy's brother was the District Champ and the State Champ from his freshman year to his senior year. The single State Champ in the history of Molly Pitcher High School. In fact, the only four-time state winner ever in the state of New Jersey. Get the picture. His name is plastered all over the Wall.

Randy smiles at Diggy. Randy used to sell cars and he's got this unmistakable salesman's smile, with one side of his mouth raised and a blink at the same time. Now he owns the dealership.

"Of course I do." Diggy wants his name next to his brother's. He's thought about it ever since Nick's name was put on the Wall.

They go into the weight room, lined with mirrors. Diggy's black hair, cut in a fade, is clean and tight. He smiles at himself. He may not be ripped, but he has the look that half the high school guys would crush their left nut for. Randy sets the sit-up board on an angle. "Gimmie sets of twenty, until you reach one hundred."

Diggy hooks his feet under the cushioned bar. "It's called five sets of twenty," he cracks.

Randy smacks the back of his head with his open hand. "Get serious."

"Keep your damn hands to yourself."

"That didn't hurt you," he says.

"How would you like it if I slapped you upside your head?"

"Just do them."

"I can count for myself."

"You got it, buddy. Do it your way." Randy leaves and Diggy hears his footfalls on the stairs.

Diggy bangs through a set of twenty. Randy's right. He is the 152 varsity starter. He should move up a weight class to 160, but Jimmy O'Shea has it locked. Diggy's not saying Jimmy is better than him, but at the moment he's not challenging him to a wrestle-off for a few reasons: Diggy will win more matches at 152; Jimmy will win more matches at 160 than 170; and the truth is, he could lose to Jimmy.

He rests, then cranks out another set. There's a part of Diggy that knows Randy is doing this for his own good, and then there's Nick's theory: Randy is pushing him because he's a fat-assed prick who rode the bench on his high school football team, then got cut in the first round at college. Randy never got any respect. He wasn't the big man in the gym until Nick tore through wrestlers like a tree shredder.

Diggy grabs a handful of fat around his navel. He knows where the weight came from. Taco Bell Grande Platters at the mall, definitely.

He climbs to the top of the stairs. The door is locked. "Hey, Randy!"

"That's where you're spending the night," Randy says through the door. "Because I know you. You're going to get hungry and start eating. Then when you can't make weight, whose fault will it be?"

"Mom!" screams Diggy.

"Devon, I'm here, honey," she says.

"Open the damn door."

"Your father says you need to focus."

"Now!" yells Diggy.

"Randy, I'll make sure he doesn't—" starts his mother.

"Beverly, shut up. Diggy, this is called fasting, something you're going to have to learn."

Diggy lies on a wrestling mat, angry, with tears of frustration in his eyes. Randy's right, and he has to admit it—if he weren't in the basement, if he weren't locked up, he would eat something, because he's starving.

Diggy

DIGGY ELBOWS HIS WAY PAST THE OTHER WRESTLERS AND claims his locker from last year. He throws his sneakers at the bottom, then unloads his bag: Speed Stick deodorant, anti-fungal spray powder, shampoo, triple antibiotic cream for cuts, and a crushed tube of medicine for ringworm, which developed under his arm last season. It was disgusting, oozing and itchy.

Guys shuffle in, tossing gym bags on the floor, banging fists.

"Man, I hope you guys are ready for this," Pancakes yells from a toilet stall. He likes to yell when he's in the can. Once he gets going, no one can shut him up. "Hey, Diggy," he calls, "we got some new freshmen to break in!"

"Why don't you finish dumping that deuce," Diggy calls back, cracking everyone up.

"This is our year, our senior year, while we walk the valley and feel no fear," raps Pancakes.

"Cut the rap and finish your crap," someone yells.

It continues like this. Everyone yelling. Guys holding

their noses race into the bathroom, bombing Pancakes with wet paper towels.

Diggy pulls a notebook from his bag. He's written the lineup with the new weight classes:

106 Little Gino

113 Turkburger

120 Jordan

126 Garrett

132 Mario

138 Cleaver

145 Salaam

152 Me

160 Jimmy

170 Trevor Crow?

182 Bones

195 Boyle

220 Paul

285 Pancakes

Diggy writes, "Win Districts, Win Regions, Win States, Get a scholarship, Get a one-way ticket from my house."

Fifty or so wrestlers in baggy gym clothes lean on the red foam mats that go halfway up the gym wall; incoming freshmen in the back of the gym, junior-varsity in the middle, varsity up front. Diggy heads to the varsity guys.

"Let's start the merry-go-round," yells Coach Greco. "Get the monkeys off your back. You come in with twelve monkeys on your back, you go home with no monkeys, that's a good practice."

Wrestlers circle the gym. Diggy feels the mats tilting under his feet like the deck of a cruise ship. He should have eaten breakfast today, but yesterday was Thanksgiving and his grandmother's dining-room table was a free-for-all. Randy told him to "watch it," and "no dessert," but his mother and uncles all laughed. So he ate, picked, then ate more, then packed his stomach with custard pie. And, was it really his fault? Did Greco have to schedule the first practice on a school holiday?

"Warm it up," yells Greco. "Dust off the cobwebs."

Diggy falls into a rhythm with Bones on his right and Little Gino on his left.

"Look at Crow, he's got to be first," says Bones with his beaded dreadlocks bouncing around his tan face. "I hear he's going one-fifty-two."

"He can suck my ass," says Diggy.

"He can suck my cock." Little Gino's laugh sounds more like a seventh-grade girl's than a senior's.

"If only you could find it," says Bones.

"Give him some tweezers!" Diggy slaps Bones's five.

They go around the gym about twenty-five times. Sweat runs on Diggy's forehead. He's "double shirting" the practice to cut some water weight. A pain in his side knifes through him. "Bones," blurts Diggy between breaths, "let's take a dive."

They cut from the line and zip into the locker room. The wrestlers pass, with Diggy catching his breath and Bones laughing silently, knowing no one on the team has the balls to turn them in.

Twenty laps later, they rejoin the runners. Some are grinning, some are peeved, but it's all part of the game. Diggy: One. Greco: Nothing.

Killer sprints are Diggy's nightmare. He lines up with the wrestlers, already dreading finishing with the heavy-weight wrestlers. It's like showcasing the fact that he's out of shape. Total humiliation.

On Greco's whistle, the wrestlers charge in jagged rows across the gym. The first wrestler to reach the wall sits out. Jimmy streaks from the pack and tags the wall first. Greco points to him. Smiling, Jimmy goes to the bleachers and takes a seat.

The torture continues, back and forth. Sprint after sprint. Sweaty waves of wrestlers racing from one side to the other, with the fastest guy going to the bleachers. Diggy, huffing and puffing, loses count. He just can't break from the back of the pack. He's stuck next to Pancakes's whale ass. One by one, wrestlers are eliminated. Diggy's legs are lead. He's hot, red faced, embarrassed, and the ache in his side has spread to his temples. He's still dragging butt when there are only two other wrestlers remaining.

Pancakes, Diggy, and a freshman built as wide and tall as an ATM machine, line up. Everyone is cheering and laughing at them. Laughing at their lard asses. The freshman takes off at the whistle, with Pancakes on his tail like an angry rhinoceros, followed by Diggy. How could he be behind Pancakes? Diggy can't let this happen. He comes alongside the two hundred and eighty-five pounds of Pancakes, ca-booming the mats on his cannon-ball calves, sweat flying from him like rain, passes him, and grabs the freshman's shirt, who crashes to the mat. Diggy reaches the wall first.

Greco's whistle sounds. "Diggy, you owe me for that."

Diggy falls dead on the mat and spreads his arms.

"Sit-ups, let's hustle!" yells Greco. "Ladies, today is the last easy practice of the season. At five o'clock, I want the practice in our bank and the monkeys in the zoo. No monkeys on your back, that's a good practice."

They form lines. The juniors and seniors know the routine; everyone else follows. Diggy can't bear to do sit-ups. Not only are they pointless and boring, but does anyone really think doing them is going to matter in a match? Diggy has seen plenty of guys bust their asses week after week and disgrace themselves under the light when it matters.

Instead of doing the sit-ups, he patrols the rows, wondering how long Greco will let him screw around. "Come on," yells Diggy. "Use your abs, not your elbows!"

Greco seems to be absently nodding approval; usually he's already barking, "Stop slacking or get packing!" And then it hits Diggy: *Could he have given up on me?* The sweat on his back goes cold. He looks around the room at the straining faces, then at Greco. Could someone have told Greco his weight?

Diggy jogs over to the coach. "I'm trying to get us all on the same page," says Diggy lightly, as if they were Facebook friends.

Bundles of muscles on each side of Greco's neck rise and harden. "Oh, yeah," he says suspiciously. "What's your weight?"

"Maybe one-fifty-eight, one-fifty-nine, but I—"

Greco cuts him off. "You been watching your carbs?"

"Like all the time. I'm practically anorexic."

"And I'm practically handsome." Greco bends his cauliflower ears forward, which look like wads of chewed bubble gum, and crosses his eyes. Not in a funny way, but as if to say, *I'm on to you, Diggy Masters.* He releases his ears and his eyes return to the mat.

Diggy wants to tell him *You're all bony, all muscle, angles, and sinew. You never had to cut any serious weight!* "Don't I always have to cut?" He smiles nervously, but he's dying inside because this could be the year he can't make weight. "Didn't I always make it?" he asks.

"In seven days you've got to be one-fifty-two," says Greco. "If you want me to run you from here to Lake Lakookie, then I'll run you from here to Lake Lakookie."

"Where's Lake Lakookie?"

"It's where you'll be running to." Greco hits his fingers against Diggy's chest.

"That's assault on a student." Diggy continues smiling. "Gino," he calls, "be my witness. I need a witness."

"You're going to need an ambulance if you keep it up." Greco sounds his whistle. "And Diggy, I'll get the team on the same page. You get yourself into your weight class." Greco blows his whistle again. "Braces!"

The wrestlers flip to their backs and arch their torsos into the air, supported by their heads and feet. Diggy has to show Greco that he's going to be the 152 starter. Hands folded across his stomach, he rocks forward and back, side to side, stretching his neck. He tries to tell himself that getting back to wrestling isn't so bad. *At least I'm not listening to Randy freak about me playing video games, but God, when is the warm-up going to be over?*

Next Greco calls, "Spin review!" Bones gets on all fours. Diggy lays facedown across Bones's back. Greco's whistle sounds and Diggy spins on Bone's back like a helicopter blade. Diggy goes around, pushing off his toes, spinning his body like a human gyroscope. He tries to do the drill especially quick and hopes that Greco is watching.

"Reverse!" Greco blasts his whistle.

Diggy spins the other way. Around and around he goes, until the gym is a blur and the wrestlers are blots of color. "Switch positions!" Now Bones gets top. Diggy concentrates, trying to imagine his back flat and hard as a diving board. He feels Bones's hands, his 182 pounds pressing. Diggy remains rigid. Wrestlers are collapsing around him.

"Come on, you slugs, this is the first day. Impress me," calls Greco.

Diggy's soaked to his socks. Bones's braids are plastered to his forehead. The gym is a steam room. Mats are spotted and smeared with sweat.

"Partners!" shouts Greco. "Find a partner. Come on slackers, let's move. Remember, you guys are always one shot away from a pin, one shot away. I WANT TO HEAR IT!"

"One shot away," they yell.

Diggy pairs off with Bones. The practice continues with hand-fighting, then duck-unders and sweeps. "You check out the size of Trevor's arms?" asks Bones.

Diggy doesn't have to look. His arms are ridiculous.

When the drills are done, everyone drops to one knee around Greco. Diggy checks the clock. Only an hour in with at least an hour to go.

"Guys, in case you haven't heard, you can forget the weight classes you had last season. This season starts the new classifications. Where's Gino?"

Little Gino raises his hand.

"You were one-o-three last year, this year you're in the one-o-six weight class. So tonight you can go home and have an extra chicken breast." Everyone laughs. "The only weight classes that weren't changed were the three middle ones, one-forty-five, one-fifty-two, and one-sixty, and the heavyweight at two-eighty-five. So, Salaam, Diggy, and Jimmy, you guys can keep doing what you've been doing. The rest of you, learn your new weight class. I posted them in the locker room. You got it?"

A few guys say, "We got it."

"What? I didn't hear you!"

"We got it!" they roar.

"And another thing—this year, on the line is in-bounds. So you guys have more room to wrestle. Got it?"

"Got it!"

"Good. Now today, we're going to work on penetration," says Greco.

"Worked on it last night," says Bones with a grin.

Everyone laughs.

Greco ignores him. "Let's get a definition of penetration."

The gym is quiet.

"You mean the kind at wrestling?" cracks Bones.

More chuckles. Even Greco's smiling.

"That's easy," says Jimmy. "It's when you get in close enough to a wrestler to take a guy down."

Greco pats Jimmy's crew cut. "Right, forward motion through your opponent, directed at his hips, will result in penetration. Good penetration will put you completely past your opponent before he can react." Greco looks into the faces of the wrestlers. "I need a victim."

Trevor Crow raises his hand.

"Trevor," says Greco. "Up here for a demo."

Diggy mouths the words "Kiss-ass."

Trevor takes a ready position and pushes his hair from his eyes. The only wrestler with hair past his shoulders. The only Indian not from India in the school. In an instant, Greco, in his chinos and Minute Men shirt, shoots in and is holding one of Trevor's legs in the air. "The trick is to anticipate where your opponent is going to be and then shoot in that direction," says Greco.

They pair off for live wrestling. Greco sticks Diggy with Trevor Crow. Diggy knows that Trevor would rather be wrestling anyone else. Not that Diggy could give a fat fart. Last year, Trevor was cut from the varsity squad. So Trevor has no right to pick and choose anyone or anything. Trevor was an eleventh grader on the JV team, which equals total humiliation, no varsity letter, no jacket, and no girls.

Diggy shoots in and slams his shoulder against Trevor's knee.

"Hey, watch it," says Trevor. "I wasn't ready."

"Why don't you cut your hair or wear a hair net?" Diggy doesn't wait for a response. He shoots for Trevor's legs and wonders how Trevor got so big over the summer.

Trevor holds him off. Diggy falls forward on his hands and knees.

"Hey Tonto, how much do you weigh?" Diggy wants to tick him off. Guys make mistakes when they get angry.

"One-fifty-one." Trevor wipes his forehead with his palm.

Diggy stares across the wrestling room at the Wall of Champions. "You realize I'm wrestling one-fifty-two," he says. "You got that, Chief?"

Trevor holds his ground and swallows. "I told you about that. You call me that again, I'll report you."

"To who?"

"To Coach Greco."

Diggy sighs. "Look, Trevor, the team can't have two guys at one-fifty-two. Only one can start. I'm not splitting the weight class with you."

"I know how it works." Trevor winces and glances toward the clock. "Let's wrestle."

"Why don't you start eating and go all the way to one-seventy?" Greco sounds the whistle. The wrestlers begin to grapple. "Answer me, or are you too stupid to understand?" Diggy gets right into Trevor's ugly mug. "I own one-fifty-two," he says. "So you might as well go home and eat a frickin' buffalo, because you're not taking my spot." Trevor takes a step back. Without warning, Diggy springs forward and into Trevor's knees, knocking him over. Trevor's head thumps the padded wall.

Trevor rubs his head. "What's with you?" he asks. "You keep it up and I'll—"

"You'll what?" asks Diggy. "Shoot me with a bow and arrow?"

"Diggy, cut the crap, okay?"

Diggy is not stepping aside for Trevor. He will do what he has to do. Last year he finished with 18 wins, 6 losses. His wins weren't masterpieces like Nick's, but they were wins. He smacked his opponents' faces, ears, throats. In a clutch, he used a choke hold, which was virtually undetectable. He dug his chin into back muscles, until his opponents squirmed with pain. And more than once, in desperation, he popped his knee into a guy's balls. He received cautions from referees. Greco constantly warned him to cool it. But, when Diggy put up a "W," all seemed to be forgotten and forgiven. "Any way you win is the right way to wrestle," said Randy. "A win is a win."

Diggy slaps his hands against his thighs and shoots forward with his arms extended. Trevor pushes Diggy's head down. Diggy feels an impact, a solid collision. His head springs back as his face absorbs the full force of Trevor's knee coming forward. Blood erupts from Diggy's mouth like someone turned on a faucet. He drops to his knees and covers his mouth with his hand. The blood seeps between his fingers.

Someone throws him a towel. A large blot of bright red seeps through.

"Bend your head back." Coach Greco tips Diggy's chin up. "Let me take a look at it." Greco pulls his bottom lip down. "Going to need stitches," he says.

* * *

His mother's black Land Rover speeds into the parking lot and brakes in front of the gym steps. Diggy's Mustang is parked nearby, but Greco won't let Diggy drive to the hospital. The Land Rover's tinted passenger window opens.

"I'm afraid we've had a little accident," says Greco.

"We?" Diggy speaks through an icepack. "You mean me."

"Stop with the wise mouth," says Greco, "or you'll be bleeding out the other side."

Beverly leans to the passenger window. "Stitches?"

"I'm afraid so," says Greco.

Diggy slips into the large front bucket seat. "Trevor Crow," he says to his mother. "He's dead."

"Don't say things like that," says Beverly.

"Trevor wouldn't hurt anyone on purpose," says Greco. "He's a good kid. This was definitely an accident."

Diggy rests his head against the cool leather. The car smells of hairspray from Beverly's beauty salon.

"Thank you, Coach." Beverly leans across Diggy toward the window. "I'll go get him patched up." She pulls off.

His mother drives with her palms on the steering wheel. Her painted fingernails shine like miniature shells. She taps out a cigarette with one hand. "Was this a fight?"

"You heard the coach; it was practice, an *accident*."

"Well, I'm sure, knowing you and your track record—"

"I was going in for a shot and Crow clobbered me with his knee."

"Purposely?"

Diggy removes the ice pack. Maybe he shouldn't have called him Tonto. Everyone called him that in the sixth grade, especially after Trevor approached the guys one day and told them that "Tonto" isn't a Native American word. "In Spanish it means stupid," he said. "So there's no reason to call me that." Everyone just laughed harder.

"He's in my weight class," says Diggy to his mother.

"One-fifty-two?"

"Yes, what other weight class am I in?"

"You will beat him?"

"Of course I'll beat him. He never even wrestled varsity." Diggy works his tongue into the gash on his bottom lip. It's the freakin' Grand Canyon. "Last year, he was a scrub. He must have taken steroids or something."

"Honey, you have to remember who you are. You're Diggy Masters and—"

"Don't start quoting Randy," he says, cutting her off.

Diggy

DIGGY SPEEDS DOWN THE BLOCK, THEN SLOWS HIS MUSTANG IN front of Trevor Crow's house. A single electric candle glows in the front window. Bones is riding shotgun. Little Gino's in the back, hanging his head between the front bucket seats.

"What're we doing here, yo?" asks Bones.

Even with the car's heat blowing, Diggy feels cold. His lip throbs. "Get this," he says. "I'm getting stitches, my lip is yanked to my dick, and my mom hands me her phone. You know what my father wants to know? If I'll be ready for the first match." Diggy tries to laugh, but it hurts. "Believe that?"

Gino and Bones laugh. "At least your father is into it," says Gino. "My father thinks I wrestle like the guys in the WWF."

"The WWF?" says Bones. "They have a midget league?"

"Oh, yeah, like you could be in the WWF?" says Gino.

Diggy rubs his tongue over the stitches. They feel like a zipper. "Crow did this on purpose." Diggy likes the way the words seem to reverberate. Full of menace.

"No way *that* was an accident," says Bones.

"What are you going to do?" asks Gino.

Diggy flips through the radio stations. He shivers and remembers Trevor's stiff, unmovable sprawl. "What do you think Crow is taking?" he asks.

"Taking?" asks Bones.

"Like steroids, GHB, what?" Diggy wants his suggestion to become a fact.

They are quiet. A rap song thumps in the car. The heater whirrs. Diggy moves his sneaker next to the warmth blowing near the floor. The porch light remains on. The wind rolls a sheet of newspaper past the car.

"Trevor is screwing everything up." Diggy thumps the steering wheel. He wants to be as angry as he sounds, but he's already looking forward to the time off from practice, nursing his lip. "See that deer in the front of Crow's house?" he asks. "I dare you to snap the head off." He's sure one of them will do it.

"What deer?" asks Gino.

"Not a real deer," he says. "The cement deer in the bushes. Neither of you has a hair on your balls."

"Why don't you do it, yo?" asks Bones.

"Oh, yeah, right, and rip my stitches open," says Diggy.

"Open the door," says Gino.

Bones opens his door. Little Gino bolts from the back seat and races across the lawn. He bends over the deer and yanks it forward. It's strange to see him half in the garden, twisting and pulling. The deer's head drops, then rolls onto the lawn. Gino races back to the car. Diggy pushes the door open.

"It must'a had a cracked neck." Gino holds a twisted piece of cement with a metal rod sticking from the end. "Antlers!"

Diggy throws the car into drive and leaves rubber up the block. "Bones, you're a wuss." Diggy smacks hands with Gino.

Trevor

THE "LATE" BUS BOUNCES OVER THE HILL. IN THE SECOND TO last bench, Jimmy has his long legs across the aisle, his size twelves on the empty seat. Trevor, in the rear seat next to the emergency door, leans forward over Jimmy's seat.

"What I'm saying is watch your back." Jimmy tugs apart a protein bar and gives Trevor half. "I'm not saying he's really going to do something. Maybe he's running his mouth."

"You make it sound like he put a hit out on me." A chill passes up his spine and radiates along his shoulders.

"If he does anything, it's not going to be obvious," says Jimmy. "He's not going to jeopardize his season. It'll be when you least expect it."

"I told you about the cement deer in my front yard. Someone cracked the head off."

"It couldn't have been Diggy. He was getting stitched at the hospital. He wouldn't have gone driving around afterward."

Trevor relaxes. Jimmy's right.

"Isn't Diggy's old man a wack job?" asks Jimmy. "Did you see him getting in the coach's face?"

The team was warming up. Mr. Masters crossed the mat from his usual post in the corner where he kept an eye on practices. He said something to Greco and there was a quick exchange of words. Then Mr. Masters made his point by stabbing his finger six inches from the coach's face. Diggy was stretched on the bleachers with his Yankees cap tipped over his eyes as if he were snoozing. His lip was the size of a cocktail frank.

"I'm surprised the coach didn't take his legs out and tie him in a pretzel," says Jimmy. They laugh.

"You really think Diggy's going to do something to me?" asks Trevor.

"I know he's not letting you take his weight class without a fight."

Trevor considers the possibilities: Diggy could throw a rock through his window, give his mother's car flats, set his house on fire, push him down the stairs at school. Endless scenarios, but none of them fit. Nothing except a face-to-face confrontation with Diggy on the wrestling mat seems probable.

Wrestle-off. Varsity spot. 152. Trevor doesn't have many alternatives. He can't wrestle at 170, he'd be slaughtered, and he can't beat Jimmy at 160. Dropping weight isn't an option. He has to beat Diggy.

"Diggy can be scary," says Jimmy. "Nick taught him

moves we've never seen before. And he's dirty. Everyone knows it."

"That makes me feel a lot better," says Trevor.

"But I think if you wrestle him off smart for one-fifty-two," says Jimmy, "you could beat him."

"What if he came after you, at one-sixty?"

"He won't."

"But what if he did."

"I wouldn't be looking forward to it, but I'd have to beat him." Jimmy turns to the window. "This is my year. You know that."

Trevor does know it. He's read about it in the newspapers. He's talked about it at the lunch table. Jimmy was undefeated last year in the regular season. His only loss was in Atlantic City at the New Jersey State Tournament. He placed third.

"Maybe this has been coming for a long time," says Trevor. "I remember watching Diggy on the mat, and my father saying, 'he's all *show* and no *go.*'"

Jimmy smiles. "My pops says Diggy spends more time running his mouth than running the track."

"But he still wins," says Trevor.

"Yeah, that's the part that sucks," says Jimmy.

Over the past three seasons, Trevor studied Diggy's wrestling techniques, and his limitations. Diggy uses his lower body to topple his opponents, then he scrambles for points. Most of Diggy's matches are decided by a one- or two-point margin in the third period with Diggy watching the seconds on the clock tick down, trying to hold his lead. The bus approaches Trevor's stop.

"Later, bro," says Jimmy.

They pound fists.

Harry London and Trevor's mother are waiting for him in the car with the engine running. "Hop in," says London, like it's a happy occasion.

Trevor shuts his eyes, remembering he agreed to see the motel. "I'm dead," he says. "Go ahead without me."

"Honey, this is important to me and it should be to you," his mother calls, lowering her window.

The deer's head is still sideways on the lawn with a black eye gazing into the sky. Trevor drops his bag on the cement walk and lifts the head onto the body. His father liked this deer, frozen as if it spotted a hunter. Trevor would have to find a way to fix it. There has to be some kind of epoxy for cement animals. He rolls the head behind the azalea bushes.

"Come on Trevor, it's getting pitch-black," calls his mother.

Trevor gets in. Dammit!

Harry London pulls out. He takes his eyes off the road and looks at Trevor in the rearview mirror. "I know what you've been thinking," he says. "House to a motel. What a comedown. But I've already dumped ten grand into the place and I've got another five to back that up."

They drive on the truck route to the outskirts of town. They pass under the turnpike and follow a service road.

"No one lives around here," says Trevor.

"Not yet," says London, "but this town is growing." He talks about some zoning change and his mother listens like it's interesting, like he's interesting.

Finally, London swings a left turn over double yellow lines and hits a driveway hard, bouncing into a parking lot. "Don't worry, this thing's a tank," he says.

The motel is a one-story, open-ended rectangle with pea-green doors and a faded sign that reads SECRET KEEP-ERS, AC, POOL, VACANCY. London rolls in next to an old car with the hood lifted. An orange extension cord snakes from the engine into a motel room door.

"Whose car is that?" asks his mother.

"Oh, the battery is probably dead," says London. "This isn't the Marriott."

"It's not even Motel Six," says Trevor.

London smiles. "And I'm not Donald Trump."

His mother wears a blue dress and stockings with black shoes. She clutches a pearl-colored purse that Trevor hasn't seen in years. "Camille, that's the office where you'll work." London looks toward a door marked "Office."

A drape parts in a window and an old man peers out.

"He's one of the permanents," says London. "He's harmless."

"I hope," says Camille.

"That's the pool." London points to a tarp weighted with bleach bottles and buckets of sand enclosed by a cyclone fence in front of the motel. The middle of the tarp sags under a brown puddle clotted with cans and fast-food containers. Someone swimming could wave to the traffic going by on the road. "Hasn't had much use. I'm not going to kid anyone," he says.

"I'm sure it would be cute if it were fixed up," says his mother.

Trevor, standing a foot behind London, makes googly eyes at his mother. *Hasn't had much use?* Are you kidding?

Under a tin awning, which shelters the room doors, London separates a key from dozens of others on a large ring attached to a belt loop on his jeans. He pushes a door in with his shoulder and flicks on a ceiling light. The smell of paint hangs in the air.

His mother enters on the toes of her shoes, as if the floor is swarming with mice. The room has a love seat and a double bed with a tan spread. Opposite the far window is an efficiency kitchen with a speckled Formica counter seared with gold burn marks from forgotten cigarettes. His mother leans over the counter and turns on the sink's faucet. Water trickles and spits. She shuts it off, then lights a burner on the stove. "Electric ignition," says London.

Trevor wonders when he is going to wake and learn that this is a giant screwup. He can't be moving to this place, off a highway, with old men peeping from the windows.

"Camille, this is the bathroom." London takes her hand. "It's been cleaned since you last saw it."

The green enamel is worn off the tub. The toilet is missing a seat. "Don't worry, I'll make it cozy," his mother whispers to Trevor.

"Beyond those doors is your own room," says London with a smile.

"Go ahead," his mother says quietly. She is also smiling.

"Right through that door," says London.

Trevor opens the door and faces another door.

"Keep going," says London.

He pushes the inner door open to the exact same room, the same couch, bed, and lamps.

"Go look," says London urging him on.

Newspapers are scattered around the narrow space in front of the stove. Some are soaked with urine. A tan puppy races between his legs, then runs a circle around the room.

"He's half lab and half terrier," says London.

"He's yours," says Camille.

London catches the puppy and picks him up. "Look at this, look at the size of his paws. He's going to be a monster." He hands him to Trevor.

The puppy is as firm as a punching bag. His coat is like rabbit's fur. "You didn't have to do this," says Trevor.

London says something about every boy having a dog. Trevor follows them from his room into the courtyard with the puppy licking his cheek. Trevor knows he's just been bought off but feels something come alive inside him, some happiness he didn't know was there.

Late that night, the puppy is whining in the kitchen. Trevor finds his mother in her pajamas at the table with the puppy on her lap. Her eyes are red. She's been crying. He pulls a chair next to her and sits. "We're moving on Saturday," she says.

Black bags for the Goodwill drop box are piled against the cabinets. Already their essentials—pots and pans, dishes, bedding, photo albums, clothes—are stacked in the living room.

Trevor takes the puppy from her.

"What are you going to name him?" she asks.

"Maybe Whizzer. It's a wrestling move Dad taught me. It's used to counter a single leg takedown."

"Whizzer," she smiles. "That's a good name for an untrained puppy." She takes his hand. "I'm taking a chance on Harry London. He's a businessman, but he's not a bad man."

"I don't want this messing with wrestling. I've got to make varsity."

"Last year your father had to talk you into going to practice."

"Because I was a loser."

"No you weren't."

"But I was, I am. Dad would look at me and his chin would wrinkle, and I knew what he was thinking: 'Why is my son on the JV team? Who's this loser?'"

"Trevor, he never thought that. You have that in your head."

"Did you know the JV matches are held in the freshmen gym? There aren't any bleachers in that gym, not even a scoreboard. Instead of a time clock, someone throws a rolled towel on the mats when the periods are over. Dad had to stand with the fathers whose sons couldn't make varsity. JV is for scrubs, and we were treated like scrubs."

"You're father never complained."

"He didn't have to, he'd just look at me."

"He was proud of you. You're a good student."

"But he wanted me to be a good wrestler," says Trevor, his voice choked with disappointment. "A real wrestler."

She puts her arms around him. "Then show him and I'll be there for you." Whizzer licks Trevor's ear. "Who bought him?" he asks.

"I chose him because he looked like he needed love," she says.

"London paid for him?"

"That doesn't matter." She squeezes his thigh.

"Don't you see, London is getting into our lives. That's what this is all about. He likes you."

"He's not as terrible as you make him sound."

"I don't trust him."

"I don't have anyone else to trust."

Her words hurt. He wants to say, *You have me.* "Don't take anything else from him," says Trevor. "What we get from here on, we earn."

Jimmy

POPS RUMBLES UP IN HIS PICKUP AND BRAKES IN FRONT OF THE gym steps. Jimmy, still sweaty from practice, opens the door and hops in. The cab reeks of beer and cigarettes. Elvis's "Blue Christmas" plays on the radio. "Made captain," announces Jimmy.

"Was it unanimous?"

"No, Diggy probably voted for himself and then you've got Bones and Gino."

"Captain Jimmy O'Shea!" Pops's smile shines in the dark truck. "I like that." He punches the headliner of the truck and dust falls like snow. It feels good to make his father smile. "Now all you have to do is win them all and you'll be on your way to the States."

"Geez, Pops, you make it sound like there's nothing to it. I don't even have win number one under my belt."

"Don't worry. You will."

But Jimmy is worried. At his height, he can't pack on muscle and stay 160. Sometimes he feels too skinny, almost breakable. He'd like to explain to Pops that going undefeated again with every wrestler in his weight class gunning for him is going to be intense to the max. Bones called it "Mission-NOT possible." Nick Masters did it, but he was a machine; the perfect height, the perfect weight, a natural.

Jimmy leans back, knowing explaining this to Pops is like trying to tell him to clean up his truck. All Pops knows is Jimmy went undefeated last year, until the States. That's all anyone remembers. Now the team, the school, even Greco expects him to do it again.

They cut through a new development of suburban homes, with three-car garages and brick mailboxes shaped like Egyptian pyramids. Pops slows the truck. "I put the roof on that monstrosity."

Jimmy barely glances at the high-angled roof; instead he pictures a thick muscle-head wrestler waiting on the other side of the mat.

Pops speeds through an industrial park where the air smells like the inside of a new sneaker, then passes the faded sign for Bruney Town. Everyone in Molly Pitcher calls the square mile of identical aluminum-sided houses "Puny Town." The O'Sheas' house is concealed behind overgrown hedges that block the sidewalk.

The house has five rooms, not counting the bathroom and the hall closet. His brother Ricky's bedroom doesn't have a window or a door. They call it "the alcove," but his mother says it still counts as a room, that she "couldn't live in four rooms." She tacked a carpet with camels, pyramids, and obelisks over the opening to give Ricky some privacy. He used to be into King Tut.

Oil stains shine in the street where Jimmy's mother's minivan is usually parked. Pops pulls in the driveway. "Give me a hand with some stuff in the truck."

Jimmy jumps from the truck and heads for their house.

"Don't you dare," yells Pops.

Jimmy whacks the front door open into the wall, sending his mother's framed Bruce Springsteen T-shirt crashing to the top of the television. He picks it up.

"Is it broken?" Ricky's face glows in the television's blue light. He's eating Cocoa Puffs from the box, one hand tapping on his laptop. He's nine, in the fourth grade, a cool little brother, smart and everything, but he stays in the house a lot.

"No." Jimmy hangs it back on the nail.

Pops pushes the door open. "Thanks," he says loudly.

"Don't thank me," says Jimmy. "That's your mess."

"Ricky, where's your mother?" asks Pops.

"I don't know."

Pops puts his hands under Ricky's arms and snatches him off the couch like he's made of twisted pipe cleaners. Face to face, Pops says, "Think!"

Ricky's eyes are wide and white. "She didn't tell me."

"Was she all painted with makeup?"

"Pops, stop." Jimmy wants to grab him. "Please."

Pops goes into his bedroom. Boots hit the wall and his mattress groans. Soon he'll be snoring. "That's the drink talking," says Jimmy.

"I don't like when he picks me up. He's always picking me up. I think he does it to show me he's bigger than me."

"Pretty soon you'll be too heavy. You'll give him a rupture."

"What's a rupture?"

"That's when your balls hit the floor like a B-fifty-four, that's a rupture." Jimmy messes his hair. "Did ya eat?"

Ricky shakes the cereal box.

"Come on. I'll make you something." Jimmy finds a can of spaghetti and meatballs in the kitchen cupboard. He dumps the contents on a plate and sticks it in the microwave. After a minute, he smells the canned sauce. His stomach growls. He checks the refrigerator: pickles, applesauce, ketchup, an ancient-looking Tupperware of mashed potatoes.

On the bottom shelf is a strip of lutefisk. It looks like a slab of bloodless putrefied zombie meat. "I got it for nothing," Pops had said, opening a wax paper package. "It's a Norwegian specialty. You cook it the right way and it's supposed to be delicious." None of the O'Sheas were big fish eaters except their mother, Trish. She found a recipe online and boiled the white gunk. The house stunk like a cat died in a toilet. No one could eat it.

"Ricky, you want some lutefisk?" asks Jimmy.

Ricky grabs his throat as if he's choking.

Jimmy serves his brother a steaming plate of spaghetti. With a butter knife, he chisels a package of hot dogs from the freezer.

"Those are from the Ice Age," says Ricky.

Jimmy melts the freezer frost in the microwave. He tries to read the nutritional chart on the package, but the gluey price tag makes it impossible. "How many calories are in a hot dog?"

Ricky shrugs. "All I know is if you eat a hot dog every day for a year, you'll die."

"Who told you that?"

"Urban legend." He smiles.

They eat under the round ceiling light. Headlights from the highway behind the house flash across the cabinets.

"You made it too hot," says Ricky.

"Wait for it to cool."

"Could you make some toast?"

"You make it," says Jimmy.

Ricky doesn't move. "You still like Roxanne?"

"Yeah."

"I like a girl and she doesn't like me."

"That's because you're too young to like girls. You're supposed to be torturing them."

"Like how?"

"I used to take their hats and run around the playground with them chasing me."

Ricky laughs. "That's dumb. The girls in my class don't even wear hats."

"You could invite her over to do homework," says Jimmy.

"She lives in the new development. The one they built over the sunflower fields."

Jimmy pictures the new development, with winding Belgian-block curbs and juiced-up houses that cost over a million each. "Meet her in the library then."

Ricky bites on his pencil. "I guess I could." He goes back to his social studies book, open on the table. "I don't see why I have to know this," he says. "I mean the Magna Carta happened in twelve-fifteen."

"You mean it happened right after lunch?" asks Jimmy, smiling.

"Yeah, funny, right. So funny I forgot to laugh."

Jimmy finishes his hot dogs and pulls his chair next to his brother's.

"I have to write a full page, actually write it with a pen," says Ricky. "The teacher won't let us print it off the computer." Snores from the rear bedroom make them glance at each other. "I smelled weed from Ma's bedroom today," says Ricky. "She was talking in her baby voice about taking us to Disney." Ricky grunts. "Like we're ever going to go."

Another long snore. Ricky shuts his eyes and starts in on his pencil again.

"Don't worry, Pops is passed out for the night," says Jimmy.

Ricky shakes his head. "He could get up, right?"

Jimmy

A BREEZE RUFFLES THE LEAVES ALONG THE CURB. THE AIR IS CRISP and cold. Jimmy shivers and raises his hoodie. Today at Greco's weigh-in, he was three over. Six-foot two. 163. He spits into the street. He once spit off a quarter pound. If only he could move up to 170. He'd be able to eat. Diggy could take 160, and Trevor would fit right into 152. But Jimmy could lose at 170. One weight class makes all the difference. At 160, Greco says Jimmy's height is an advantage. "You're lean, stripped, and ripped." At 170, he's screwed.

He needs to play it safe. In ninth and tenth grade, his seasons were just above average. Then last season happened. On the mat, there was nothing except the next move, the strength he needed, the possibility of winning. In the battle, he spun, grabbed, twisted, cranked, and listened for the whistle. His father made protein powder concoctions in their blender, mixing skim milk, ice, bananas, and strawberries. And Jimmy grew stronger. His muscles popped like rolls in an oven.

He settles into a jog and tries to imagine his weight melting off his body. Coach Greco says wrestling is cerebral, physical, and strategic. The right weight makes the difference between winning and losing. Jimmy spits.

He jogs into Roxanne's development, named Washington's Crossing, then into her cul-de-sac. Brick towers rise on each side of the driveway, topped by brass carriage lamps with real flames. Her Volvo, square and expensive, reflects the moon.

Jimmy jogs around to the back of her house to a sweeping deck with redwood furniture. He calls her cell phone.

Roxanne lets him in through the kitchen slider. She wears baggy sweats, a soccer shirt with faded numbers, and slippers. She looks fresh from the shower. Her naturally curly hair is wet, almost straight. Roxanne is like one of those American Girl dolls Jimmy's seen in her room, except for a chipped front tooth that happened when she was mountain biking. Her parents want her to fix it, but she says she's keeping it as a souvenir.

The kitchen is as large as his entire house. Copper-bottomed pots hang from a rack above a granite-topped island.

"Who is that?" yells her father.

"Don't tell him I asked you to come over. Act like you just showed up, unexpectedly, okay?" she whispers.

"Am I talking to myself?" calls her father.

"Jimmy," she says, answering him.

"Bring him in here."

"My father doesn't like surprises," she whispers.

Jimmy follows her into the den and faces a humungous flat-screen playing the news. Her father mutes the sound, then gets up off a leather couch. Her mother reclines in an easy chair, pen in hand. Her lap is covered with papers. She's an English teacher at the junior high. Ricky could have her in a couple of years.

"Jimmy," he says, thrusting his hand forward.

"Hi, sir." Mr. Sweetapple's hand is almost mushy. "Hello, Mrs. Sweetapple," he says.

"To what do we owe the pleasure?" She smiles. "I hope nothing's wrong?"

Jimmy glances at Roxanne. "I was running and figured I'd say . . ."

"You do realize this is a school night." Mr. Sweetapple raises his bushy eyebrows.

"Yes."

"Well, then let's not make it too late." He sort of smiles.

Roxanne tugs him from the room, down the hall. "My parents, they're like my private Volturi," she whispers. "They ask me what I'm doing, where I'm going. Why are you wearing that? Who's on the phone? What time are you coming home? Blah, blah, blah, blah, blah, but they already know the answer."

"Volturi?"

"From Twilight, the vampire coven."

"Oh, right." Jimmy only saw the movie. "Maybe they just really care."

"That's what they both say. It's really annoying."

She leads him into a wood-paneled room. The walls are coated with law books and framed degrees. "These are all your father's?" asks Jimmy.

"Yeah, he has a PhD in economics. Sometimes people call and ask for Dr. Sweetapple. It's totally weird." She smiles.

"My father has his PhD in Post Hole Digging."

She laughs, then shuts the door. The floor is covered with photos, pages of stickers, colored paper, and scissors arranged around a large album. "I'm into scrapbooking," she says. "I'm doing our entire senior year."

He is about to kneel and look, but she takes his arm. "No one sees it until it's done, that's my rule." She puckers her lips and kisses him. She smells like strawberry shower gel. "It's not completely safe in here," she breathes in his ear. "I'm not allowed to lock the door."

They share a desk chair. He twists his body until she's half on his lap. Her laptop and schoolbooks are spread across the desk's glass top. "I heard you made captain. Are you going to get it sewn on your jacket?"

"I haven't thought about it."

"You should. I mean, I wouldn't mind showing it off. I know a place that does embroidery. I could get it done and make it our one-month anniversary present."

"Is it one month?"

"Next week." She sprinkles his face with kisses, then gently kisses his mouth. "I guess I should get you something," he says.

"Your jacket is enough." Her cheeks are already red from his shaved face. His leg is falling asleep, but he doesn't care. He goes on kissing her, running his tongue across her chipped front tooth. Roxanne is so soft and delicious.

A door closes somewhere in the house. Roxanne freezes. "You better pull up another chair."

He sits on a low stool next to her.

"I was checking on my early applications," she says, turning on her laptop.

"To college?"

"Yes, to college." She laughs. "Did you apply?"

"Not yet."

"You want to do it?"

"Now?"

"Yes, now. I'll show you."

He presses his lips on her neck. Having her help is like God coming down from heaven and showing him the secrets to the universe. Half of her classes are advanced placement, the other half are honors courses. He's always studied just to earn his B-minus average.

"What's your dream college?" she asks.

"East Stroudsburg," he says.

"Really? Isn't that a Pennsylvania state school?"

"Coach Greco went there. He's writing me a recommendation letter. It's division one wrestling," says Jimmy. "If I can win like I did last season, I'm in." Saying these words out loud makes his stomach feel heavy.

"What major?"

"Physical education."

She smiles. "What are you going to do with a degree in physical education?"

"Teach phys ed and coach."

"Do you know what a teacher makes? Don't you want nice things?"

"What's that supposed to mean?"

"I don't know, like a house with four bedrooms."

He wonders if she's seen his house. "I never thought about it."

"If you're good at math you could major in accounting." She says this like she has it all figured out. "Undergrad, my father majored in accounting."

"Too bad I suck at math." He wants to say that in his family being a gym teacher would be like being elected president.

"I guess all I'm saying is, I wouldn't be able to major in phys ed." She looks at the PhD degree. "But forget it. We can do the entire application tonight and save it. Okay?" She finds the college site and clicks "Applications." They go through all the biographical questions, then read the essay question aloud together:

"Imagine yourself at the end of your freshmen year in college. What do you see? How do people see you? What are you doing?"

"I see my father driving up in his rust-bucket truck," says Jimmy. "Probably drinking a beer."

"Let's make it a BMW and we'll sober him up." Her fingers fly over the keys:

Finally, the end of my freshmen year has arrived. In the distance I spot my father's BMW coming onto the campus.

"How's that?" she asks.

"Cool."

She goes on typing:

By Thanksgiving of my first semester, I was ready to start my wrestling season. I had developed study habits and forced myself to stay in the library until all my college work was completed. Near the holiday break, I looked forward to the next semester.

"See," she says. "It's easy. You just have to give them what they want to hear."

She goes back to the keyboard. In five minutes it's finished. She reads it back to him, ending with:

On the ride home, I tell my father about my professors and how interesting my pre-law classes are. His face glows with pride. I explain that my four years in high school wrestling really paid off. I learned the importance of teamwork and dedication. Wrestling at Stroudsburg enabled me to make the college proud. My father takes my hand

and squeezes it. "It's going to be a great summer," he says.

Jimmy laughs. "Pre-law?" The essay and her efficiency blow him away, but she has taken his ramblings and turned them into something that sounds like some character in a Nickelodeon show. "My father's never held my hand in my life," he says.

"That doesn't matter. It's a college essay, not your life story." She clicks to another website.

"You're going to need a credit card to submit the application," says Roxanne. "You go to this screen, and then you press 'Apply.' It will take you to the cashier and you can add your attachments here." She clicks the mouse and opens a box marked "Your essay here."

No one, not even his guidance counselor at school, had explained how to complete the online application.

She stares into his eyes. "James O'Shea, did I ever tell you I like you?"

He smiles. "Oh yeah, and why's that?"

"You're my work in progress and you're going to look great in a tux," she says, laughing.

"Me, in a tux?"

"The prom," she says. "It's only like four months away."

"I didn't even ask you yet."

"I'm hoping that you do." She kisses him. "Besides, I've already told my parents I'm going with you. You're my decision."

"Would you go with me?" asks Jimmy.

"I'll think about it," she says, then laughs.

They sit on a love seat that faces another flat-screen television. She turns on VH1's "Top 100 Songs of the Nineties." Number 26 is Eminem doing his Slim Shady video. She slides her hands over his back. Her face in the dim light is pink and glowing. He slips his hand beneath her T-shirt. She's not wearing a bra.

The door opens. Jimmy scrambles across the couch.

"We were doing college. . . ." Roxanne's voice drops to a whisper then disappears.

Mr. Sweetapple narrows his eyes on Jimmy. "Let's go, it's late. You can see each other at school tomorrow."

Trevor

A U-Haul truck backs into the driveway, close to the walkway. Trevor watches from the porch rail, knowing in a few hours he will no longer be living in this house. His room will be empty. His window over the yard will be bare. The house is already rented to a couple with no kids. The rent has been raised by $200. None of this seems fair.

London arrives in his pickup truck. He slams the door, then walks straight to the stoop. "Your mother got a call from the police," he says. "Did she tell you someone wrecked your father's truck?" He places his hands on his hips and cocks his head. "The truck is virtually worthless now, good for the junkyard. Do you know anything about it, maybe something you're not telling me?"

"Is it any of your business?" Trevor stares at him.

London grinds his teeth, then pounds across the lawn to the U-Haul.

After a huddle in the driveway, the movers follow London into the house.

Trevor walks Whizzer to the lawn and glances at the

headless deer. His father touched up the deer with paint every year. Now the deer will never be fixed.

A skinny mover clomps down the stoop carrying the television, the trailing wire clicking against each step. They slide the television onto the bed of London's pickup.

"Why isn't that going in the U-Haul?" calls Trevor.

"Everything in the U-Haul is going to auction," says London.

"What?"

"Your rooms are furnished, but I can use the TV as a spare. I'm giving half the money from the auction to your mother and putting the other half toward back rent."

Trevor feels like he's just been struck. The kitchen furniture and Trevor's maple dresser wait to be loaded into the U-Haul. The movers maneuver through the front door with a china closet that once belonged to Trevor's grandmother.

Trevor remembers his father's tools in the garage. Some of the carving chisels and stone-splitting hammers must be a hundred years old. He jogs the driveway and lifts the garage door. He lugs a bucket of tools from under his father's workbench.

His mother is at the back door wrapping a box with tape.

"Mom, we can't leave these," he calls.

She straightens, then shakes her head. "We can't take them."

"I'll put them in my room. I don't care."

"Leave them for now," she says. "We'll figure something out with Harry." Trevor knows it is hopeless. Harry will sell them for back rent. Trevor carries the bucket back. This cannot be happening.

"What about grandpa's trunk?" he calls. The trunk, battered and unpainted, is piled with newspapers in the back of the garage.

Camille shakes her head. "I don't think there's anything in it. Your father was going to have a locksmith look at the lock. He thought the lock might be worth something."

Trevor pushes the newspapers to the floor. The wood is dark from age. The lion-faced lock has a mouth that serves as the keyhole. He tips the trunk one way, then the other. Nothing rolls or bangs around inside. He drags the trunk to the driveway. "It belonged to grandpa," he says.

"But it's filthy." Camille wipes her finger in the dust.

"I'm taking it!" He storms into the back door and karate-kicks the kitchen wall. His foot cracks the plaster. He stares at the shoe-shaped impression and doesn't feel any better. He leans over and grabs his kneecaps with his hands. Nothing here was perfect, but now things are going to be plain wrong. *My father is dead.* The words pummel his brain. *My father is dead. Joe Crow is dead.* After Trevor and his mother leave the house, there'll be no trace of his father.

The puppy jumps on Trevor's leg. London's idea. A spoonful of sugar to make the medicine go down. Trevor kicks a box across the room. Whizzer runs into the living room.

Trevor flips on the lights in the basement. The weight-lifting gym casts a shadow on the cement floor. He slides two forty-five-pound plates on each side of the Olympic-size bar and leans back on the bench press. He can hear his father telling him, "You do back and abs, rest a day, then work chest and biceps."

Trevor lifts the bar off the rack. His last set in this basement, in this house.

Jimmy

JIMMY PACES FROM THE KITCHEN INTO THE FRONT ROOM, remembering the gleaming copper pots in the Sweetapples' kitchen. He stops at the Bruce Springsteen T-shirt under glass. "Ma, you sure this shirt is worth something?" he asks.

"I saw one on eBay for fifty dollars." She sticks her tongue out at him.

He puts his hands up. "Okay."

His mother did the dishes, vacuumed the living room, dusted, sprayed the bathroom with Lysol, and cleaned the kitchen floor on her hands and knees. Jimmy packed as much junk as he could into the pantry and shut the door, but it hardly makes a difference. It's still four rooms and an alcove.

The doorbell sounds just after seven o'clock. Roxanne enters with a big smile, holding a pumpkin pie covered with plastic wrap. "I made this for you." She hands him the pie and pecks him on the cheek.

Jimmy knows he can't have a piece.

"Don't worry, it's low fat," says Roxanne. "I made it with a fat-free crust, egg whites, and I used half the sugar."

"He'll have to keep this away from his brother." Trish takes the pie from Jimmy. "I've heard so much about you," she says.

This isn't true. Jimmy barely spoke of Roxanne.

Trish winks her approval at Jimmy over Roxanne's shoulder. Jimmy takes Roxanne's coat and lays it across the back of his father's recliner. She's wearing embroidered Lucky jeans and a sweater that shows off her flat belly.

"Did Jimmy tell you we finished his college application?" asks Roxanne.

"No, he didn't," says Trish dramatically.

"I was going to tell you," says Jimmy.

"He should be applying to more than one college," says Roxanne. She takes Jimmy's arm.

They sit on the couch that's covered with a brown woven blanket. Trish places a plate of cheese and crackers on the coffee table. "Help yourself," she says.

Roxanne smiles and takes a cracker. She seems to be glowing in the grayish light. "Is that your room?" She takes his hand and pulls him off the couch. "You have to show me."

She goes around his room, lifting his dried piranha fish off his dresser, touching its white teeth, looking at his framed Derek Jeter rookie card that Pops bought him for his tenth birthday. "This is cool," she says, touching his replica of the Trade Center.

"I made it in shop after 9/11," he says.

"I thought it was made in China or something." She laughs. "I mean that as a compliment."

The floor under his window is lined one end to the other with wrestling trophies on marble stands. "You won all these?"

"Yeah, my father and I were supposed to build a shelf. You want to see something else?" He pulls a shoebox from under his bed, then lifts the top. The box is almost filled with gold- and silver-colored medals.

"You should display these." She touches the medals as if they were really gold and silver, then carefully places them back in the box.

"And it all comes down to this season," he says.

"You sound worried." She comes into his arms. She presses against him.

"I just have the preseason dreads."

"You'll be fine." She takes his hand and places it on her sweater over her breast. "Have you ever had a girl in your room?" Her voice is dreamy, but she's smiling.

"Just my mother."

The doorbell buzzes. Jimmy looks over Roxanne's shoulder. "Ma," he calls. "Could you get that?"

"I'm putting the laundry in. Just see who it is."

Jimmy opens the front window drape a few inches. Two

men in suit jackets and loose-fitting neckties wait on the stoop. They are square-shouldered and clean-shaven. One is bald—his head shaved so close the streetlight reflects off it. A dark four-door sedan with no hubcaps and black wall tires is in front of the house. Police. The stolen lumber smashes into his brain. Jimmy feels a line of sweat rising on his spine.

Trish sneaks a quick view of the stoop.

Jimmy backs into the kitchen. He's trying to breathe normally.

"What's the matter?" Roxanne takes his hand.

His mother opens the door. The bald detective is a bull with a thick neck, a large nose and mouth. He's holding up a gold badge. The other detective is young with a dark crew cut. Trish invites them in.

"I'm Detective Barnes," says the bald detective. "This is Detective Santos. We'd like to ask your son a few questions about some missing building supplies."

Roxanne stands next to a cutting board hung on the wall that says "Bless This Mess." Her green eyes flash from Jimmy to the detectives.

"Maybe you should go," whispers Jimmy in her ear. He walks her to the stoop and shuts the door behind them.

"Jimmy, what's this about?"

"I don't know. Just don't tell anyone about the cops being here, okay?" He presses his cheek next to hers.

"You're trembling. Are you in trouble?"

Jimmy takes her hands in his. "Don't worry and don't tell anyone."

"Is it something serious?"

He shakes his head. "I don't know yet. I'll call you later." They hug.

Jimmy takes his place at the table. His hands have turned to ice.

"James, right?" asks Detective Barnes.

"I go by Jimmy."

"You're eighteen?" he asks.

"Next week," says his mother.

"You're a wrestler," he says. "Varsity, right? What weight class?"

"One-sixty."

"That's light for your height. I figured you were heavier."

"Varsity squad for three seasons," says his mother.

"I've seen your son's name in the paper," says Detective Santos. "You have a lot to be proud of."

Detective Barnes writes the date on the top of his pad. He raises his eyes. "Do you help your father on carpentry jobs?"

The question thumps Jimmy like a blow on the head.

"If this is about my husband, why don't you ask him the questions?" His mother's lips flatten on her teeth.

"It's about your husband and your son. They were pulled over with a load of lumber in his truck. Your husband didn't tell you about it?"

"He mentioned it," she says.

"Your husband told the officer that they were on their way to a job site. Jimmy, do you remember that?"

Jimmy swallows.

"Where was that job?" asks Detective Barnes.

Jimmy considers the lies his father told to the policeman. He doesn't want to repeat them.

"Your father was transporting lumber for a job, right?" he asks again.

"Right," agrees Jimmy.

"What did your dad do with the lumber?"

"I don't know. He dropped me home."

Detective Barnes writes something in his pad. "Where did he pick up the lumber?"

"I'm blanking out. I've been starving myself to make weight."

Detective Barnes smiles. "You do remember being pulled over by the marked unit?"

"Marked unit?" repeats Jimmy.

"The police car, the officer?" he asks. "Your dad failed to display a warning flag on the lumber. Do you remember that?"

"I was sleeping through most of it." His palms are soaked. Jimmy wipes them on his jeans.

"Dead to the world, huh? Not according to the officer," says Detective Santos. "He said you looked nervous.

He said he didn't write your father a ticket because he knew you wrestled for the high school and you looked like a good kid."

"He is a good kid," says Trish.

"We're trying to learn what happened that night," says Detective Barnes.

"It's obvious Jimmy doesn't know, or he doesn't remember," she says.

"Nothing is obvious." Detective Barnes leans back and crosses his leg. He places his large hand at the top of his sock and massages his ankle. "I used to work highway patrol," he says. "If I pulled someone over in a stolen vehicle, ninety-nine percent of the time they couldn't keep their story straight because they were lying. They'd try to hand over their driver's license and I'd watch it in their hand, shaking like a leaf."

"What's that supposed to mean?" asks Trish.

"I've heard a lot of stories." He uncrosses his legs and folds his arms.

"Is my son going to be arrested?" she asks. "Don't you have to read him his rights?"

"Whoa, hold on." Detective Barnes raises his palms. "That's TV, this is a simple interview. We're trying to connect the dots. No one is getting arrested, at least not tonight."

At least not tonight! The tiny hairs on Jimmy's arms stand up and he shivers.

"At the same time, you should know, this is a

grand-larceny investigation. A felony. If your son were arrested, he could do time in prison," says Santos. "He could forget wrestling and whatever came after." He looks at Jimmy. "So why don't we start from the beginning?"

"I'd like to talk to a lawyer," says Trish.

"Ending this interview now wouldn't be the best thing for your son," says Santos.

"I'm asking you both nice." She fixes her eyes on Detective Barnes.

"Could we look around?" asks Detective Santos.

Jimmy wants to take a shower, pull his bed covers over his head. He wants them gone from the house.

"Why?" His mother's face is unyielding.

Leave, please leave.

"Well, if you let us take a look around," he says, "we'd be that much further with the investigation."

"No." Trish shakes her head. "It's late, and everyone's tired."

The detectives stand. "What does your husband keep in the shed in the backyard?"

"What does anyone keep in a shed? Stuff."

Detective Santos is looking in an ashtray on top of the stereo cabinet. Jimmy follows his gaze to a joint with his mother's rose lipstick on one end. The detective pokes the joint with his pen. "Who's smoking marijuana?"

His mother holds her hands in front of her face like someone praying. "Oh, come on, that must have been there for six months. We had a party and someone—"

"It's not yours?" Detective Santos asks.

"No," she laughs. "I've got kids here."

"You could get charged for this."

"For one lousy joint? Oh, I get it—if I let you look around, I don't get arrested." Neither detective budges. Trish searches their faces. "Then go ahead and take a look," she says.

"We'll start with the shed," says Detective Barnes, moving toward the back of the house.

"I told you that's my husband's. I can't give you permission for the shed."

"What does he keep in there?"

"It's not my stuff. I don't bother with it. He told me it's off limits."

"Off limits? A shed in your yard is off limits?" Detective Barnes smirks. "We can start with the house if you want, but we will get to the shed eventually. If not today, then someday soon. We could get a warrant."

"I don't think so." She's not blinking. She's almost daring them.

The detectives walk through the rooms and poke their heads in the alcove. They open the closet door.

"Make this easy and get it over with," says Detective Barnes. "All that's left is the shed."

"Enough," says Trish. "We're done."

"Not quite," says Detective Santos. "Flush the joint."

Trish opens her mouth an inch and takes a few short breaths. She grabs the joint from the ashtray and strides into the bathroom. The toilet flushes.

Roxanne's Volvo idles across the street. Jimmy is flooded with relief. She waited for him. He jogs to the car. Roxanne turns the radio off. "Are you all right?"

Should he tell her about stealing the lumber to pay an overdue mortgage, about his mother spending money on pot? That he didn't know his father was a bona fide thief? "I'm okay." He takes her hand. "Thanks for not leaving."

"Jimmy, I know it can't be anything terrible, right?" She brings his hand to her lips and kisses it. Her confidence in him is overwhelming. He wipes his eyes on the shoulder of her coat and buries his face in her honey brown hair. All he wants to do is hold her.

"No, it's not that bad," he says.

"What did they want?" She's wide-eyed and serious. "I mean, if you want to tell me."

Jimmy considers laying it out to her, describing the night moment by moment, the wet earth, the guard, the police lights. He wants to trust her, but should she know? What would she think of him? "It's my father. He's always getting into trouble at work."

She bites her bottom lip, waiting for more.

"I don't even know what it's really about." He tries to smile.

"Is that the truth?"

"Yeah."

She lets go a breath. "Close your eyes."

"Right now?"

"Yes, right now."

He hears some rustling, then something is placed on his lap. "Open," she says.

It's his jacket. Above his name in thread script it says "Captain."

"It's perfect, really, thank you." He didn't buy her a gift.

"Can I wear it?" she asks.

"Of course." She climbs over the bucket seat and almost falls on top of him. He feels her warm body. Her weight. The firmness of her breasts on his chest.

"Move the seat back," she says.

He finds the control and floats the seat back, until she's lying on top of him with their noses touching. Their mouths come together. It is the longest kiss. When they come up, the windows are fogged and the streetlight is blinking on and off.

Diggy

DIGGY COULD HAVE PRACTICED, BUT HIS LIP IS STILL SWOLLEN.
So after warmups he settles on the corner of the wrestling
mat, his Spanish book on his lap, thankful that he's not
sweating to Greco's whistle. Diggy fell behind in Spanish III. Señora Rodriguez is relentless on verb tenses. She
doesn't allow anyone to move to a new tense until they
master the last one. He's stuck on the imperfect. He could
never memorize or concentrate on anything for very long.
Names, dates, and events become tangled in his head like
wrestlers in a giant heap. Words and letters leap around
the page like frogs. In grammar school, he was tutored in
math and English. Diggy once overheard his mother use
the term "learning disability" while she was talking to his
tutor. Afterward he confronted her. She became flustered
and said he was just a slow learner; "You'll outgrow it, don't
worry."

He reads lines in his text: *Yo estaba hablando.* I was
speaking. *Estabamos comiendo.* We were eating. *Estabas ley-
endo un libro.* He closes his textbook. He nods to Jane, who's

lounging in the bleachers across the gym. She nods back. Jane's been watching him for almost the entire practice. She's the team's groupie, sort of an obsessed one-girl wrestling fan club, officially called "manager" by Coach Greco. At matches, she keeps the time clock, the score, and mops blood off the wrestling mat with a rag soaked in Clorox. There were two other girl managers last year. The guys called them the Lemming Sisters because they'd basically run off a cliff if you told them to. Both graduated.

Jane's tall and scrappy, with slim hips, C-cup tits, and abs hard as a wrestler's. She's got dull brown hair that falls past her shoulders. Diggy considers calling her over, but there's this thing about Jane: she's got a birthmark around her right eye, covering half her forehead. It looks as if it could be peeled off like dried Elmer's glue. Even in grammar school, when Diggy lived on the same block as her, she was Jane the Stain.

Jane hops off the bleachers and crosses the wrestling mat in shredded jeans and a tight wrestling T-shirt. "Studying?" She has one of those gargantuan smiles with lots of teeth and gums.

"More like procrastinating."

Guys say Jane's doable, not dateable. According to one story, she snuck into an away wrestling camp and blew half the team. His brother was there but said don't believe everything you hear.

She leans against the padded wall, then slowly slides to

the floor next to him. Her tan thighs show through holes in her jeans. "How's your mouth?"

He pulls down his lip and shows her the gash.

She winces.

"Crow wants my weight class," he says. "Trevor *no es mi amigo*." They watch the practice. Trevor is matched up with a kid named Turkburger, who's about as coordinated as a penguin. Trevor executes a ball and chain move and has Turkburger on his back.

"Crow's weird," says Jane. "Walks around like he's tripping on something. You ever notice that?"

"I guess it's an Indian thing," says Diggy. "You know he sleeps in a teepee?"

"He does?"

Diggy laughs. "Yeah, and he shoots buffalo from the school bus." They watch Trevor tie Turkburger in a human knot.

"Trevor got jacked over the summer," she says.

"Oh, really? I didn't notice." He looks at her cross-eyed.

"You better stop being such a wiseass know-it-all." She squeezes his thigh a few inches above his knee and it tingles all the way up his leg.

Across the mat, Trevor gets in a takedown on Turkburger. It's clean, completely awesome. Trevor never apologized, never said the collision was an accident. Diggy wonders if Trevor will have the balls to challenge him to a wrestle-off.

"So how's living in the Hills?" she asks.

"What?"

"Gateway Hills, what's that like?"

"It sucks, it's great, who cares. It's a place to live."

"It's got to be better than our old neighborhood."

"Better? Maybe quieter, more spacious, but not better."

"You have a pool and a hot tub, right?"

Diggy shrugs. "You know what, no one ever goes in them. All we do is pay all these people to take care of the chemicals, vacuum the pool, cover the pool. Right now there's a sycamore branch sticking out of the pool. Went right through the pool cover. My old man saw it, and do you think he cares? You know what he cares about?"

She shrugs a shoulder.

"Coach Randy has this idea that I can be half as good as my brother."

"I've seen your father at practices. He looks intense."

"Coach Randy thinks he's my 'real' coach. He's not doing it because he's trying to win father of the year. He wants his last name on the Wall again." They look up at the names. Last season, Jimmy O'Shea's name was added as a District and Region winner. Diggy was relieved when Jimmy lost at the State tournament. He didn't need Randy ragging on him about that.

"I wish we could go back to when we were kids just, like, for a week. You ever think about that, when we used to live on the same block?"

"I think about it." Diggy used to ride minibikes with her brothers. They reduced their front lawn to bare earth from circling the house. He considers sneaking out of the gym with her. He watches the wrestlers, waiting for the right moment.

Diggy

In the summer, customers line the parking lot for Mr. Freeze's ice cream and Italian ices. Tonight the outdoor ice cream window is shuttered and locked. Diggy follows Jane's firm little butt through the side door under a plywood cutout of a giant French fry with a long nose and a stupid grin. The restaurant has no customers, which is fine with him. He should take her home now, before he spends any more time and effort, but he has to admit, he wants a girlfriend. He's tired of beating off to his brother's porn stash and more tired of beating off to his father's vintage Penthouse mags in the basement. He even crashed his laptop looking for porn.

Everyone in school thinks he's the master of poon, the Molly Pitcher babe magnet. He's got the face. He's got the attitude. No one would believe he only did it one time with a chubby girl on a pile of coats in an upstairs bedroom at his cousin's engagement party. By the time he lifted her dress and pulled down her panties, he was already half over. He rolled off her and wiped himself on a mink coat. A few weeks later, at his cousin's wedding, the girl approached him on the church's walk and said, "Scope out your aunt Dotty." His aunt was wearing the mink.

Diggy chooses a corner table. A waitress with vampire eyes and poufy hair falling to the side like a ruined soufflé appears from behind the counter. Her turquoise uniform is splattered with mustard. "We're closing soon." She slides menus on the table and fills their water glasses. "You know what you want?"

"A turkey burger, no roll, and a diet Sprite," he says.

"So just the patty?" she asks, squinting.

"Right."

The waitress writes on a small pad. "It comes with fries, you want fries?"

"No."

"Onion rings?"

He shakes his head. He hasn't had an onion ring in this century.

"I'll have his French fries and a vanilla soda," says Jane. The waitress collects the menus. "Be right back."

"This is cool," says Jane. "I like it when it's quiet."

"You eat here a lot?"

"Sometimes with my sister. They have specials."

"I never come here," he says. "I can't eat anything greasy, so what's the point?" In the stark light, her birthmark reminds him of a violet-colored balloon floating across her face.

"I think you're a good wrestler." She places her elbows on the table and folds her fists under her chin.

"My brother was a lot better than me."

"How's he doing?"

"He hurt his back. He had to quit."

"I know that—the whole town knows that."

"He left Iowa State and transferred to Springfield College in Massachusetts. He's a computer science major. He never opened a book and now he's always in the library studying. It's got Randy crazy. He had plans for Nick to go to the Nationals, and then the Olympics." Diggy closes his eyes and sees his father in the dark family room drinking scotch, playing Nick's wrestling tapes over and over. They have stacks of them, marked and categorized. Every match ends the same way: Nick's arm raised in victory.

"I remember Nick's one-hundredth win," says Jane. "There had to be two thousand people in the gym."

The match was moved to Rutgers University. The high school provided bus transportation. "Sometimes I think my brother's better off now. At Iowa State, he was majoring in basket weaving and bowling."

"None of my brothers were into sports. Frank plays guitar. He's in a hillbilly rock band. They call themselves Whiskey Tango. You ever hear of them?"

Diggy shakes his head.

"Whiskey Tango is what the police call the white trash people in this town." She puts her hand to her mouth as if holding a radio head. "I've got a Whiskey Tango pushing a shopping cart on Main Street." They laugh. "I know, it's so lame, right?"

"And your other two brothers?" he asks.

"Willy's into cars. He fixes them and sells them. My oldest brother, Hank, well, you heard about that, right?"

"He got in trouble?" Diggy guesses.

"He's in prison for drugs. It was in the paper."

"For how long?"

"You ever hear of the Federal guidelines? They suck. He has four years left." She looks at the table. "At home, it's me and my little sister, Gloria. She's in the ninth grade."

Gloria's a mini-version of Jane, slim, tall, long neck, pissed-off facial expression, proof that without the birthmark, Jane would have been as pretty as any of the popular girls, even Jimmy's girlfriend.

The food comes. Diggy pokes the small gray burger with his fork. It reminds him of something he's seen on the Discovery Channel. He douses the meat with ketchup. The smell of her French fries drifts across the table. "Have one," she says.

"I can't. Those things are fat bombs."

She smiles and munches another fry. "I went on my mother's diet once. Cigarettes and desserts. I lost ten pounds in a week."

"What desserts did you eat?"

"That was a joke," she says. "I heard it on Comedy

Central. It was a lot funnier."

He's hungry and tastes the burger.

She pokes at her fries. "How is it?"

"Tastes like ass," he says, and she laughs.

"Don't eat it then."

"You don't know how hungry I am."

"Some girls in the school, they think you're, like, totally stuck-up," she says.

"Do you think I care?"

"Absolutely not." She reaches and takes his hand.

"You ever hear anything about me?" she asks.

"Nothing that big." Diggy thinks of the wrestling camp gossip. He tries to picture her taking on half the team and wonders if she would put out for him. She could be his "friend with benefits." Hookups only. He smiles and wipes a spot of ketchup off her chin with his napkin.

Diggy

JANE'S COMPLEX IS BEHIND THE WEEKEND FLEA MARKET, A QUAR-
ter mile of crooked wooden tables and corrugated iron buildings. In grammar school, she worked at a stand behind the gray building selling umbrellas and cheap toys from China. Diggy bought yo-yos and invisible-ink pens as an excuse to say hello to her. Talking to her now reminds him that he always felt comfortable with her. They drive past a group of Mexican teenagers hunched over stingray bikes, wearing bandanas around ball caps that are tugged so low, they bend their ears.

"Don't worry," she says. "They're all a bunch of wank-sters." She waves to one of them and he waves back. They yell something in Spanish, and she yells something back in Spanish.

"What's a wankster?"

"You know, a wannabe gangster."

He finds a spot, gets out, and follows her to the concrete walkway that runs along the front of the apartments. Each steel door has black peel-and-stick numbers. The apartment windows have metal mesh cages over them. In front of apartment 16, a hoodless Saturn's hoses and wires dangle from the engine compartment like an aborted surgery. "My brother's leftover project," she says. "They thought they could make that old four-banger into something." A dead poinsettia, decorated with a red bow, is tipped over on the doorstep. Its branches are stiff and dry. She sets it upright. "It's like a private joke. My mother told me to get rid of it, and I told her to do it herself." She turns her key in the lock and opens the door. He doesn't know what to expect, but he already has a hard-on.

Jane's sister sits cross-legged on the living room carpet playing Xbox.

"That's Gloria," says Jane.

Gloria glances at Diggy. On the television screen a cartoon man in a blue leisure suit with black button eyes approaches a car and drags a driver into a 3-D street.

"Grand Theft Auto?" he asks.

"No, it's Ms. Pac-Man." She smiles.

"She's an annoying little wiseass," says Jane.

"And you suck," says Gloria.

Dishes are piled in the kitchen sink. An unidentified cooking odor hangs in the air. A black cat stretches across the stovetop, his head resting near the handle of a frying pan. "This is Ezra. He was my brother's. He named him after the guitar player in Leftover Smack. They're totally, like, amped, off the hook." She pets the cat. Ezra purrs.

They enter a short wallpapered hall, pass a bathroom, then enter her bedroom. "Sorry, it's a mess." She removes a pile of folded clothes off a chair and places them on her dresser. "My mother doesn't like boys in my room, but she's working tonight and Gloria's cool." Clothes bulge from the closet. A pair of pink pajamas with a cat-paw print is tangled in her rumpled blankets. "Mom gets off at eleven." She raises her thin eyebrows at Diggy. "So, chill."

She unzips her jacket and tosses it on a pile of clothes. Heat is pumping from somewhere. She places her hand on Diggy's jaw, eases him gently toward her, and kisses him. Her mouth is soft and warm and tastes like French fries, which isn't a bad thing. He's sweating and crazy excited. They lean back on the bed. Her hair falls away from her face. The birthmark is the color of a plum, a light plum. Not so bad. He slips his hand between her thighs. He rubs the denim, wondering if he's at the spot he read about in his mother's Cosmopolitan magazine.

She pulls away from him and he's ready to apologize, but she lifts her sweatshirt over her head. She wears a black bra with foam cups. He unsnaps the top button on her jeans. Strings of a red thong ride her hipbones.

"I'm boiling." His cheeks are heated and his mouth dry. "Is it hot in here?"

"We can't control the heat. The landlord cooks us for the entire winter."

His stomach rumbles.

She lifts her hips and pulls down her jeans, so that all that separates his fingers from her is a two-inch-wide thong. His belly makes a noise that sounds like a door closing in a horror movie.

"Are you all right?" Her voice is breathy and distracted.

His throat bubbles. "I feel like I'm gonna heave. That turkey burger." He stumbles from the room. Food is coming up fast. He spins into the bathroom doorway and drops to his knees. Oh, God!

Jane comes to the doorway. She's already dressed. Gloria stands behind her. He waves them away, but they watch as he retches into the toilet. He wipes strings of spit from his mouth and stands.

"Are you okay?" asks Jane.

"Do you have mouthwash?"

She pulls a bottle of blue mouthwash from the medicine cabinet.

Embarrassed, he gargles, feeling weak, but better. "I'm not eating there again."

Gloria backs down the hall toward the kitchen. Diggy follows Jane into her room. The urgency has drained out of him. Part of him wants to go. Part of him hates her for luring him to this room. Now he's screwed either way. If he stays, she'll believe this is more than just a hookup. She might jump right to boyfriend/girlfriend status.

Her vanity table is crowded with makeup and creams. He imagines her looking into the mirror trying to cover the birthmark. She begins picking up her laundry from the floor. Each time she lowers her head, the birthmark darkens to purple, then lightens as she stands.

Her eyes narrow. "You're looking at me funny."

"No I'm not."

"It bothers you, right?" She touches the lower edge of the birthmark.

"I didn't say that."

"But it does."

He can't tell her. Of course it bothers him.

"Believe me, you're not the first guy. I know what those dimwits at school call me." She is a foot from his face. "Jane the Stain, right?"

"You ever see that plastic surgery show on MTV?" he says. "They had a girl with no jaw. . . ."

"Do you really think I'd keep this on my face if I didn't have to?" Her lips are hard, eyes set.

He feels ridiculous and mean. He's living in the Hills with his pool and Jacuzzi and he hurt her already, without trying. "I'm outta here," he says.

"I know you heard the stories about me," she says. "Are you here because you think I'm easy? Is that why you're here? Don't lie."

"What if I am?"

"If you are, then you can leave, because I was drunk. Nothing weird happened."

He doesn't know what to say. She sits on the bed with

tears filling her eyes. "Diggy, I was in the tenth grade. I was the only girl there. The guys had beer in the rooms."

"You don't have to tell me," he says.

"They wanted me to do funnels. To this day, I don't know why I agreed. They put the tube in my mouth." She shakes her head. "I shouldn't have done it. My mother took me to the emergency room and had my stomach pumped." Jane looks up at him. "Then I heard the rumors." Her cheeks are wet with tears.

"Did they, you know?" he asks softly.

"No. Diggy, I swear, nobody raped me, if that's what you're asking." She wipes her tears on her sleeve.

He thinks about her on a bed in a darkened dorm room, boys mocking and cheering.

"Diggy, no one forced me to do anything. I swear nothing really bad happened."

But how could she know? And maybe nothing *really bad* happened, but what happened must have been bad for her all the same.

"I have to make dinner for my sister." She stands and opens the bedroom door.

"I'm sorry," he says. "I'm a jerk."

"You definitely are." She smiles at him.

Before he can stop himself, he leans in and kisses her. Their noses bump. She turns her face, and then it's okay, amazing, a kiss he's thought about a dozen times, but never had the nerve to complete.

He follows her past the kitchen, through the living room.

"Feeling better?" asks Gloria.

Diggy nods. "Bad turkey."

Gloria opens her mouth and sticks out her tongue. "Gross!"

Jane and Diggy step into the night. Music pumps from a Civic with its hatch open. The cool air feels refreshing.

"I always thought you were beautiful," she says.

"Beautiful how?" He feels himself getting hard again.

"Like in every way." She takes his hand. "You can call me," she whispers, moving her face toward his. She slips her tongue in his ear and turns it around, then they are kissing again and he's holding her incredibly hard butt.

He trots to his car. Inside, he releases a breath and starts the engine. What did he just do? She's *Jane the Stain!*

Trevor

IN THE HALLWAY, BOYS STUDY THE PRESEASON MATCHUP BRACK-ets printed on eight-and-a-half-by-eleven paper, taped at the corners with masking tape. Fourteen weight classes, 106 to 285. Today is when Greco gets to see who's for real and who's a skater.

Trevor finds his bracket. Damn! Greco put him at 170, and damn, he pulled Armbrewster.

170-Pound Matchups

Match 1: Trevor Crow vs. Richie Armbrewster

It's insane to think that he can beat Richie Armbrewster. Last year, Armbrewster came in second in the districts, while Trevor had a pathetic JV season. Why would this year be different? He'll be pinned in the first period.

"Hey, Crow, you got lined up with Arm-buster right out of the gate," says Little Gino.

"Awesome," shouts Bones. "We're gonna have ourselves an old-fashioned ass kicking," he says with a country drawl, cracking everyone up.

Trevor shrugs and moves away from the crowd. At the

end of the hall, he pulls his cell from his sweatpants pocket and calls his mother.

"Secret Keepers, can I help you?"

"Mom can you get away for an hour to watch me?" If he loses, she'll be able to give him a ride home. He won't have to wait around like a humiliated loser.

"Honey, we have three rooms that turned over and I've got two check-ins. Harry is fixing a roof leak, so I'm flying solo in the office."

"Flying solo? Is that one of London's stupid expressions?"

"Trevor, I can't talk now."

"When can you talk?"

"This is my first weekend here."

"How's Whizzer?" he asks.

"Harry had to tie him up."

"Why?"

"He was chewing the paneling."

"Tied where?" he asks.

"He's outside the office under the awning. He's fine. He has water and his blanket. Listen, someone's here checking in."

"Mom, I'm wrestling one-seventy." He hears her shuffling papers. "The guy I'm wrestling, he's all sucked down. He probably weighs one-eighty during the week."

"Trevor, just do your best."

"You don't know anything about wrestling!" He clicks

off the phone. He walks to the end of the hall and presses his cheek against the cold window glass. Snow falls softly and is sticking to the grass. He calls his mother back and says he's sorry.

"I know you're under a lot of stress."

"No, I'm not. I just want to win my warmup. That's it." Silence. "And Mom, it's snowing. Bring Whizzer inside."

"Hold on."

He takes a deep breath. She's talking to someone in her phony cheerful work voice. He watches the snow blow across the parking lot.

"Okay, I'm back," she says.

"Just let Whizzer in, okay?" He doesn't care that he sounds annoyed as hell.

"You're right, I will. Honey, don't get hurt. Okay? That's the most important thing. Good luck, love you."

Luck? Wrestling has nothing to do with luck. His father never wished him luck. Wrestling is skill, strength, and determination, even courage, not luck.

Diggy struts up with his headgear hanging from a shoulder loop on his pulled-down singlet. His T-shirt says "Pinners are Winners."

"How's the lip?" asks Trevor.

"Healed. The mouth heals about three times as fast as the rest of your body." He looks up the hall, then at the posted matchups. "You're going one-seventy today. I'm glad you wised up. I told you there can only be one wrestler at one-fifty-two and everyone on the team wants me to be it."

"Today doesn't count against my record," says Trevor. "I don't mind wrestling one-seventy."

"You don't mind." Diggy smirks. "That's funny. You don't have a choice. Greco set this up. You're the one-seventy wrestler so suck it up."

"I may have to wrestle you off," says Trevor. "It's my senior year too."

"My dad's already contacted some of the big wrestling colleges. Do you think they're interested in me because I'm Thomas Edison splitting atoms?"

"Edison?"

"Whoever the dickhead is." Diggy turns, then stops. "You know what your problem is, Crow? You think that someone owes you something. You think that because your dad died, everyone is going to treat you different. Well, count me out. Do whatever you have to do, call on some of your Indian spirits, I don't care."

"Keep your mouth shut about that." Trevor's heart rages in his chest. He places his palm flat on Diggy's chest.

Diggy's eyes soften. "Forget it. You're not worth it. You're always going to be the no-friends weirdo." He stares into Trevor's eyes. "Right?"

"Get out of my face."

Diggy wiggles away. "Let's just wrestle today." He extends his hand. Trevor automatically goes to shake it. Diggy pulls it away. "Sucker," he says in a singsong voice.

* * *

The team forms two lines into a clap tunnel. Diggy charges through the Minute Men, slapping five with everyone.

Kevin O'Malley waits on the other side of the mat. Trevor heard Greco tell Diggy "not to take him lightly."

Diggy shakes O'Malley's hand. The ref sounds the whistle. It's on.

Diggy starts his normal routine. Hand tap, move. Hand tap, move. Trevor's suffered through it in practice. Diggy strikes O'Malley's head and face again and again. Diggy pushes O'Malley's head, slaps at it, paws it, then dances away. Diggy continues the punishment, until the referee blows his whistle and holds his fist up, issuing Diggy a caution.

Trevor knows it's all strategy. Diggy is blowing O'Malley's game plan. The ref sounds his whistle, restarting the match. O'Malley is wild with frustration. He leads with his arms, trying to grab Diggy's head and shoulders. Diggy shoots in and under for a two-point take down. The match continues like that, Diggy stepping away, O'Malley off balance, struggling for a point.

Diggy wins, six to two. The applause is subdued. Diggy's father smacks a newspaper in his hand. He comes down from the stands and rubs Diggy's shoulder. Diggy pulls away and points back at the stands.

Jimmy's up next.

Trevor finds a team chair next to Pancakes. "I give that

guy eighty seconds," says Pancakes.

Jimmy steps to the center of the mat. Mr. O'Shea and a few of the Minute Men Varsity Dads clap loudly. Jimmy's wrestling Bobby Longo. Trevor's seen him before. He's hardcore. One knot of muscle from shoulders to calves.

At the whistle, Jimmy attacks like a praying mantis with quick stabs of his hands, trying to get a good hold on Longo. Jimmy comes in low. Longo's sprawl is too late. Jimmy has a double-leg takedown. Two points.

"You see?" says Pancakes.

Jimmy "throws legs," winding his legs around Bobby Longo's legs. Jimmy extends and holds tight to Longo's shoulders, stretching him like he's on a medieval torturer's rack. Jimmy wedges his arm under Longo's elbow, then reaches and grips Longo's neck, achieving a solid half nelson. He makes it all look easy, like it's something that needs to be done quickly, without fanfare.

Jimmy tests his weight on both sides of Longo's back by flipping his legs to one side then the other, then begins cranking the half nelson by walking his legs around in a flat circle. Longo's face clenches in pain and resentment. It's like watching a snake squeeze a mouse. No escape. Jimmy flips him to his back and immediately goes for the pin.

"Lift the head," yells Greco.

Trevor stands. Everyone is screaming. Jimmy slips his arm through Longo's leg and his other arm around his neck. It's pin time. Longo is trapped in a cradle.

Students stomp their feet. "Pin him," can be heard all over the gym.

Bobby Longo struggles, twists under Jimmy's weight. The referee scrambles around the mat on his stomach, trying to get into position to see Longo's shoulder blades. The referee slaps the mat. Pin. Jimmy springs to his feet. He struts to the center of the mat, shoulders back, chest out. Jimmy shakes Longo's hand. The referee raises Jimmy's arm in victory.

"Seventy-five seconds," says Pancakes, smiling. "You owe me a Coke."

"We didn't bet."

"Yeah, we did," he says with the same stupid smile.

Trevor glances across the gym at Armbrewster, who's skipping rope like a prizefighter.

"You got Armbrewster." Pancakes shrugs. "I saw him lose once when he was in the fourth grade. So, it can be done." Pancakes cracks himself up.

"He looks bigger," says Trevor.

"He is. Last year, he wrestled one-sixty."

"Okay, Crow, show us what you got," shouts Greco.

Trevor reaches for his toes, stretching one last time, then jogs through his teammates' clap tunnel. "Crow, Crow, Crow," they chant.

On the mat, he skips in place like Jimmy had done. The crowd is quiet. Armbrewster jogs onto the mat. Trevor pictures him at weigh-ins towering over the other wrestlers. Trevor needs to stop thinking, needs to relax. His heart pounds.

"Feed him to the lions," yells someone from the other team.

"A stack of bricks," yells Jimmy. "You're a stack of bricks!"

The referee signals them to the line. The whistle blares. Trevor circles, then shoots under Armbrewster's arms toward his legs, but instead of clasping the legs, Trevor remembers the Fireman's carry and seizes Armbrewster's arm with one hand and thrusts his hand between Armbrewster's legs. Trevor drops to his knees and throws Armbrewster over his shoulder to his back. It's quick, and Trevor can't believe it worked. Suddenly he's in pinning position, chest on chest, with Armbrewster struggling, arching. Trevor locks his arms around Armbrewster's neck and squeezes.

Armbrewster struggles, arches high with his head and feet on the mat. Trevor hangs on with his bicep crushing Armbrewster's face. Trevor's not letting go. He's riding a wild animal, but he's got him. Armbrewster is pushing himself out of bounds. Trevor sees the line and tightens his grip around Armbrewster's arm and neck.

Armbrewster flips and hurls Trevor almost to the center of the mat. The power is shocking. Trevor hangs on, but now he's on his back with Armbrewster crushing him!

106

Trevor struggles, rocking his shoulders. Armbrewster's rough beard scratches Trevor's forehead. Armbrewster's stale breath is in Trevor's nostrils. Armbrewster powers down for a pin.

Everyone is cheering. The Minute Men leap in the air screaming. Trevor can't arch, can't move. He glances to the clock, thirty seconds left.

Then, it's over. Pinned. Armbrewster runs to the side of the mat for high fives from his team. Trevor rises slowly. He stumbles off the mat in half a daze.

Trevor

THE LATE BUS LETS TREVOR OFF AT THE SIDE OF THE HIGHWAY, past the motel's sign, blazing with new light bulbs. He carries his wrestling bag and books into the parking lot. His room door is wide-open. He enters and tosses his stuff onto the old trunk. His mother and London are looking at a hole, about six inches wide, scratched through the sheetrock wall. Chewed plaster lies on the carpet.

"You're going to have to train your dog," says London sternly. "I'm planning to sell this place someday, and I'm working on a margin, a thin margin. You get what I'm saying?"

Trevor ignores him and turns to his mother. "What are you doing in here and where's Whizzer?"

She frowns.

"You see this?" London moves the drapes off the windowsill. "The molding is gnawed. Who's going to fix this? Me, that's who."

"You just come into my room, uninvited?" asks Trevor.

"Trevor, I opened the door," explains his mother.

"Whizzer was barking."

Trevor glances toward the courtyard. "Where is he?"

"If he can't be in this room unsupervised, then he'll have to be outside." London drops the drapes.

"What did you do with him?" demands Trevor.

"He's fine," says his mother.

"Where is he?" Frustration rises into his throat.

"In the lot, out back," says London. "Tied up."

Trevor runs down an alleyway to an empty asphalt field dotted with stiff straw-colored weeds and broken glass. He looks toward the road and the streaming head-lights. Whizzer is chained to a fence post at the corner of the building. He stands alert, attentive, straining on his chain as if hoping someone will take him home. Trevor unhooks the chain from his leather collar. He carries his puppy back toward his room. Whizzer licks his face. His nose is ice cold.

Trevor pushes the door open. "I don't want him chained like that!"

"He was perfectly fine," says London. "Dogs like fresh air."

"You're full of it," says Trevor.

"He's half Lab," says London. "He doesn't mind the cold. Feel his coat." London tries to touch Whizzer.

Trevor stiffens and backs away.

"You're making a big deal out of nothing," says London.

"Maybe I am," he says. "But you gave him to me. He's

mine, and I don't want him chained outside."

"Trevor," says his mother. "Harry didn't mean any harm."

"Mom, can't you for once take my side?"

"I can't have him ripping this room apart," says London. "And your mother can't be in here all day."

Trevor wants to scream. He sits on his bed and raises his eyes to the rusted exposed pipes. Whizzer continues to lick his neck and face.

London puts his hand on Trevor's shoulder.

"Get off me." Trevor shrugs him off.

"You're not going to wake up one day and discover Whizzer knows how to do everything," says London. "It won't happen. Dogs don't work like people." He looks around his room until his eyes settle on a puddle of pee that missed the newspapers spread on the floor.

"I'll clean that up," says Trevor.

"Let me show you something." He snatches Whizzer by the neck. Whizzer's nails scrape on the peel-and-stick tile. London presses Whizzer's nose into the urine. "No!" he shouts.

"Harry, that's enough," says Camille.

"I'm showing Trevor something. If a puppy wets off the paper, you've got to rub his nose in it, otherwise he thinks my motel is his toilet."

"Just keep your hands off him." Trevor pushes London and seizes Whizzer by the neck, snatching him from

London. They lock eyes. Trevor's heart somersaults in his chest.

"That's enough," shouts Camille. "Enough."

"Dogs are animals, that's all I was trying to teach the boy." London's face is red and he's huffing.

"Leave." Trevor holds Whizzer tightly. "You too, Mom."

"I can't have him pissing and ripping apart my motel!"

"Come on, Harry, that's enough for tonight," says Camille. "Whizzer is a smart dog, he'll learn." She takes his arm and they step out of the room.

Trevor closes the door. He looks around his jail cell, his own personal rat-hole motel room. He wants to punch the wall.

Diggy

RICKY O'SHEA IS PERCHED ON THE CONSOLE, BETWEEN THE front seats of the minivan, bouncing like a bag of groceries. Diggy's sitting in a captain's chair in the back seat. Jimmy's kneeling on the floor. Trevor Crow is in the other seat, with Little Gino on his lap. Bones is squished in the rear compartment under the hatch. Jimmy's father is driving like a nut, frogging lanes, riding every car's ass. Jimmy's mother has one hand on the dashboard and the other across Ricky.

"The early bird special is over at five-thirty and it's five-twenty," says Mr. O'Shea. "I'm not paying eleven bucks for chicken parm." He presses the gas. "Not for these savages."

"If we have an accident on the way there, we're not going to eat anything," says Mrs. O'Shea. Steadying his phone, Diggy reads another text message from Jane. In the past hour, she's sent him six texts. He didn't text back. He presses through them:

Text 1: **Dig where r u? want to hang tonight? i get off at 8:30**

Text 2: **movies then TGIFs**

Text 3: **TGIFs has ½ priced appetizers tonight**

Text 4: **u alright**

Text 5: **do u want me to call u at home**

Text 6: **if u don't want to go to the movies, tell me**

The movies on a Saturday night? Every dating couple in the high school will be there. People will be looking at her face. He's not ready to go public yet. He likes her, yet when he's with her, he feels messed up, buzzed, and weird, all at the same time.

Every evening for the past week, Diggy stopped at Jane's apartment after practice. He told his mother he was doing a class project. They played backgammon or rummy in the front room with the television on MTV. They made out and joked around while her sister did homework at the kitchen table and her mother drank white wine and talked on the phone. Jane made fat-free microwave popcorn and cut celery and carrot sticks for him. In her room, they kissed and did some serious DH-ing—that's what she calls dry humping. Then, it happened. They had their clothes off and they went all the way. After, he was lying next to her covered in sweat, thinking this is what it's supposed to be like.

"Jimmy, where are we going, anyway?" asks Diggy.

"The Naples."

"For real?" asks Diggy.

"What's the matter, you don't want to see Jane?" says Gino.

"Jane the Stain, yo," yucks Bones. Everyone cracks up.

Diggy reaches over the seat and punches Bones in the head. Bones puts Diggy in a chokehold.

"Now stop it!" yells Mrs. O'Shea.

Diggy wonders what it would be like to have Jimmy's mother. As far as moms go, Mrs. O'Shea is the double bomb. So cool and real. No makeup. No beauty parlor hairdo. No maids necessary. Not like his mother. She never leaves her bedroom without two layers of lipstick and a mushroom cloud of hairspray around her head.

"Hold on, I'm hanging a U-ee!" Mr. O'Shea makes a u-turn, sending all of them into a heap. The car swerves. A driver, eyes popping, whizzes by, flipping the bird. Everyone is laughing. Diggy extracts Jimmy's bony shoulder from his side. Finally Mr. O'Shea straightens the car and hangs a quick left into the Patriot Shopping Center.

"Artie, what the hell do you call that?" yells Mrs. O'Shea.

Naples Pizza is slotted between the Protein Punch Juice Bar and the Sew Clean Laundry. Diggy stares at the red curtains and the menu scrawled on the window, wishing he'd stayed home. They've come here to celebrate Jimmy's birthday. What's the big deal? He's eighteen, can't drink legally, doesn't have a car, and probably will be pumping Regular at the Shell across the street in a year. Diggy will be eighteen on January 8th. Elvis's birthday. Nixon's birthday. One drug addict. One liar.

Everyone piles from the car like clowns in a circus. Mr. O'Shea leads the pack across the parking lot.

The place is practically empty, except for Roxanne, who must have parked behind the restaurant so she wouldn't ruin the surprise. She's wearing Jimmy's varsity jacket, all hyped up, shrieking like an eight-year-old at her first sleep over. She holds a gift bag over her wrist, the ones with the little nylon rope handles. "Omigod! Are you surprised? Are you?" she asks. Jimmy plays along, acting astonished by shaking his head. They touch lips and hold hands. The thing Diggy hates about Roxanne is she's too cute. She's like a stuffed poodle you win on the boardwalk. All bright and perfect.

Jane's clearing dishes from a table. She wears a short top, hip-hugger blue jeans, and an unbuttoned red waitress jacket. Roxanne and the guys follow Jimmy's parents past the counter toward the rear dining room. Tables are set with tablecloths, red napkins, and vases with cloth flowers.

Diggy meets Jane's eye. Her smile spreads across the room. She winds through everyone and gives him a hug. "Diggy! I don't believe this. What are you doing here? I texted you like five times in the past hour." She kisses him on the lips.

He's like a ventriloquist's dummy without a hand up its ass, dead and playing dumb. He neither kisses her back, nor pulls away.

She backs off. "What's wrong?"

Jimmy, Trevor, Bones, and Gino wait with their jaws dropped open. Diggy knows he owes Jane. He was with Jane last night, all over her, and he wants to continue being with her. He's trapped. He raises his palms to the guys as if to show them he's not hiding anything and remembers a line he's heard Randy say. "Must be my new cologne." He grins like he's too cool.

Confused, her eyes go from Diggy's grin to Little Gino's, Bones's, Jimmy's, and Trevor's. Splotches of pink appear on her checks and her birthmark deepens. They are all waiting for her to slap his face or curse him out. She grabs a stack of stiff menus and heads to the back of the restaurant with Jimmy's parents following.

"What's up with that?" asks Jimmy.

"Nothing." Diggy cracks his neck, one side to the other.

"That's not nothing," says Jimmy.

"Come on, what's up with that, yo?" Bones shoves him. "You must be hitting that butter face."

Diggy stiffens at the description and draws in a breath. "No, she just likes me."

"I'm talking to the Dig Master General," says Bones. "You're telling me she lip-locks you like you just got back from the war, and she just likes you?"

"That's what I'm saying." He grins, hoping to end it.

"Jimmy, do you get this?" asks Bones. "He's got to be doing her."

"That was some kiss," says Trevor.

"Yo, Chief Sitting Bullshit, butt out," snaps Diggy. "Your dog face never had a first kiss."

"Chief?" asks Trevor. "I told you about that." He pushes Diggy in the chest. Diggy could knee him in the balls, but takes it. He's not going to throw down here at Jimmy's party.

"Trevor, cool it," says Jimmy. "Everyone, cool it."

Diggy follows the guys to the table. Stone-faced, Jane flings the menus at the wrestlers, then strides through the swinging kitchen doors. Mrs. O'Shea plops her leather pocketbook on the table.

Mr. O'Shea removes his jacket, revealing a "Molly Pitcher Raceway" T-shirt with a dragster kicking up dust across his chest. He leans in next to Diggy. "I've got to give you credit," he says in a whisper. "When I was your age, all I wanted was the prom queen type, and I never got any."

"I'm not dating her," Diggy exclaims. "And what's that supposed to mean?"

"Well, hooking up or whatever you call it."

"Mr. O'Shea, with all due respect for you and every-thing, don't assume that about her, okay? Because it's not true."

Trevor has taken off his denim jacket. All he's wearing is a black wifebeater. In December! What a first-class jerk. He's beyond pathetic.

"Trevor, you're as big as the Hulk," says Mrs. O'Shea.

Diggy has to admit, Trevor is jacked to the max.

"Green teeth and all," says Jimmy. They laugh.

Mr. O'Shea grabs Jimmy around the neck. "When I was eighteen, my father took me to a bar."

"And they had no trouble finding one," says Mrs. O'Shea.

Mr. O'Shea kisses her neck. She grabs his face, moves it away, then she kisses him on the mouth. Ricky sticks his finger in his mouth as if he's going to barf. But Diggy thinks it's kinda sweet. Last time he knew his parents touched was when they conceived him.

Diggy doesn't bother following the conversation. He's too busy watching for Jane, waiting for some eye contact. He owes her an apology. Yet he's not at all ready to announce that they hooked up.

Jane comes to the table holding her pen and order pad. "Technically, I'm not supposed to offer the special in its last fifteen minutes. And Trevor, technically, you're supposed to have on a shirt with sleeves."

"He's got to show off his muscles." Jimmy punches Trevor in the arm.

"But I'll let it slide," says Jane.

Mr. O'Shea has his paper bag on the floor beneath his chair. He rummages around it and removes a can of beer, then a wine cooler for the Mrs.

The Early Bird has three choices: chicken parm, shrimp parm, and spaghetti and meatball; in parenthesis it says "one meatball." Everyone goes for the chicken parm without the cheese, except for Roxanne. She orders the house salad that's not one of the specials and doesn't come with a soda.

Jane scribbles all of this on her pad.

"And garlic knots." Mr. O'Shea smiles. "How's that sound?"

Everyone groans. "What are they," asks Bones, "a billion calories each?"

Jane raises a menu to her face and mouths "bastard" to Diggy, then goes to the kitchen.

"I'd like to make a toast," says Roxanne. "To Jimmy." They raise their glasses. "To the sweetest guy. Happy Birthday."

What a suck-ass toast. Diggy can't imagine Jane saying anything that lame. Everyone touches glasses.

Jimmy opens Roxanne's gift bag and pulls out a tiny teddy bear wearing a red wrestling singlet and headgear. Mrs. O'Shea goes on about it being "so, so cute." Diggy thinks it's about the stupidest gift he's ever seen.

"The team is going to have a good year," says Mr. O'Shea. "All we need is Trevor at one-seventy." Everyone's eyes go to Trevor.

"Don't look at me," he says. "You saw what happened to me at one-seventy."

"But that's all that's open," says Diggy.

"It's too heavy. I was one-fifty-two this morning."

"You had Richie Armbrewster on his back, didn't you?" asks Diggy.

"I can make one-fifty-two without trying and you're starving yourself. There's something wrong with this picture." Trevor looks around the table. "Besides, my chances are a lot better at one-fifty-two."

"Are you saying you're going wrestle me off?" asks Diggy.

"Are you saying that, yo?" Bones leans forward.

"Hey, come on," says Mrs. O'Shea. "Easy, let's leave it for the coach." She puts her hand on Trevor's bare shoulder. "He's not saying that."

"Well, then what is he saying?" Diggy wants an answer, now, in front of everyone. "Trevor, you couldn't even make varsity last year. You get lucky with that fireman's carry and now you're talking smack about taking my spot." Diggy wants some support. The guys nod at him.

"It's like a brotherhood respect thing," says Bones. "Diggy wrestled varsity at one-fifty-two last year. Right, yo?"

Hearing this makes Diggy smile inside.

"Besides," says Bones, "Trevor, you're going to be awesome at one-seventy. You can eat all you want and keep packing on the muscle."

Everyone waits for Trevor to say something. He stares at the tablecloth.

"You see," says Diggy. "All the weight classes are set. I told you before, I have the one-fifty-two spot."

"But you're more like one-sixty-five," says Trevor.

"How do you know?" asks Diggy.

"How many days did you starve yourself?" asks Trevor.

"That's not your business." Diggy hasn't eaten anything but two apples and baked chicken breasts for two days. Last night, Randy took him to their county club. They sat in the sauna until Diggy almost blacked out.

"You could wrestle one-seventy easier than I could," says Trevor. "You'll be one-seventy when we leave here tonight."

"Oh, snap," says Gino.

"How can you talk about anything? Last season you were a scrub. Then you knee me in the face." Diggy points his finger across the table. "You've got to earn your spot. You wrestle like somebody doing a bad robot." Diggy stares defiantly at Trevor. "Am I right?" No one says anything. "You better start eating, because I'm not giving up my weight class."

Bones whispers a chant, "Wrestle-off, wrestle-off," and the guys join in. "Wrestle-off, wrestle-off."

"Cut it," says Mr. O'Shea.

"Trevor, you definitely have gotten bigger," says Mrs. O'Shea. "You could probably handle one-seventy."

"You might as well start eating," Diggy says. "No one is going to survive a wrestle-off against me."

"I used to have a gym in my basement," says Trevor, ignoring Diggy. "I couldn't bring the weights when we moved."

"How is that working out?" asks Mrs. O'Shea. "I see that they're doing work on the motel."

"I'm getting used to it," says Trevor.

Jane brings two loaves of hot bread, a basket of garlic knots, and a dish of butter pats.

"Get the butter off the table," yells Jimmy.

Jane picks it up.

"He can't resist butter," says Mrs. O'Shea.

The garlic smells so good. Diggy grabs a hunk of bread.

Mr. O'Shea shoves garlic knots inside his cheeks. "My imitation of Jimmy getting his wisdom teeth pulled." He frowns. "Ma, it hurts. Ma, it stings."

Jimmy punches his father in the arm.

Mr. O'Shea laughs so hard he spits the garlic knots into his napkin.

"Honey, act respectable." Mrs. O'Shea pats her husband's hand.

Everyone is ha-ha-ing their asses off. Everyone except Diggy. He's watching Trevor, burning his eyes into his skull, hoping he realizes a wrestle-off is a major disrespect. A bitch slap. Trevor's announcing, *I'm going to take your weight class.*

Jane sets the food on a stand and serves the steaming dishes of pasta. Diggy only has half a chicken cutlet on his plate. The guys have two each. Jane gives him a defiant stare and whispers, "Choke on it."

They begin hoovering up their meals as if they haven't eaten in a week, which in Diggy's case is almost true. He shouldn't be eating, but he can't stop. Besides, it's a special occasion.

Jane moves around the table, filling water glasses. She's good at her job. Diggy's never had a job, not even something part time. It has always been wrestling.

When Diggy comes up for air from his chicken, Jane is holding the kitchen door open, pointing toward the rear of the pizza parlor. His phone buzzes with a text.

Text 7: **Meet me—bathrooms**

Jane leaves the kitchen and walks by without glancing at Diggy or the table. Ricky is left holding up his empty soda glass. Diggy counts to ten, then gets up. "Gotta drain," he says.

She's standing next to the ladies' room. "Must be my new cologne?"

"That was stupid."

"You're just like all the rest of the cocksuckers. Why did I think you'd be different?" Hurt simmers in her eyes.

"You're making a big deal out of nothing."

"Oh, am I? You've been at my house like every night this week."

Shame rises from his half-full stomach.

"In my bed."

"I'm sorry," he says.

"You don't have to be sorry," she says. "I know it's not

all your fault. I know I'm *Jane the Stain*." A single tear rolls down her cheek.

"I never had a real girlfriend," he says. "I'm not good at it. I didn't know if we were, you know, really going out."

"You mean, or just hooking up?"

He searches for a plausible excuse. "When you kissed me in front of the guys, I was, you know, like, shocked, that's all. It had nothing to do with you."

"Really?"

"I swear."

She wipes her eyes with her palms. "Shut up and kiss me."

He puts his arms around her and looks into her eyes. Maybe he could date her. The guys would have to get used to it. The bathroom door swings open. The light shines across Jane's face and all he can see is her purple birthmark.

Diggy

TODAY IS THE FIRST WRESTLE-OFF OF THE SEASON. DIGGY MASters vs. Trevor Crow. It's going to be a war. Diggy sucked weight to 156. Four pounds to go. A couple of Ex-Lax and that will be gone too. His stomach is tearing him apart, begging for food. If he loses today . . . Diggy smacks himself in the head. He can't lose. There is no losing.

Jimmy is on the center of the mat working with Trevor, showing him how to bend from his hips. Trevor takes his stance in front of Jimmy, lowers himself by bending his knees. He shoots and wraps his arms around Jimmy, lifting him off the mat.

"Jim, can I talk to you?" asks Diggy.

"Sure." Jimmy follows Diggy to the pull-up bars.

"What are you doing?"

A bead of sweat rolls from Jimmy's crew cut. "You mean with Trevor?"

"No, with Pocahontas."

"I was showing him—"

Diggy tries to laugh. "Believe me, nothing's going to

make any difference. I'm not going to go easy on him."

"He doesn't expect you to."

"What's that supposed to mean?"

"You should do the team a favor and move up," says Jimmy.

"How am I going to move up? You've got one-sixty."

"You'll have a better chance at winning at one-seventy than Trevor. He's never been on varsity."

"Jimmy, come off it. You know my record at one-fifty-two. I'm just about unbeatable. Why should I risk going to one-seventy?"

"Then you could eat."

Diggy juts out his chest and chin. "You've been at one-sixty for how long, since the tenth grade? Why don't you wrestle one-seventy?"

"You're not your brother," says Jimmy. "You can't expect to win them all."

Diggy wants to hit him so bad.

"Diggy! Get over here." It's Greco. He's standing next to his office.

"I thought you'd have some loyalty," says Diggy to Jimmy.

"I do," says Jimmy. "Loyalty to the team."

Greco closes the door and pulls the shade over the window, blocking the view of the mats and the main entrance. Diggy's eyes roam over the posters of beefy wrestlers and their captions: "They call it obsession. I call it dedication," and "Train to near death, rest, repeat." One book is on the desk, the same one that's always there: *The Winners Manual*, by Jim Tressel.

"Sit down," says Greco.

Diggy perches on the edge of a chrome-legged bucket chair. Last time he was in here, Greco lectured him about throwing his headgear at an opponent.

"What was that with Jimmy?" asks Greco.

"Nothing."

"What's your weight?"

Diggy folds his arms across his chest. "I'm almost there."

"I didn't ask you that."

"One-fifty-four," lies Diggy.

Greco heaves a sigh. "Did you ever think that winning matches is a short-term goal?"

Diggy groans. "No."

"What do you want from wrestling?"

"To win, to get a scholarship."

"How about getting prepared mentally and physically for life? How about becoming a good sport? How about leaving this program in better condition and a better person?"

Diggy raises his eyebrows. "Yeah, right."

Greco leans back in his chair. "I've been coaching ten years. I've had two wrestlers go to college on a full scholarship. One quit his freshmen year because he couldn't keep his grades up. One was your brother. Ten years, thirty wrestlers a year. Two out of three hundred."

"Coach, are you telling me that I'm not going to get a scholarship?"

Greco hesitates. "I'd like you to take one-seventy. I think you'll be as effective and it will give your body a chance to grow stronger."

"I knew it." Diggy leans forward, anger rising in his chest. "You think Randy's going to agree?"

"I think this should be our decision."

Diggy smiles.

Greco reaches over the desk and grabs his arm. "Come on, Diggy, cut the crap. I need someone at one-seventy or we forfeit the weight class. I have two wrestlers at one-fifty-two, you and Trevor. I think you're the one to move up."

"You mean I'm supposed to volunteer?"

"I'd cancel the wrestle-off. You build on your current weight."

"Everyone would think I wimped." Diggy stands.

"I'd rather settle this without a wrestle-off," says Greco. "I think it's better for morale."

"Morale? This was never about morale. It's about Trevor. You feel sorry for him. Well, I don't, and I'm not jumping two weight classes." The room is quiet. Greco's face reddens. Diggy pulls the door open and flees into the gym. Randy is standing next to the emergency entrance.

128

His hair is gelled. His face is all business.

Diggy trots over and spurts, "Greco just tried to talk me into going to one-seventy."

"What?"

"Trevor Crow is one-fifty and . . ." Diggy doesn't finish his sentence. With his shoulders hunched and his chin protruding like a hood ornament, Randy beelines across the red wrestling mats. His black leather shoes make perfect impressions, then disappear.

Greco lets his whistle fall from his lips.

Randy points his finger in Greco's face. "My son is not going up two weight classes for anyone. It's that simple. He'll pin that kid." His voice echoes off the rafters. Wrestlers freeze and turn to watch.

Greco pushes Randy's finger away from his face. "Off the mat!" orders Greco. "This is MY gym right now."

"My son might be on your team, but he's my responsibility!"

"Off the mat!"

Randy drops his shoulders. He crosses back to the emergency doors.

"You're an asshole," says Diggy with his eyes on the floor. "Please, go back to work, or home, just get out of here."

"No, you go wrestle like a Masters and there won't be a problem."

* * *

At Greco's whistle, Diggy steps forward in a staggered stance, head upright, knees bent, arms dangling like a hyperactive raptor he's seen on Animal Planet. He leans right, feints left. Trevor stalks him, flatfooted and deliberate. His muscles knot under his tan skin. Diggy smacks Trevor's head. He needs to get on the inside. He tries another head smack. Trevor snags his fingers and squeezes them tight.

Diggy pulls back, momentarily off balance, and feels his finger pop from the knuckle. Searing pain. Diggy sees the beast in Trevor's eyes roaring. Trevor shoots into his legs. He wraps Diggy's knees in his arms, pivots, and power lifts him in the air. The team cheers. Diggy is over Trevor's shoulder, kicking, twisting, fighting. Trevor's muscles feel hard as iron. Randy waves his arms over his head, screaming something. Everything feels upside down. Diggy rakes his fingers across Trevor's face. Once. Again. Trevor spins around. Diggy sees his teammates' faces flash by, all of them are screaming, rooting for Trevor.

At the edge of the mat, Trevor drops Diggy down hard on his back. Diggy's brain vibrates in his skull. Trevor drives his shoulder into Diggy's gut. In that instant, Diggy knows what he should have known all along—he underestimated Trevor.

"That's a slam," screams Randy from the side of the mat.

Diggy wishes Randy would back off, give him some

space. He listens for the whistle, hoping Greco will halt the match, but Trevor is on him, chest-to-chest, face-to-face. Trevor extends his legs in a push-up position and balances on his toes. Head up. Diggy knows it's perfect pinning position. Trevor locks his arm around Diggy's arm and head.

Diggy goes wild, shifting his weight, arching his back, rolling his shoulders, ripping at Trevor's face, his neck, any exposed flesh.

"Trevor, lift his head, lift his head," yells Jimmy.

Hearing Jimmy makes Diggy's entire body go numb. They are all rooting for a scrub, for Crow. Diggy twists right, then left. Trevor's arm crushes Diggy's chest and shoulders. Diggy's fingers press into Trevor's eye socket, because there is no playing fair. Nothing is fair. He doesn't care if he is penalized. But Trevor doesn't let up the pressure. He grabs Diggy's free arm by the wrist and straightens it on the mat. Trevor jams his chin into Diggy's shoulder, just above his collarbone. The pain is shocking.

Greco, watching for the pin, lies flat on the mat getting a good angle on Diggy's shoulder blades. Trevor jerks Diggy like a rag doll, forcing his shoulders to the mat. Greco's hand slaps the mat. Pin. The whistle sounds. A cheer bursts into a roar. Headgear is flying in the air. Guys are slapping five.

Diggy sits up and spits his mouthpiece into his hand.

"Crow was out of bounds," shouts Randy. "You didn't see that?"

Greco ignores Randy and meets Trevor in the center of the mat. Trevor toes the centerline, a mass of flexed, glowing muscle. Tufts of his black hair stick out of his headgear. Blood seeps from the corner of his left eye, down his cheek. Greco raises his arm. Victory!

Diggy cradles his hand. "I think he broke my finger," he yells.

Randy follows Greco around the mat. "You didn't hear me? I said he was clearly on the line. Coach, you're not going to let that stand as a win?"

Greco spins around, making fists with his hands, cutting Randy off. "Trevor was in-bounds! On the line is in-bounds. I was looking right at the line! It's over!"

"Believe me," says Randy. "This isn't over." He smacks Diggy in the back of the head. "What are you sitting there for? Get up."

"Keep your hands to yourself." Diggy gets up. "And go back to work or go home. I don't care, just get out of here. Do you understand me! Get out of here!" he yells.

The guys are quiet. Trevor takes a knee with them. Jimmy holds out his hand and Trevor slaps it.

Diggy looks at his father, then at the team. All traitors! Randy pushes open the emergency door. A crack of light shoots into the gym, across the red mat. The hell with it. Diggy holds his throbbing hand and passes by the team. "I'm gonna destroy you," he mouths to Trevor.

Diggy

DIGGY LOCKS THE BATHROOM DOOR. HE RUNS COLD WATER over his throbbing finger. It's definitely dislocated at the base of the joint. He grabs the tip with his good hand and pulls gently. Pain. Nothing like on the mat, but enough to make his eyes tear. Groaning, he pulls harder, then pushes the joint back into place with steady pressure. It clicks.

He sits on the side of the hot tub and calls his brother.

"What's up," says Nick.

"Hey, bro."

"I'm on my way to the library. I have a multivariable calculus test tomorrow."

"I lost my wrestle-off."

"You what? You lost, to who?"

Through the walls, Diggy hears his father. "He never wanted it bad enough! You don't give something away, just give it away!" Diggy imagines his mother holding her breath, afraid to say a word.

"Randy's going nuts," says Diggy.

"What happened?"

"I lost. I didn't have it." Diggy can't tell him Crow lifted him in the air, that he was on Crow's shoulders, then pinned in 46 seconds.

"You didn't get pinned, did ya?"

"Nick, yeah."

"When?"

"In the first period." His throat is closing. Diggy can't let himself cry, not with Nick on the line. The Masters brothers don't get pinned. "I should have beaten him."

"Do I know him?"

"You know him. Crow, the scrub."

"Trevor Crow, the kid who couldn't make varsity to save his life? That kid? The one that's Native American or something?"

"It wasn't fair. And the whole team was on Crow's side." His voice cracks. "Even Greco was against me." Diggy can still hear them cheering for Trevor.

"Was Randy there?"

"Same as always, standing there with his *White Men Can't Jump* body, wearing his Range Rover jacket."

"I wish I could tell you what to do."

"Nick, come home this weekend."

"I can't, I've got papers due, labs, and exams coming up."

"What the hell am I going to do, Nick? You know I can't wrestle one-seventy. You know that? Sucking weight, that's my whole game." Diggy's middle goes into a knot.

"Diggy, you're a good wrestler. Remember you and me in the basement rolling around on the mats? You were tough as hell."

"Come home," begs Diggy.

"I will."

"When?"

"Soon."

Diggy looks at the phone, then presses End. "Soon? When is soon?" he screams into the shower stall.

Randy holds a bourbon in his monogrammed glass. Beverly sits on a leather-cushioned barstool sipping wine from a long-stemmed glass. Randy's eyes slide from the glass to Diggy. "It feels like we've had a death in the family. My son's season just croaked."

The words are a blind whack on the side of Diggy's head.

Randy swirls his drink with his finger. "A junior-varsity wrestler pins you like you're nothing, like you're a rag doll."

Diggy massages his knuckle. It's pulsing like it has its own heart.

"I took off a half day of work to witness that mess!" The cords in his neck strain. "Say something. Do you think sitting there like a dope is proving anything? I'm not one of your idiotic friends walking around with their caps on sideways and their pants falling off."

"It was one match."

"It was *the* match! You don't do well in school. You don't do anything around here."

"He really doesn't have much time to help," says Beverly.

His father stares angrily at her. "Your mother and I, we don't ask for much. All we ask is that you give one hundred percent. That's what separates us from them. We give one hundred percent. I built my business from nothing, from nada. Your brother started a tradition. So how do you let that second-rate little . . . little . . . "—his face trembles—"pin you right in front of me, your coach, your team? How?"

"Maybe he should move up a weight class," suggests his mother.

"Bev-er-ly, you would think after all these years you'd understand the team dynamics."

"I-I thought . . ." she stammers.

"Mom," says Diggy, "Jim O'Shea's one-sixty."

"And my son can't beat O'Shea," says Randy.

"No one can," says Diggy.

"Your brother would have made O'Shea look like a hundred and sixty pounds of candy-ass."

"I'm. Not. Nick." He spits the words. "I wish I was, but I'm not."

"No, you don't give anything your all. Your brother put his heart in it."

"And where did it get him?" asks Diggy. "Huh?"

"Don't insult your brother. Don't you ever think for one minute that he wasted one drop of sweat." Randy's finger wags in Diggy's face.

Diggy knows what his brother did was exceptional. Everyone knows it.

"Diggy, you get the seriousness of this?" yells Randy. "Or am I the only one around here who's got a half a brain?"

"I couldn't tie up with him," Diggy says. "He grabbed my fingers. I thought he was trying to break them." Diggy shows him his swollen knuckle. It's the size of a golf ball.

"Why couldn't you have pushed yourself out of bounds?" asks Randy. "I mean, come on, it was basic, Wrestling 101. Were you afraid of him?"

"No, sir."

"The worst part is you made that kid look like a wrestler." Randy finishes his drink.

"Crow's built like a damn ox," says Diggy. "They call him 'the stack of bricks.'"

"And why aren't you a stack of bricks? What are you a stack of?" Randy reaches to cuff him on the head.

Diggy ducks.

"You've got your own wrestling room and weights in the basement. You live on a damn golf course. Did you run this summer like I told you? Do you ever do one extra ounce of training?" His father drops his hand. "Beverly, what did his personal trainer say? What were his exact words?" Diggy knows these words, and knows his mom remembers them. When Randy is in a mood, the personal trainer comes up like a dinner of bad shrimp.

"You don't have to go there," says Beverly. "I think you've made your point."

"He said, 'Your son has the potential, he just needs the drive.' That's what he said." His father's face is tomato-red.

"What are you going to do, tape me to the bench press again?" asks Diggy.

"What?"

"You think I forgot that?"

"Enough." His mother waves her hands.

"I did that for your own good. It was a lesson." His father returns to the bar and finishes his drink. "And that was a long time ago."

"Three years ago," shoots back Diggy.

It happened during a father and son training session. Nick was out with a girl or his friends. Workouts always started with the bench press, something Diggy still isn't good at. With him struggling under the weight bar, Randy grabbed a roll of duct tape and wrapped him to the bench, around and around, pinning him. "Now, give me a set," he yelled. Diggy pushed one rep, then the bar sank to his chest, crushing him. He was screaming for Randy to get it off him. Then his mother came in and smacked his father's face. She cut the tape, freeing him.

"Let me show you something." His father crosses to

the Persian rug in the sunken living room. He bends his knees and holds his open hands in a wrestling stance. "Why didn't you jerk the damn kid's arms up and come under like you usually do?" His father lunges and tackles an imaginary opponent.

Diggy can't look at him anymore, can't hear his complaints and his insults. He has to get away from Randy or he will do something crazy.

Trevor

His mother knocks softly, then pushes his door open. Trevor lies on his stomach in bed, watching the motel television with the lights off. Whizzer is curled next to him. A videotape of a snowstorm recorded at his old house plays in the VCR. Snow blows past the camera, obscuring Trevor, eight years old, wearing a snowsuit with a zipper up the front, boots, and a ski hat. His dad shovels the sidewalk. Wind whistles in the camera microphone. He sticks the shovel in a snow bank, shoves his hands in the front pockets of his jeans, and smiles.

"I remember that day," she says. "Your father gave me that camera for Christmas. You had the day off from school. We all stayed home."

She strokes Whizzer's neck. He rolls to his back and she scratches his belly.

His father tosses a shovel full of snow into the storm. The camera zooms past his dark eyes and wavy hair. Trevor falls back into the snow and flaps his arms, trying to make a snow angel, but it's snowing too hard. Then the tape cuts directly to their old kitchen. His father is at the stove melting a large chocolate bar in a saucepan. His mother is slowly pouring in milk.

He shuts off the VCR. He doesn't want to cry but feels it coming. He's glad his mother can't see his eyes. She massages his shoulder as if she feels the pain radiating off him.

The day his father died, and for weeks after, his chest hurt from crying. But crying didn't bring him back, or do any good. After the wake and the funeral, after the casseroles and cakes sent over by the neighbors were gone, after the visit from his aunt and uncle from Florida, after all this, the summer heat set in and the house was quiet. On the Fourth of July, Trevor stayed in his room looking at photo albums and videos. He broke down and sobbed, cried more tears than he thought possible. His mother came to the door, but rather than open it, he raged at her, "GET AWAY FROM ME! LEAVE ME ALONE!" She said they could still walk to the fireworks, like other years. "DIDN'T YOU HEAR ME? GET AWAY FROM ME!"

Trevor stretches on the bed, sore from the wrestle-off. He pictures Diggy standing on the edge of the mat, clutching his hand with pain as bright as red paint on his face. Trevor doesn't want to feel anything for him. Diggy doesn't work hard in practice. Trevor's father would have called him a slouch. He gets by, doing as little as possible. He knows Greco and some of the guys think the wrestle-off should have been avoided, but if Trevor accepted the

170-weight class, he would have a losing season. He would be humiliated again. If he's ever going to prove anything, he needs to win.

"I want to talk to you about something," says his mother. "Harry asked me out, sort of a date."

"You mean like boyfriend and girlfriend?"

"No, not exactly, more like two people with things in common. We might see a play in Red Bank." Her eyes turn up at the edges and her mouth does something like a smile.

"Why would you do that?"

She removes her hand from his shoulder. "He's a friend."

"I'm your friend."

"Trevor, I know you're there for me, but I don't want to lean on you. I need someone to confide in, someone my age."

London is using her. She changes beds, empties the trash baskets, works the desk, all for free rent? Why doesn't he pay her enough for them to get an apartment?

"I see something in Harry," she says. "We might just end up friends. I don't know. He's a hard worker and he takes risks, big risks. He took one on me."

"No, he didn't. You're someone he knew he could depend on. You never let anyone down. You always work hard."

"You're my son. You see things that way."

"No, that's the truth. London needs you. This was his

plan from the day Dad died."

"Well, I wanted you to know what I was doing."

"Mom, London's not Dad, and he's never going to be. You shouldn't date him. Dad died in June." Trevor feels sick just thinking about his mother with London. "I don't see how you can look at London." Trevor knows it's not what she wanted to hear, but he's not going to take back his words. He doesn't want to make her suffer, but he doesn't want her to feel anything for London, or any man, at least not yet.

She begins to cry into her hands. "I know it's too soon," she says.

He puts his arm around her. "I'll take you to a play. We can borrow London's truck."

"Stop calling him London," she says hotly. "For once, try calling him Harry!"

"Stop being used by him!" he yells.

Trevor swings his legs off the bed and turns on the light. He doesn't want to hear anymore and he doesn't want to argue. "I'm taking Whizzer for a walk." He snaps the leash on Whizzer's collar.

"What happened to your face?" she asks.

"It's nothing."

"Your eye. You're all cut and bloodshot."

"I wrestled-off Diggy Masters."

"Can you see all right?" She stands. "Oh my, you're a mess."

"I won," says Trevor.

"I don't care if you won. All I ever asked is for you not to get hurt. We don't have health insurance. You know that. You could have lost your eyesight."

"Mom, now I can wrestle at my real weight. It's a big deal." He smiles.

She opens his eye with her fingers and examines it. "I hope you didn't damage your cornea."

"Mom, you don't get it. If I didn't win today, I don't think I'd have anything going for me. Nothing. I'd be that same loser I've always been. I'm going to do something that I should have done when Dad was alive. So get used to it."

Diggy

BONES TROTS DOWN HIS STOOP, CARRYING A BROWN PAPER BAG and his bass guitar. He shoves his bass into the backseat of Diggy's Mustang, then climbs in beside it. He pulls a half-empty bottle of vodka and an orange Gatorade from the bag. "Check it out, fellas."

"Your old man isn't going to miss that?" asks Gino.

"He'll scapegoat my mother's ass," says Bones.

"Barnstorm?" Diggy says, reading the label.

"Hey, yo, it's alcohol," says Bones.

Diggy puts the car in gear and peels out, screeching the tires.

Bones leans forward. "What did Randy say about the wrestle-off?"

"Compared it to a death in the family." Little Gino and Bones laugh and shake their heads. "Then he tries to show me a wrestling move. Me? You believe that?"

Bones lowers the rear window and pours half the Gatorade out. He refills the bottle with vodka. "Cocktails are served," he says with an English accent. He takes a gulp

145

and smacks his lips together. "Scrumptious!" He passes the bottle to Little Gino.

They drive to the man-made beach at the lake. Diggy stops diagonally across the white parking lanes. They leave the car doors open with the music pumping. Standing in the lot, they pass around the vodka-Gatorade. "You know how Greco's always saying he's going to run us to Lake Lakookie?" asks Bones.

"Yeah, what's with that?" asks Gino.

"The place doesn't exist," says Bones. "I Googled it ten different ways."

"I thought it was in Brazil or somewhere." The alcohol burns into Diggy's stitched lip. He wipes his mouth on the sleeve of his jacket.

"Yo, I'm going to ask him someday," says Bones. "Where the hell is Lake Lakookie? Put up or shut up."

"Then you'll be running to Lake Lakookie!" Diggy slaps five with Gino.

"Greco thinks he's so funny with his cauliflower ears," says Bones. "He ought to get some seat covers for them." They laugh.

Diggy takes another swig. "He should have had some loyalty to me. Without my brother, no one in this state would have even heard of Molly Pitcher." Diggy burps loudly. The booze has gone right to his head. The town's lights, a half-mile across the lake, blur and start to revolve.

"Some people say you're making booty calls to Jane's," says Gino.

"Who?"

"My sister swore me to secrecy. Need I say more? She says you're over there like every night."

"Word is, Jane gives primo head," says Bones.

Diggy wings his hand at Bones and catches him on the forehead. "You must be getting her confused with your sister."

"No, my sister doesn't have the continent of Africa stamped on her face." Bones laughs and raises his hands in a boxer's stance. "And she didn't blow the wrestling team and have to get her stomach pumped."

Diggy throws the empty bottle at him, just missing his head. He gets in his car and starts the engine. He doesn't need them. He doesn't need anyone. He turns the car around and starts driving at them. They both run. He jams on the brakes. "Get in," he says. "And make sure I don't crash my ride."

"Listen, yo," says Bones. "You start heading for a tree, I'll exit with a chain saw."

Diggy speeds through downtown Molly Pitcher, past the closed stores. His head buzzes from the vodka. At least his finger doesn't hurt as much. He veers down a side road lined with swamp maples and little houses into Puny Town.

"Where we going?" asks Gino.

"Nowhere," he says.

Diggy slows the car in front of a cottage with a single picture window and a brick stoop. Lights are on inside the house. The mailbox is the same, still bent forward into the street. The bushes in front of the house grew above the windowsills. His father always kept them trimmed. Living in Puny Town was better than living in the Hills. Randy thinks owning a big house and earning a fat paycheck makes him better than everyone. But he's still Randy from Puny Town and Diggy doesn't forget this. "I used to live there," says Diggy.

"Imagine that," says Bones. "Diggy Masters living in the ghetto."

"Why don't you blow me." Diggy passes Jane's old house. The fence is overgrown with vines and the windows are boarded up.

"Did you have a wrestling mat in your basement back then?" asks Gino.

"We didn't have a basement."

They wind around the block. "That's Jimmy's house," says Diggy. "We used to hang like every day of the week."

"Can you believe he's getting a piece of Roxanne Sweetapple? I bet she craps cherries and whipped cream," says Bones.

"I could be dating her if I wanted," snaps Diggy. "Last year she was blowing up my phone with texts."

"But this year she lost your number!" Bones laughs.

Diggy slams the gas. His eyes are heavy. Keep moving. Keep driving. He speeds south on Tennant Road, wishing it was Jimmy in the front seat, not Bones. He trusted Jimmy. He could tell him stuff. Not like Bones. Everything is a joke to him. Once Jimmy and Diggy tried to cross the ice-covered lake. Twenty yards from the shore, they fell through. They both panicked, until they felt the soft bottom and then laughed with relief. They told that story for about a year and it was always funny.

He turns at the police station and passes the weekend flea market, hangs a right, and enters Jane's complex. He stops next to the Saturn with no engine and dials her number.

"What are you doing, a booty call?" laughs Bones.

Diggy tries to ignore him. "Hey," he says into his cell. "I'm outside with Bones and Little Gino." He shuts his phone. "You guys act like asswipes, I swear to God you'll never get another ride from me. I don't care if it's ten degrees."

Jane emerges wearing skinny jeans, a black T, and a short denim jacket. Her hair is parted in the middle.

"Hey, Diggy." She leans into the window.

"Hey."

She looks at Gino and Bones. Both of them are grinning. "You guys smell like a freaking brewery," she says.

"Gatorade screwdrivers, yo," says Bones and burps. They laugh.

"Where'd you cop 'em?"

"That's for us to know," says Bones.

Jane squeezes into the middle of the bucket seats, half on Bone's lap, and half on the console. She smells like cigarette smoke and vanilla icing.

Diggy drives into the back of the deserted flea market. Sometimes high school kids park near the fence, but tonight it's empty. He passes the wire trash cans and the plywood remnants of the weekend stands. Facing the lines of empty tables, all in straight rows, he shuts off the engine and turns the key to ignition. With Z-100 on the radio, they pile out with the bass pumping. A jet streams overhead. "Got any more of those screwdrivers?" asks Jane.

"Gone," says Bones.

"Well, what'd we come here for?"

"I'm not driving anymore with half a buzz on," says Diggy.

Bones takes Jane's hand. "Let's go see if anyone left anything on the tables."

"Get off me." She yanks her hand away. "You must be drunk."

"What, all of a sudden you're too good for me?" asks Bones.

"Not all of a sudden," says Jane. "Since the beginning of time."

"Come on, little man," says Bones. "Let's leave the lovebirds alone." Gino follows Bones toward the yellow building, cutting through the tables. "We'll be back, don't make a baby," shouts Bones.

"Assholes," mutters Diggy.

"Most guys are," says Jane.

They sit there swinging their legs. Diggy hates the silence. He positions his arm behind her and considers resting it on her shoulders.

"My brothers have found some amazing junk here. If people don't sell their crap, sometimes they chuck it in the trash," says Jane.

"Are you cold?" he asks.

"Not really."

"The alcohol is keeping me warm." Diggy removes his varsity jacket and puts it on her shoulders. His heart pounds in his ears. "You can wear my jacket if you want to."

"Really?"

"I may need it sometimes, but yeah." He can hardly breathe.

"At school?"

"Yeah."

She kisses him, slowly, deeply, her tongue working against his. Then they hug with her head on his shoulder. "I'm going to feel so tough," she says in his ear.

"I'm not as hardcore as everyone says I am." He smiles.

"I could have killed Trevor for wrestling you off," she says. "One match doesn't make him a better wrestler than you."

"I'm not going to hear the end of it from Randy." His finger sends a wave of pain up his arm. "And look at this. Dislocated again."

She brings his hand to her face and sucks his skin.

Diggy

DIGGY GETS RID OF BONES FIRST. "IT'S BEEN REAL, YO," HE calls, pulling his guitar from the back seat. "Stay in touch with yourselves."

Next Diggy wants to drop off Gino, so he can be alone with Jane, but Gino cries like a little emo-bitch, saying he can't go home until after his father's left for the graveyard shift at the nuclear plant. "He sniffs my breath," says Gino, "makes me blow into his face." Gino's father isn't an engineer. He's a square-badge guard.

"I should get home. I'm really tired anyway," says Jane.

So Diggy drops Jane off instead of Gino. Diggy holds her for about five minutes in front of her door, knowing Gino's watching. Diggy feels his eyes, but tries not to care. Finally, he decides he'd rather hold her than worry about what Little Gino thinks. "So, I'll see you tomorrow at school," she says, pulling her lips off his. "Are you sure about the jacket?"

"Keep it. Wear it tomorrow."

In the car, Gino lowers the music and says, "You gave her your jacket?"

"You got a problem with it?"

"The first time I saw her," says Gino, "I thought she'd been hit in the head with a hockey puck or something."

"Is that supposed to be funny?"

"I'm just surprised, that's all I'm saying."

"Like your little hobbit ass is ever going to have a girl-friend," says Diggy.

"Mention her name to anybody and what's the first thing they think of?" asks Gino.

"You short little turd," shouts Diggy. "Shut the eff up." Diggy head slaps Little Gino; the same way Randy smacks him. "You never got past first base and you're cracking on me?"

At the fork, he veers onto Iron Ore Road. He presses hard on the gas pedal. They zip by the plank fence that surrounds the horse ranch, then past long stretches of dry corn stalks.

"Where to?" asks Gino.

"I have to check something out."

At the Lobster Mobster Restaurant, he turns onto Route 33. They fly by the used car lots, then the hot tub place. "Where're we going?" Gino asks again.

Diggy doesn't answer. He's almost there. Little Gino brings his legs on his seat, curling into a ball. Diggy slows and pulls off the highway. Fifty yards ahead, a spotlight shines on the SECRET KEEPERS sign.

"Crow lives here." Diggy pulls into the parking lot. "Can you believe this?" Some of the rooms are lit. He drives to the edge of the lot. Television screens flash behind the curtains. A puppy is chained to the cyclone fence. The dog stands and trots forward, dragging the chain toward the headlights.

"That's got to be Trevor's new puppy," says Gino, opening his door. "Come 'ere boy," he calls.

Diggy positions the car so that the dog is at Gino's door. The dog steps forward.

"If I had a puppy, he wouldn't be chained in the cold," says Diggy.

"Ditto that," says Gino.

"Unhook him," he says, leaning over the console to see the puppy.

"Why?"

"Just do it."

Gino unhooks the chain from the dog's collar.

Diggy reaches across Gino's lap and snags the collar, yanking the dog into the car. The puppy twists and braces his legs against the front seat. His tail whacks the dashboard.

"What if we take him?" Diggy looks into the animal's brown eyes.

"And do what with him?" asks Gino.

"Keep him for a while." Diggy pictures Trevor in the

155

parking lot, lifting the chain, then looking up the road. How is that going to feel? A surge of power rushes through Diggy.

"Crow's not the same guy he used to be. He'd kill you."

PART TWO

Trevor

TREVOR IS WASTING HIS FREE PERIOD IN THE LIBRARY WITH HIS feet on a radiator. He squints at the athletic fields, hoping Whizzer might emerge from the pin oaks and maples beyond the fields. School is a long way from the motel, but maybe Whizzer is completely lost. It's been three days of riding around with London and his mother searching for Whizzer or his body on the side of the road. It's hit Trevor like a bad virus. He can't focus. He hasn't done any homework. He's skipped wrestling practice. He can't think of anything else.

He walked the highway calling Whizzer's name, imagining him trotting from an alleyway with his tongue hanging from his mouth, scared and anxious. Trevor's roamed all over town, down Main Street, through parking lots, around the flea market buildings, circling the elementary schools. He's peered into backyards and over fences. He's stopped people coming from the train. Holding Whizzer's picture, he's asked them if they'd seen his lost puppy. "A Lab mix," he said, "about four months old."

Jane sits two tables away. When their eyes meet, Trevor looks past her toward the main desk. He's seen her sucking face with Diggy in every hallway.

Trevor's phone vibrates in his pocket. "Hello." Shuffling, noise in the background. "Hello." He looks at the phone, a private number. "Hello?"

"Trevor?"

"Gino?"

"Yeah."

"What up?" Trevor tries not to smile. Gino has never called him.

"What are you doing?" Gino's voice is high.

"Nothing. What's the matter?"

"You going to practice?"

"I suppose. Why, is something going on?"

"No, I just was thinking. . . ." Gino's voice trails off. "You hear anything about your dog?"

"Nothing new."

"Okay, listen." Gino heaves a deep breath.

"What?"

"Ah, forget it, I'll see you at practice." The call disconnects.

Trevor puts the phone on the table and looks at it. He wonders if Diggy and Gino have devised some type of revenge. Are they going to give him a "lights out" party, and jump him in the locker room?

Jane gets up, shoves her fingertips into her hip-hugger

pockets, and approaches. She's wearing a tight shirt that says "Jersey Girl, 'Nuff said."

She slides into the seat across from him. "Heard anything about your puppy?"

He shakes his head. "Gino just asked me the same thing."

"I saw your flyers. You named him Whizzer?"

"Yeah."

"Like the wrestling move?" Her eyes are hard, unblinking.

They've always been aware of each other. He's the Indian. She's the girl with the birthmark. They pass each other in the halls with small nods of recognition or "Hey," then "Hey" back. But they've never been friends and it wasn't the birthmark that stopped him. Trevor knew, and he imagined Jane knew, the two *different* kids in the school shouldn't hang out. It would have been unpleasantly weird.

"Did you ever think your dog could have slipped his collar?" she asks with an edge.

"I would have found the collar hooked to the chain. Right?" He says this as if it's her fault.

"I think someone checking out from the motel must have taken him," she says. "Did you check the ASPCA?"

"Twice."

"I'm sure he'll turn up." She doesn't take her eyes off him. Still doesn't blink. Jane folds her arms across her chest. "Your mother is the motel manager?"

Why is she interested in his life? Is she going to tell this to Diggy? "She works the desk." And cleans rooms. They get free rent. Bug off, Jane.

Trevor turns to the window. Rain is coming down at an angle. Some winter track guys run across the field with their sweatshirts pulled over their heads.

"Your father was Penobscot, wasn't he?"

Trevor's surprised. Everyone knows he's Native American, but no one in the school knows the tribe. "How do you know that?"

"A presentation you gave in the fifth grade. You said a bunch of Indian words. The teacher thought it was extremely badass."

The Wabanaki Confederacy: Abenaki, Micmac, Penobscot, Passamaquoddy, and Maliseet tribes run through his mind. His father taught him the names of the tribes. He used a stick and drew a map in the dirt. With the stick on the landmasses he chanted, "Passamaqouddy, Maliseet, and Micmac Nations." He circled them and finished with "The Wabanaki Confederacy." He made Trevor repeat the words with him.

"How's Diggy doing?" he asks.

"How do you think he's doing? First he gets your knee in his mouth and eighteen stitches, then you dislocate his finger and take his spot at one-fifty-two." She glares at him. "You know what I think? I think the knee-lift to his face was on purpose."

Trevor remembers the feel of it, the impact. Diggy asked for it, and he got it. Trevor leans back, surprised at himself, pleased that he's not apologizing and making excuses.

"You know, one-seventy is not going to be easy for Diggy," she says.

"He'll have it easier than I would."

The bell rings. She gets up and slams the chair in against the table.

Diggy

At lunch, Jane's getting extra help in geometry, so Diggy has no choice but to sit at the wrestling table. He can't sit alone. As he approaches, Gino's eyes flash at Diggy, then dart over to Trevor. Diggy knows Gino's a walking, talking time bomb. Diggy sits and lets out a long, slow breath.

"To what do we owe this honor?" asks Jimmy.

"Is the little lady on the rag?" asks Bones. "Or maybe she's trying to wash Africa off her face." Everyone erupts into laughter.

Diggy grabs Bones's sandwich and squishes it until wheat bread squeezes between his fingers. "Next time, that's your face."

"You ever touch my lunch again, I'll break your jerkass hands." Bones isn't laughing. "You've got to learn how to take a joke."

"You're a joke." Diggy dumps his own lunch, turkey sandwich, an apple, a protein bar, and a slice of cake, from a brown bag onto the table.

"That's like a week's worth of food," says Jimmy.

"If you'd move up a weight class"—Diggy bites his sandwich—"then you could eat too."

Pancakes holds a "lost dog" flyer with Whizzer's picture on it. Bones snatches it from his hand. He cranes his neck around to Trevor. "Sorry to say this dude, but he's got to be roadkill by now. Why would anyone steal a mutt? He was a mutt, right?"

"He was half Lab," says Trevor.

"That's a mutt, yo," says Bones. "And a mutt is a mutt, right, Gino?"

Gino fixes his eyes on his square of cardboard pizza from the cafeteria kitchen.

"Who made you the expert?" says Gino.

"If he was going to be a big dog," says Jimmy, "maybe somebody needed a guard dog. Trevor, you ever think of that?"

"Yeah." Trevor nods. "The police mentioned that."

Diggy chews his sandwich, barely tasting it. His stomach feels like it's on a seesaw. He looks at Gino, who has tears pooling in his eyes.

"Principal Anderson is going to make an announcement tomorrow during homeroom," says Trevor.

Diggy puts his sandwich down. He's lost his appetite. "Trevor, he'll probably show up when you least expect it," he says.

The wrestlers look at Diggy.

"He was a puppy," says Bones. "How's a puppy just going to show up?"

"I don't know, anything's possible, right?"

"Thanks," says Trevor. "I'm not giving up either."

Everyone, except Gino and Diggy, leave the table to play handball. Gino's wide-eyed and worrying like a three-year-old on his first day of nursery school. "Give him back," he says.

"Or else what?" Diggy hunches over the table.

"You've got to give him back," says Gino. "Chain him somewhere and somebody can drive by and find him." A tear leaves the corner of his eye.

"It's a dog," says Diggy. "Not a person. When I'm ready, I'll give him back."

"You better give him back now," says Gino.

"You didn't tell anyone, did you?"

"No, but I can't think about anything else."

"Just chill."

"I can't. It's freakin' me out."

"You told someone, didn't you?" Diggy's eyes narrow.

"I almost told Bones last night."

Diggy reaches across the table, grabs his shirt, and twists it in his fist. "Stop worrying. I'm going to take care of it."

"Only a prick could do a thing like this."

"You took him too. We get caught, you're going down as hard as me."

"You pulled him in the car! I didn't know what you were doing."

Diggy releases him. Taking the dog was dumb, and he wants to give him back. But no one suspects anything. It's perfect revenge. Trevor's moping around at practice. Greco's probably already wishing Diggy was back at 152.

"What are you doing with the dog anyway?" whispers Gino. "You want a dog so bad, get your own."

"This is a lesson. Every time I drove by that motel, the dog was chained up. It was animal abuse."

"That's baloney and you know it. You wanted to get back at Crow for taking your spot. You need a shrink," says Gino. "You've got issues."

Diggy shoves Gino's shoulder. If anyone finds out, nothing will ever be the same for Diggy. He could be arrested, and no one would hear his side. His heart crashes in his chest. "You open your mouth, you're going down, same as me."

Diggy

DIGGY CARRIES THE PUPPY FROM THE POOL HOUSE AT THE BACK of the property. The leafless sycamore branch, about two feet around, rises from the green mesh pool cover. Twenty feet up the trunk of the tree, he spots the gash where the tree branch snapped. The water is coated with translucent new ice. He wonders if the puppy could break through and drown.

The puppy slurps his ear. "Happy to see me?" he asks.

His parents are at the county club for the night. Diggy puts Whizzer in the family room. Whizzer tears around the rug, running up and over the couch, around and around. He charges into the kitchen, stops, then charges back toward Diggy.

Whizzer wolfs down a porterhouse steak cut into tiny pieces, then laps up an entire bowl of water. After he's finished, he looks at Diggy as if to ask, Is that all? "You're a rowdy one, aren't you," says Diggy.

He snuggles with the puppy on the leather wrap-around couch and watches one episode after another of

Survivorman. He TiVo'd an entire week. In the first episode, Survivorman roasts scorpions over a fire and pops them in his mouth like potato chips; in the next he cuts the meat off a dead elk and cooks it on a fire, then he builds shelters with pine branches.

Diggy likes the smell of the puppy's fur and the feel of the puppy's solid body. "Trevor was looking for you," he says to the dog. "But he couldn't find you, could he?" Diggy wants to feel in control, but the truth is he never intended on taking the puppy. It was just the way it went down. Trevor needed to learn a lesson about respect and there's the dog hopping into the car. Diggy may have gone too far.

He microwaves popcorn and tries to teach the puppy to roll over. It's no use. He feeds the dog popped kernels, which are swallowed without chewing. After four episodes of the show, he leads the puppy back to the pool house. For the fifth night, Diggy locks the puppy in and examines the dark sky, knowing Trevor is lying awake in the motel, wondering if his dog is roadkill. He has to give the dog back. He rubs his tongue across the scar tissue forming on his lip. "But you didn't have to wrestle me off," he says aloud. "So don't try to make me feel lower than whale crap."

Jimmy

JIMMY AND POPS SIT ON METAL FOLDING CHAIRS FACING A BAT-
tered wooden door labeled "Franklin B. Scales, Attorney
at Law." Jimmy bites and tears tiny pieces of flesh where
his skin meets his fingernails. He considers going to the
police and telling them the truth, but would they arrest
him? He was there. He stole the lumber too.

Pops leans on his elbows, his sandy-blond hair hanging
over his forehead. He's got his "good" clothes on: black
jeans, scuffed dress shoes, and a worn leather jacket. He
looks like a goon in a gangster movie, squeezing the fil-
ter of his stubby cigarette, sucking it like it's his job not
to leave one bit left. "When this is over"—suck, puff—"I
promise you"—suck—"I'll make this up to you."

And how are you going to do that, wonders Jimmy. *How are
you going to give back the practice I'm missing today, or all my
sleepless nights?*

The attorney's door opens. A man in gas-station cov-
eralls emerges. "He's all yours!" The man pushes out the
door.

The attorney, white faced, with a wispy comb-over, looks like he just rose from a coffin. He's got to be in his seventies. His office is packed with boxes filled with files and papers.

"This is my boy," says Pops.

"The wrestler, tough guy, huh?" The attorney laughs at his own joke. "Frankie Scales," he says, "like the scales of justice." He pushes a pile of green and yellow files, tagged with names, to the side of his desk. He rifles through the contents of a cardboard box on an overturned milk crate and pulls a file. He reads for a minute, then gazes at them with his saggy old eyes. "Okay, let's set the ground rules. Jim, you're eighteen?"

Jimmy nods.

"Don't talk to anyone but me and your dad about this. Any police show up on your doorstep, you say, 'Talk to my lawyer.'" He leans forward. "From today on, I'm your lawyer. You got that?"

Jimmy nods again.

"I hear you got yourself a little girlfriend, is that true?" The attorney grins. "Well, you don't tell her anything either. You start talking to her, you might as well go chalk it on the blackboard in school. You got that?"

"Yeah."

"Remember, Frankie Scales," he says. "Like the scales of justice."

Jimmy doesn't feel reassured. Nothing his father does

ever turns out right.

"I don't want either one of you talking about your case on the phone. Not on your home phone or your cell phones."

"They're bugging my phone?" asks Pops.

"Artie, you're a big fish in a small town. The police could indict you and your son, or they could come and pick you both up, or they could drop the whole thing."

"What do you think they'll do?" asks Jimmy.

"All they have is circumstantial evidence," says the attorney. "They don't have a witness; they don't have the wood; and they can't verify the sale of the wood. Now, what they do have is you and your son in a truck filled with, what'd you call it?"

"Lumber," says Pops.

"Right, lumber." He scratches his head. "What, like two-by-fours?"

"Like that, yes." Pops coughs.

Jimmy shuts his eyes. Stealing wood. It sounds moronic, like stealing rocks or dirt.

"So, the police have a truck with lumber leaving the approximate area of the theft on the night of the crime." The attorney cocks an eyebrow. "That's all they have?"

"Right, that's it." Pops looks at Jimmy.

"I guess," says Jimmy.

"Could they find a witness?"

His father lifts his eyes. "A witness?"

"Someone who saw you. A guard or a citizen out for a midnight stroll?"

Jimmy's heart jolts. "There was a guard."

"He let us in." Pops's knee is vibrating so hard, Jimmy can feel it in his chair.

"Pops, tell him the truth," says Jimmy.

Pops clears his throat. "I paid him two hundred to turn his back."

"Well, stay away from him," says Frankie Scales. "The police may have already flipped him. He could be talking."

"I don't think so," says Pops. "That old guy . . ."

"You don't know and I don't know, so stay away from him."

They sit for a moment in silence.

"How do you think it looks?" asks Pops.

"With you getting stopped, and now you tell me about a co-conspirator, who may or may not have been approached." Frankie Scales shakes his head. "We'll see and hope for the best."

Jimmy shuts his eyes. Hope for the best? What does that mean?

The lawyer stands. "I'll need a check for five hundred or four in cash."

Pops yanks his wallet from his back pocket. He places a stack of bills on the desk. "It's all there," he says.

"I'm sure it is." They shake hands.

Jimmy follows Pops from the office. He's numb.

Trevor

TREVOR ENTERS HIS MOTHER'S ROOM FROM THE ADJOINING
door and freezes. London's shirtless, sitting on the edge of
his mother's unmade bed, pulling on his socks. His dark
hair sticks up, uncombed. Their eyes meet.

"Morning," he says.

"I thought my mother was here."

"She's taking care of a mess. The toaster oven in nine
A caught fire." He shakes his head. "Ruined all the work I
did in that kitchen."

Trevor can't think of London's hairy chest in bed next
to his mother without being nauseated. "I'll come back
later," he says.

"No, no, please, come on in," says London.

Trevor goes behind the counter in his mother's
kitchenette. He plugs in the blender. He needs something to fill his stomach after the weigh-ins. He removes
a package of protein powder from the cabinet. His
phone rings. He says, "Hello," but there's no one there.
He checks the phone: "private number." Last time Gino

called, it was a private number.

"I fixed the clog in your sink," says London. "You don't want to know what was in the drain. First, I remove a wad of crud, looked like something from the black lagoon, and then I find a nail file. Believe that?"

Trevor dumps the powder into the blender. He's trying to concentrate on making the protein shake. He doesn't want to look at London, or hear him. Trevor opens the refrigerator for skim milk.

"You missing a nail file?"

"No." Trevor clenches his teeth with his tongue against the roof of his mouth.

"Well, it was there." He slips on a pair of work boots. "It would help if you'd get a little more involved around here. I could put you on the payroll." He pulls on a shirt.

Trevor studies the back of the protein package. Forty-four grams of protein. London is sleeping with his mother. Fat calories 30, total fat 3 grams. London is sleeping with his mother. Does she have real feelings for him?

"How about some painting tonight?" asks London. "I need the ceiling in five A painted pronto. I had the roof fixed, and there's a water stain right over the bed."

"Tonight?" Trevor's already painted four rooms at ten dollars a room. That's below minimum wage. He doesn't want to paint any more rooms. Especially not tonight, a Saturday. Maybe the team will get together, or he and Jimmy might do something.

London folds his arms. "This is a motel. That room could be making money."

"I never wanted to move here in the first place," says Trevor.

"What's so bad? You have a roof over your head, your own room, not to mention a mother who would do anything for you, anything in the world."

"She regrets it, and I hate it here."

"She regrets it? Are you sure? Because she told me things were finally coming together for her." London steps closer, cornering him next to the microwave. Trevor feels his height and weight. "I'm asking you man to man, give this a chance. Your mother is a good woman."

"You don't have to tell me that. I've known her a lot longer than you." Trevor tries to pass, but London doesn't budge.

"I know you're having a hard time."

"You got us here and you chained my dog outside when I told you not to. Now you're messing with my mother."

"What was I supposed to do, let your dog eat my motel? Remember, I'm not a rich guy. I couldn't let you live in that house for free. But I did the next best thing."

"Get away from me!" He's trembling.

"I ask you to paint one room, one room."

"I've already painted four rooms. I have a match today. I'm not painting anything!"

The door opens. Camille's carrying a bouquet of

flowers. "Look what I found in seven A," she says, then frowns.

"We were talking." London straightens the blanket on the bed.

"About what?" Her eyes narrow on London.

"About everything," says Trevor.

"Har-ry," groans Camille.

London grabs his coat and goes out the door.

"What happened?" she asks.

"You're sleeping with a manipulating asshole," yells Trevor. "That's what happened!"

She follows him into his room. "I wanted to talk to you. I'm so sorry sweetheart, so sorry."

"Sorry about what? Living here? Sleeping with London? What?" Trevor faces the window. A blonde girl he's seen a few times slips out of a room and enters a taxi. She's got to be a hooker.

"Sorry about everything," she says.

Jimmy

THE FIRST MATCH OF THE SEASON IS ALWAYS AGAINST THE COLTS. The gym will be standing room only. Jimmy should be warming up with the team. Instead, he's in the locker room, slumped over on a bench, shirtless, barefoot, wearing a pair of green boxer-briefs covered with shamrocks. He hasn't slept a full night since going to the lawyer's office. A feeling that something bad is going to go down is cemented in his brain. He can't shake it.

He examines his reflection in the mirror hanging in his locker. His eyes are half closed. His cheeks are hollow. His lips gray. He needs to go back to bed for a week.

Diggy bursts from a stall, smiling. "I just killed a mule in there."

Jimmy tries to laugh, but can't release the ache in his chest.

"What's the matter?" asks Diggy.

"I'm over. A pound and a half."

Diggy finishes washing his hands, then sits next to him. "You can run that off."

"I know, but I'm already burnt. I haven't eaten since yesterday at three o'clock. I had a protein bar and I can't even take a crap." Jimmy opens his bag, revealing a pair of silver-colored rubber sweatpants. "My father gave me these to sweat off water weight." He looks around to see if anyone else is watching. "These suits are illegal."

"Illegal?" asks Diggy.

"You know, against the regulations. I've got to go run in the basketball gym where no one will see me." Jimmy pushes the silver suit back into the bag. He walks to the electronic floor scale, which sits on a block of marble next to the toilet stalls. Over it hangs a drawing of an orange, with the words "Remember the Five-Pound Orange." Greco's anecdote about a wrestler, who after weighing-in five pounds over whined, "All I ate was an orange," is told at the start of every season. Greco finishes the story by saying, "Everything you do counts. Everything."

The scale shows 161.

"One pound," says Diggy. "You put that spaceman suit on and you can drop it in five minutes."

Jimmy leans against a locker and tugs on the aluminum-colored pants. "I don't know if I can do this. I'm hungry, and I'm wiped."

Diggy pulls the top of the suit from the bag. "Man, you can do it."

"It takes about thirty minutes to burn off a half pound, and my mind quit like five minutes ago." His face runs with perspiration. He sits and hangs his head above his knees.

"You don't look good." Diggy steps back. "You're hands are shaking. You want me to get Greco?"

"I don't have the flu, if that's what you're thinking. I'm just tired of pretending. I'm the team captain. I'm supposed to have things under control, but nothing's right." Jimmy shakes his head at the floor, then looks up with a sudden thought. "If things go the wrong way for me, you'll be captain."

"What are you talking about? You're captain. I got three votes." Diggy folds his arms. "Did you knock up Roxanne?"

"No." Jimmy heaves a deep breath. "But I probably already lost her." He doesn't want to tell Diggy anything else. Strong people don't advertise their problems.

Diggy sits next to him. "Jimmy, what are you bugging about? You can tell me. I'm the Dig-Master General, remember?"

He used to call Diggy that. "All I can say is my father put me in a bad place and I'm gonna have to suck it up."

Diggy doesn't budge. "Look, Jimmy, I got secrets of my own. You don't have to worry."

"Diggy, if I do tell you, it's got to be in the vault. Don't go blabbing it around, especially not to Greco."

"One thing I can do is keep information underground," says Diggy.

"It's something bad," says Jimmy. "This is for real."

Diggy grabs Jimmy's shoulder. "Look, I won't tell anyone."

"I can't trust my own father." Jimmy's voice quavers. "That's part of it."

Diggy laughs. "Once you know that, it's not a problem anymore. I don't trust mine either."

"He talked me into stealing some stuff with him and the cops already figured the whole thing out. I could be arrested today, tomorrow, the next day. I could leave the gym and detectives could be waiting for me."

"What kind of stuff?"

"That doesn't matter."

Diggy is silent. He looks stunned.

Trevor

GRECO LOCKS THE LOCKER ROOM DOOR, SEALING OFF THE noisy crowd in the gym. Trevor waits with the Minute Men, all dressed in matching hooded jackets and sweatpants. Greco looks them over. "Today is the season's opening day," he says. A few guys clap. "You've all put in the work to get here. I saw you all at the practices. I ran you from here to Lake Lakookie and you made it there and back." A few guys laugh.

"Wherever that is," says Bones.

"You put sweat equity in at the summer program," continues Greco. "Trevor, you were there. How hot was it in the gym?"

Trevor looks up.

"Hot as J. Lo," pipes up Bones. Everyone laughs.

"The practices are in the bank, and you've made weight. You've already earned a win today. Do you understand that?"

"Yeah."

"What was that?"

"Yeah!" they shout.

"And don't let me see you give up. If you're down ten points, you can still get a pin. You're just a shot away from a pin at any point in the match. Do you understand that?"

"Yeah!"

"One shot, one properly executed shot, is all it takes. Think about what you've done in practice. Let's put them in." The guys stand and toss their headgear in a small pile on the tile floor. Trevor drops his on the others and they form a circle around the pile.

Greco grips a hockey-stick handle, painted red and white, the school colors, and mixes the stick around the headgear, stirring them. Guys place their hands over the headgear as if they are warming them above a fire. So, this is the team's tradition, thinks Trevor. He's heard that they stirred "the soup" before every match, but never understood it. Now, he's in. It feels good. He searches the pile of new and battered headgear until he finds his. Last year, his father taped the straps of his headgear with cloth first-aid tape. "Now it should stay where it belongs," he said.

Greco grabs as many hands as he can, cupping them into a large mass. Trevor peers around the circle: Pancakes, Bones, Jimmy, Gino, Diggy, Turkburger, Mario, Cleaver, Salaam, Paul, and the rest of the guys. He feels good about all of them. Even Diggy. Maybe he'll win today at 170 and the wrestle-off will be behind them.

Trevor has to prove he can hold his weight class. "That's

Crow," he imagines Greco remarking to another coach. "He can go the distance with anyone at one-fifty-two."

"God, keep us safe today. Help us do our best," says Greco. "Let's show everyone what we are made of!"

They line up in the locker room—lightest to heaviest. Trevor looks down the row of red warmup jackets.

"Let's get stoked!" shouts Bones.

"Show them some attitude," yells Diggy.

They charge from the locker room into the darkened gym and jog around the mat to their team song that blares over the loud speakers. Fans are cheering and clapping. In unison, the wrestlers bend over backwards, hands extended over their heads into neck bridges. They flip over to front neck bridges. They rehearsed the warmup routine a dozen times, and now with the music, under the spotlight, Trevor feels it was all worth it, all of it, all the practices, the sweat, the hunger, and the wrestle-off.

Jimmy slides on his stomach to the center of the mat and slaps his hand on the red vinyl. All of them, all fourteen, dive onto their stomachs, creating a giant pileup of gray sweats and red jackets. Trevor feels a knee in his back and Jimmy's hot breath on his face.

"Are we gonna kick some today?" yells Bones.

They roar.

"Minute Men on three! Let's do it," he yells louder. "One, two, three!"

They roar again.

Jimmy

JIMMY DANCES ON HIS TOES LIKE A BOXER, SHUFFLING SIDE TO side in the corner of the gym. He made weight. At least that's over. Six foot two. 160. He swings his arms in circles. He breathes in and out, in out, in out, in out, hoping that telling Diggy wasn't a mistake.

Pops, shouldering up with the Varsity Dads, laughs about something. Why isn't he worried? How can he act like nothing's happened, like nothing will happen, when nothing between them is ever going to feel the same again?

This morning, Pops stuck his head into the bathroom. "You gonna win today?"

"I'm not thinking about winning today. I'm thinking what you did was really stupid," said Jimmy.

"Stupid, how?"

"Stupid because you thought you could get away with it. Stupid because it was me in the truck with you!"

"What are you worried about? If something goes wrong, I'll take the heat."

"It already went wrong," said Jimmy.

Pops stepped behind Jimmy and placed his large hands on Jimmy's shoulders. An inch of Pops' pinky finger is missing on his left hand. A work accident. In the mirror, the stump was whiter than his knuckles. "You shouldn't be talking like that. First, you're not showing me any respect, and second, I already told you, it's being taken care of."

Jimmy shivered.

Trevor is on the mat crushing his opponent. He is going to be hard to beat at 152. He does a knee drop to a single leg grab and earns a quick two points for a takedown. He looks quicker and slicker than Jimmy remembers. It's Trevor's strength. He's not the JV wrestler from last year.

Jimmy trots to the locker room and into a stall. He's sweating. He swallows the burning bile in his throat and tries to puke. Maybe then he'd feel better. Nothing comes up. He's still nauseous. He splashes his face with water. A roar sounds from the gym. Trevor's match must have just ended.

Jimmy stretches under the spotlight. He checks the scoreboard. Trevor's win has put the Minute Men up 2 points, 24 to 22. Fans pound the bleachers. Roxanne and her girlfriends chant "Jim-mee, Jim-mee." His opponent, Rafael Sanchez, twitches his head on his bull neck. He looks thick, impossible to knock down. Jimmy slaps the sides of his headgear. Wake up. He jumps high in the air, touching his knees to his chest. He can feel his muscles tensing in his lower back, neck, and jaw.

The referee signals them to the toe lines in the center circle. Jimmy bites down on his mouthpiece. The whistle blares. Rafael's stance is staggered, with his right foot forward. He's surprisingly light on his feet. Jimmy tells himself to be lighter. Which would work better, a low single-leg takedown or a v-pop of the arms to a double-leg take-down? He angles for the double.

They tie up. Jimmy has one hand reaching over Rafael's neck, the other on Rafael's wrist. He jerks Rafael to the left and shoots. He wraps his arms around Rafael's calves try-ing to yank him off balance. Rafael sprawls hard on top of Jimmy. Caught, stretched out, on his knees, Jimmy fights to stay off his stomach. He pulls his knees under him.

Jimmy slides his hands down to Rafael's ankles and muscles the legs in. In one quick motion, Jimmy pops up and takes top position over Rafael's back. Takedown! The referee waves two fingers, awarding Jimmy the points. Now Rafael is on his knees. Jimmy drives his shoulder into Rafael's back and grabs Rafael's wrist, sending him to his stomach. Jimmy checks the clock. Twenty-two seconds left in the first period. Damn, that was a hard two points.

Jimmy tries to turn Rafael over to his back, but he slips from under him. The ref awards Rafael one point for the escape. Two seconds left. The buzzer sounds.

Greco grabs Jimmy's arm. "How did he escape?" he yells. "Come on, work it, wake up!"

"Coach, I got it," he says.

The ref's whistle sounds.

Jimmy wins the coin toss for starting position. Top or bottom? Greco points down, so Jimmy has to choose the bottom. He'll earn a point if he escapes. But Jimmy hates being down against a short, heavy opponent. He has a lot to worry about: legs, cradles, and getting the crap cranked out of him. He kneels on the mat and puts his fingertips lightly on the mat, ready to spring up. Rafael takes top position, on one knee, with his arm around Jimmy's midsection.

The ref blows the whistle.

Rafael shoves Jimmy forward and coils his body around Jimmy using a spiral breakdown. Jimmy collapses to his stomach, arms tight to his chest. Greco is screaming something, but Jimmy can't make out the words over the cheering crowd. Jimmy looks into the stands. Behind the cheering Varsity Dads, Jimmy sees Detective Barnes.

Is it possible? Is he seeing things?

Greco yells, "Concentrate!" over the roar of the crowd. Jimmy searches the faces, trying to find the detective again.

His opponent tugs his arms, trying to lift them off the mat.

"What are you doing?" yells Greco. "Get up! Get to work!"

Jimmy rocks his body and pushes up with his free arm. He kicks his left leg free. On his side, he rolls and catches

Rafael's wrist, twisting it. Jimmy's free. He springs to his feet. One point.

The buzzer sounds. The period is over. Jimmy is winning 3 to 1. He searches the stands for the detective but can't locate him.

"What's going on?" Greco's face is red from yelling. "Are you hurt?"

"No."

"Then focus and wrestle."

Rafael gives the ref a thumbs-up, picking top position.

"Block the leg," calls Greco, slamming his hand against his thigh.

Could the police be waiting for me, wonders Jimmy. *Could Detective Santos be in the parking lot?*

Jimmy is in the down position again. He searches the faces in the stands.

The whistle blows. Rafael's leg shoots under Jimmy's body, locking him in, then the other leg follows in and under. Jimmy's facedown, flat on the mat, with Rafael's forearm on the back of his neck. *The detective could have just come to see the meet, or he could have come for me. He could be waiting for me!*

Rafael works in a half nelson. The crowd yells. "Get up, Jim-mee! Up!"

I could be arrested today, thinks Jimmy. Arrested in front of the team, in front of Greco. Rafael cranks Jimmy's shoulder up, trying to turn him to his back. Jimmy's arm is on fire, but he won't go to his back. He won't allow it. He kicks his legs and rocks side to side. Thirty seconds left.

Rafael is riding Jimmy's back. Jimmy has to get off his stomach. In a flash, Rafael pulls Jimmy over onto his back. The referee signals a three-second back turn. Jimmy fights his way back to his stomach. He lies there, no longer hearing the crowd. His head is buzzing. The lights seem to be pulsing. The referee awards three points for Rafael's back turn. And then the buzzer rings. The match is over. Jimmy lost by one point, 4 to 3. Is it possible?

Jimmy shakes Rafael's hand. Rafael's arm is raised.

He staggers off the mat. Greco grabs Jimmy's shoulder. "I don't know what you call that," he says.

Jimmy looks into the stands. Was it the detective? Was it? He can't find Detective Barnes.

"What the matter?" asks Greco.

"I'm sorry, Coach. I don't know." He pulls away. He's let down Greco, destroyed his chances of being undefeated. He's 0 and 1. Zero and 1!

"Jimmy, are you all right?" asks Trevor.

Jimmy pushes past him. He jogs to the gym door and sprints down the hall. Outside, it's snowing. Someone bangs him on the shoulder. Trevor again.

"What happened?"

Jimmy looks across the parking lot at the frozen cars. Nothing. No one. Everything is as it should be. The detective's car is nowhere in sight.

Diggy

JIMMY LOST! GRECO LOOKS LIKE HE JUST WITNESSED ARMAGED-don. The score is Minute Men 30, Colts 25. Crap. If Diggy's pinned, the team will lose by one point. His name is announced over the PA system. Fans thump their feet on the bleachers. He should be warming up, but he doesn't want to wrestle at 170, doesn't want to have the crowd whispering that Crow took his weight class, doesn't want to be the deciding match for the team! He bumps through the doors into the hall.

He paces to the bulletin board. The last thing he needs to see is staring him in the face. "Tan, mixed Lab puppy, answers to 'Whizzer.' Under a phone number someone scrawled "REWARD" in red magic marker. He doesn't want to think about the dog before the match, or about Gino telling someone, but he can't stop. He pictures the puppy in the unheated pool house with a blanket and a bath towel on the floor and realizes he isn't treating the puppy much better than Trevor did.

The weird thing is, Diggy really likes the dog. He didn't

think he'd like him so much. The puppy's wild and stronger than he expected. He runs circles around the yard, quick and agile as a greyhound. For now, he nicknamed him Mr. Burly, after his seventh-grade gym teacher, who played tennis while eating a slice of pizza. Besides, Mr. Burly is a better name than Whizzer.

Beyond the wire-webbed school windows, snow swirls above concrete sidewalks and settles against curbs and car tires. Diggy spots Jimmy and Roxanne sitting on the curb. Steam rises from Jimmy's bare head. Trevor stands over them as if he's listening. Diggy feels his face heating up. Trevor. The guy doesn't know boundaries. Always in the wrong place at the wrong time. A guy like Jimmy doesn't need a loser like Trevor Crow following him around. Diggy wonders what Jimmy and his dad stole. A car? Did they rob a bank? Diggy hopes Jimmy isn't telling Trevor. That would suck.

"You're wrestling next," calls Jane from the gym doors. "Greco is looking for you." She's wearing a Santa hat with a white pom-pom that Diggy bought her at the mall. Her name is written in sparkle script on the white furry brim. "Are you sick? What's wrong?" she asks.

"I like your hat." The hat half covers her birthmark and the rest is almost hidden with tan makeup, which makes her look older, like the MILFs who get their hair cut at his mother's beauty salon.

She touches the hat. "You don't think it looks random?"

"No, it looks cute."

"Thanks." She smiles. "What's the matter? Get in there and get psyched. You're wrestling like in thirty seconds!" She puts her hands on his shoulders, smiling into his face. "Come on Diggy, get pumped!"

"Crow was lucky," says Diggy.

"I wouldn't call a pin lucky."

"I didn't think he had it in him." Diggy turns to the window. Bb-sized hail shells the cars. Jimmy, Roxanne, and Trevor are still there.

"Can you believe Jimmy lost?" she asks.

"Yeah, I can believe it." Diggy wonders if Jane could keep a secret.

"Come on." She takes his hand. "You're going to be fine."

In the gym, Randy is coming down from the bleachers; his features, large as a puppet's, glow in the sea of faces.

Diggy feels like running.

"Did you see the score?" barks Randy. "You get pinned, your team loses. All you have to do is stay off your back."

"Like I don't know that," says Diggy. He walks to a dark corner with Randy following.

"So pull your head out of your ass." Randy's lips are thin and white.

Spectators stamp their feet on the bleachers, louder and louder. His teammates line up for a clap-tunnel. "Give me some space," says Diggy, pushing Randy in the chest. "Like, now!"

"Just stay off your back," says Randy.

Greco, ignoring Randy, places his arm around Diggy's shoulders. "You ready?"

"I think."

"It's just another match," says Greco. "Don't think about the weight difference or the score."

"I won't."

"That's Rudy Hunter, he likes to tie up. You ride the clock down and stay off your back," he says. "You're lower than he is. Use it. Go in low, and take him down. Use your hips."

Diggy sneaks a sidelong glance at Rudy Hunter waiting on the mat in a sphere of light. Hunter is big, manlike, and ripped. His cheeks are sucked out and hollow, his eyes two caves in his skull.

Diggy jogs between his clapping teammates, then to the center of the mat. Just another match, he repeats in his head. Just another match.

"Go Diggy!" yells Jane above the roaring fans.

The whistle blows and Hunter comes at him like a two-armed octopus, sucking him in. His grip is impossible to break. They struggle for position. Hunter shoots under him. Diggy throws his legs behind him in a sprawl, but Hunter has hooked his knee. Diggy is dragged in and under. It's like being hit by a tremendous undertow. Takedown. The ref signals two points.

Diggy is flat on his stomach with Hunter on his back. Hunter wraps his legs around Diggy's calves and twists Diggy's arm behind his back. Diggy knows an assortment of moves to deal with an arm bar, but there isn't any wiggle room. Hunter is overpowering him. Above the cheering, Diggy hears Randy's booming voice: "Get to your base, to your base." But with Hunter riding him, all 170 pounds of him, Diggy feels powerless. So this is what it's like to jump two weight classes. Impossible. The Minute Men cheer, yell, their necks strain with their mouths open. Hunter pushes Diggy's arm higher up his back. Diggy's shoulder is on fire. Greco calls it a first-class ticket on the pain train. Hunter is the conductor.

With the arm bar locked in place, Hunter works an Excalibur. Diggy knows the move. He's executed it a hundred times. The arm becomes the sword, Excalibur. The idea is to drive the arm across your opponent's back until he flips over on his stomach. Diggy can only suffer the pain, experience the burn, the humiliation. He fights, but knows Hunter will never release his arm. Instead, Hunter pushes it higher and higher, so that it feels like his arm will pop like a cork from a bottle. If Diggy fights, he could rip his arm from the socket. He's trapped. Hunter ratchets the torque on his arm. "The move is all physics," Greco explained. "There's only one place to go—on your back." Hunter is forcing Diggy over. Get pinned and the team loses. But Diggy can't stand the pain. In an instant, the ceiling light is in his eyes. A glaring, ugly white sun. Diggy's on his back.

"Bridge," yells Greco. "Bridge!"

Diggy's neck and feet brace, lifting his body off the mat, holding his shoulders inches away from a pin. The referee is on his knees, waving his open palm. The buzzer could save him. But how long can he hold this bridge?

The gym grows quiet. No one, not Randy or Greco, screams directions, because there's no way out. The clock ticks down from 50 seconds. Diggy shoves his fingers into Hunter's face. He gives Diggy a quick jerk and scoops his head with his arm, taking any hope away. Diggy rocks his shoulder blades. The seconds tick. 45, 44, 43 . . . The referee watches for that moment when his shoulders are in contact with the mat for two full seconds.

Randy's standard speech goes through Diggy's mind. "You may occasionally lose, but you don't get pinned. A pin is a complete breakdown in discipline and will. It means that you have lost your concentration, your desire, and given up on your technique."

40, 39, 38 . . . Diggy squirms from side to side. Hunter is in good position. Chest on chest. On his toes. Head up. The fans in the visitor's bleachers stamp their feet on the wooden planks and chant, "Hunter, Hunter."

The clock's upside down seconds fall, 35, 34, 33. Diggy thinks of Trevor's dog in the pool house. It's time to return him. *I shouldn't have taken him.*

The referee slaps the mat and blows his whistle. Pinned. The audience roars, hoots, and claps. The scoreboard moves the Colts up 6 points. Hunter stands and pumps his fist. Diggy scrambles to his feet. He shakes Hunter's hand. The referee raises Hunter's arm by the wrist.

Diggy pushes through his teammates toward the locker room.

Randy blocks his way. "Pinned! Pinned! You could have just lost," he fumes. "You had to get pinned like a cheerleader on prom night!" He shakes his head. "Fer Christ's sake, Diggy, come on!"

The guys hear him, everyone hears him.

Diggy shoves Randy aside. He hurls his headgear into the locker room and peels the straps of his singlet off his shoulders. Hunter overpowered him. First Crow and now Hunter.

"What was that?"

Diggy recognizes the voice and looks up. Nick is smiling under the brim of a beat-up Mets hat. He's wearing an untucked buttondown shirt, threadbare around the collar. The brothers hug hard. Nick feels like concrete, still larger than me, thinks Diggy. He smells like Diggy remembers. Aftershave and the woods. "What the hell was that?" asks Nick.

"That was me at one-seventy."

"I don't think you went balls out. I mean, who was that on the mat?"

Diggy can't answer.

"You've got to go back to basics."

"What are you doing home?" asks Diggy.

"It's a surprise. I came to see you wrestle."

"To see me get slaughtered."

"Don't worry. It's one match." He grabs Diggy around the shoulders.

"Does Randy know you're home?" he asks.

"Sure, he knows," says Nick.

"You gained weight."

"I'm lifting, even with a bad back."

They sit on a bench. The crowd in the gym continues to roar. "You don't know how good it is to see you," says Diggy. "Randy's out of control." He thinks of stealing the dog. *I'm out of control too,* he'd like to say.

Jimmy

THE GAS LAMPS IN FRONT OF ROXANNE'S HOUSE REFLECT OFF the snow. Jimmy cuts across her lawn, then up her driveway, past her Volvo, her father's Mercedes, her mother's Pathfinder, and climbs the stoop. He needs to see her, hear her voice, and hold her. At practice today he waited for the guys to say something about his loss. No one said a word. Everyone was mumbling that Diggy shouldn't have been pinned. Jimmy felt for him, but what could he say?

Greco met Jimmy's eye and said, "That's your last loss, you got that?"

Jimmy nodded.

It had to be the last loss. He couldn't recover from two losses at the beginning of the season. He could kiss his hopes of a scholarship good-bye. Diggy is the only one who knows what's really bothering him. And Jimmy has to keep it that way. If word spread, he'd be looked at like, what? A criminal?

Mr. Sweetapple holds the doorknob. His wide belly pulls his shirt stiff at the shoulders. He removes his glasses.

"Hi, could I talk to Roxanne?" Jimmy enters their foyer. Instead of his mother's supermarket calendar and half-dead houseplants, the Sweetapples have real paintings on the walls and a tree with tiny yellow fruit growing in a ceramic pot at the foot of their oak staircase.

"Jimmy!" Roxanne leans over the rail on the second-floor landing. She hurries down the staircase in sweatpants turned down low on her hips, a tight shirt, and suede mid-calf boots. Her large green eyes shine.

"Jim, let's talk for a moment." Mr. Sweetapple's voice is deep and sure of itself, like one of the Republican fatheads on talk radio that Jimmy's mother listens to when she irons.

"Dad, Jimmy came over here to see me," says Roxanne.

Roxanne's mother comes in drying her hands on a dish towel.

"Hello, Mrs. Sweetapple," he says.

"Hello, Jimmy." Her words sound like ice water.

"Why can't we talk? Right, Jim?" Mr. Sweetapple cracks a smile.

Jimmy sits on the edge of their couch. He's wondering if he's being set up for an ambush. Maybe her father had a camera planted in his office.

"Dad, could I at least talk to Jimmy first?" asks Roxanne.

"We're all here, we might as well talk." He sits opposite Jimmy wearing this phony smirk. Between them is a coffee table with a cut-glass dish filled with clear marbles with ice-blue centers.

"Dad!" says Roxanne loudly.

"For once, no," he snaps. "I'm the one who is going to be paying over forty-three thousand dollars a year in tuition."

"That's not fair," she says.

"Jim, Roxanne is turning eighteen next month," says Mrs. Sweetapple. "She's on the way to college in the fall."

"What's that supposed to mean?" asks Roxanne.

"It means exactly what your mother said," says Mr. Sweetapple.

"That's not an answer." Roxanne throws up her hands in protest.

"Your mother's saying that you need to concentrate on school and studying."

"No, she's not," argues Roxanne. "You're both being horrible."

Jimmy holds his breath.

Mr. Sweetapple glances at his wife. "Jimmy, I received a telephone call from the police department." He arches his eyebrows. "They told me you and your father were under investigation."

For a second, it feels like he's having a heart attack. He lowers his head.

"And," he continues, "the police were over at your house when Roxanne was present."

"Jimmy, I didn't tell anyone!" Roxanne clenches her teeth. "I swear."

"I'd like to hear Jim's explanation," says Mr. Sweetapple. "Go ahead son, you should tell us. I just want to get to the bottom of it."

"It's getting taken care of," says Jimmy.

"What is getting taken care of?" Mr. Sweetapple levels his gaze.

"You don't have to answer him," says Roxanne.

"It's something with my father."

"He's in trouble?" asks Mrs. Sweetapple softly.

"He could be. I don't know." Jimmy lowers his eyes. How can he tell them? They wouldn't understand. But the truth is, he'd like to tell them. He'd like them to be on his side.

"You must know more than that," says Mr. Sweetapple.

"Mom," pleads Roxanne, wiping a tear from her eye. "Make him stop."

"It's all right," says Jimmy. "It's something that happened at my father's job. He's in construction and . . . some building materials went missing. It happens a lot."

"Jimmy, you don't have to tell them." Tears run down her cheeks.

"Roxanne, it's all right," says Jimmy. "Really."

"And what's your part in all this?" asks Mr. Sweetapple.

"Nothing," says Jimmy.

"Nothing?" Mr. Sweetapple waits.

"My father has hired a lawyer. The whole thing is getting taken care of."

"Did you know that Roxanne was accepted to Villanova University? She's going bio-medical," he says.

"Premed," adds Mrs. Sweetapple.

Jimmy looks at Roxanne's face. It's burning red.

"She found out last week," says her mother. "So you can see she has a lot on the line here."

Why didn't she tell him?

"Roxanne's mother and I made sure our daughter had a plan, and we don't want"—he searches for the right word—"complications. No one's saying you're not a good-hearted person. We're not saying that. It's just that . . ." He looks at his wife.

Jimmy stands. "I've got to get going." His voice is flat. He keeps his eyes to the gleaming floor. "My mother has supper waiting."

Roxanne follows him to the front door, then to the stoop. She closes the door. "Jimmy, I'm sorry," she says. "He's a control freak and I hate him." She touches his shoulder. "An obnoxious jerk. He started on me, like he started on you." She moves her hand to his cheek.

"You could have told me about getting into Villanova."

"I thought it might be better to wait. I didn't want to make you feel bad."

"Feel bad?" He can hardly believe it. "Like I'm *not* going to college?"

"That's not what I meant. Look, I was going to tell you. You're my prom date, remember?" Her face brightens. "I just thought I'd wait until you get accepted to—"

"East Stroudsburg." He shuts his eyes and kisses her. "You still want me to call you?"

"Of course. My parents can't stop me from seeing you."

He leaves her on the stoop and takes long strides down her driveway, then up her block. He knows if the police called Roxanne's father, Coach Greco could be next.

Diggy

THEY ARE CHILLING IN NICK'S BEDROOM—NICK ON HIS BED, Diggy on the floor with his hands behind his neck. Diggy wonders what Nick would say if he told him about Whizzer, still locked in the pool house.

"Seems like a waste," says Nick.

"What does?"

"The trophies, the medals, all of it. I'd like to put them in the attic." Around the room, trophies gleam with chrome or gold-colored wrestlers in their stances, or with a hand raised in victory.

"Randy would have your ass," says Diggy.

Nick grabs a trophy and snaps the head off a plastic wrestler. He flicks it at Diggy. "Heads up."

Diggy catches it and throws it back. Nick crawls across the bed and topples onto Diggy. They turn over in slow motion, each trying to execute a wrestling move. Nick has his old strength. "You've got to get into a zone," he says. "Your last match you looked like spaghetti."

"What are you talking about?"

"All over the place. My college coach used to say that."

They roll across the carpet, folding their arms and legs into wrestling moves, half speed, half strength, until Nick bangs his head into the wall. Diggy laughs. Nick rubs his head. His brown eyes smile.

"Remember our old room in the old house?" asks Diggy.

"You mean the Legos?"

Diggy's eyes shine. Their room was covered, one side to the other, with Lego building blocks. They could barely walk without demolishing a pirate's ship, a castle, or a rocket launch. There were tiny knights on Lego horses in Lego castles. Lego spaceships with control towers.

"Remember Mom?" asks Nick. "Every time we finished constructing, she'd tell us to clean it up. Then we'd have to start over."

"Starting over was the best part," says Diggy.

Nick punches him. "You got a girlfriend?"

"Remember Jane?"

"The Stain?"

"No one calls her that anymore," says Diggy. "She's pretty awesome."

Nick looks at him like he's gone psycho.

"What?" asks Diggy.

"I'm just surprised. I didn't think you'd ever say that."

"I know." Diggy feels his heart drop.

"You were always so worried about your precious reputation."

Diggy nods. "I surprised myself." He looks out the window at the pool house. "You were there that night at wrestling camp, when she was doing funnels; why didn't you do something to help her?"

"She was drunk, what was I supposed to do."

"She was, like, fifteen."

"Like I said, people talk. She got drunk and threw up. The rest of it, I never listened to it."

He believes his brother and wonders why he ever doubted Jane in the first place.

Diggy's eyes return to the pool house. He's had the puppy too long. Maybe Nick could help him. "I'll be right back." Diggy opens the bedroom door. "Stay here, don't move." He sprints down the stairs, through the house, and out the back door. He runs across the deck and around the pool.

Minutes later, Diggy places the puppy down on the bedroom floor. The puppy sniffs a trail that takes him to Nick. "You got a dog? Does Mom know?"

"No one knows," says Diggy.

The puppy gives Nick a sloppy lick on his cheek. "Yuk." The puppy licks him again. He laughs.

"Gino and I drove to that motel where Trevor Crow lives. I saw the dog chained up outside."

"Wait! Slow down!"

"I'm giving him back."

Nick squints at him. "This is Crow's dog?"

"I know," says Diggy. "Listen, Crow bragged about him every day at lunch like he's some kind of great dog, and then I see him tied in the cold."

Nick stares at him. "Gino knows?" Nick pushes the dog away. "Who else knows?"

"No one else." The dog leans his head into Diggy's hand. He caresses his muzzle. "Every time Randy drove me past that motel, the dog was always tied in the parking lot." It's an exaggeration, but Diggy did see him once.

"Crow humiliated you by taking your weight class, so you stole his dog. You know how coldhearted that is?"

"I told you, I'm giving him back. I just need a plan." Diggy rubs the puppy's velvet ears. "Help me. All we've got to do is go to the supermarket and tie him in the lot. When the place closes, someone will see him."

"You know who you sound like, right? You ever hear Randy try to sell one of his gas guzzlers?" Nick stands and shakes his head. "Jesus, Diggy. Who the hell are you? This is like"—he shakes his head—"unjustifiable. I saw the flyers at the school. Did you get slammed on the head, or something? You're always blaming Randy for everything, now who are you going to blame?"

"We were drinking vodka."

"We?" Nick searches Diggy's face.

"I told you, me and Gino. Stop worrying. I'll tie him

up tonight and then it's over. I'm not going to get caught."

Whizzer jumps up on the bed and barks. Diggy and Nick look at him.

"No, I'm not helping you give the dog back. I don't want any part of it. What I should do is kick your fat ass."

Jimmy

ROXANNE MEETS HIM ON THE GYM STEPS. SHE'S WEARING HIS baggy varsity jacket, a tan skinlike spandex shirt, and faded jeans that have the knees blown out. She hugs him around the waist and puts her head on his shoulder as if nothing between them has changed. "I'm sorry about yesterday," she says, whispering in his ear. "My father can be an asshole. He's always talking about doing the best for me, making sure I stay on the straight path, but he never asks me what I'm thinking, or what I'm feeling."

"Don't apologize. It wasn't your fault."

She puts her hands in his front pockets and leans into him. Her breath smells like peppermint.

"Did you tell anyone about what happened?" he asks.

"No."

"Don't, please."

"Jimmy"—she touches her lips to his—"what's really going on with the police? Are you in trouble?"

"I could be."

"Can you tell me?"

"Your father probably already went to the police station," he says. "You should ask him."

"I don't care what he thinks. I want you to tell me."

"Roxanne, I can't."

They sit on the steps. The sun is melting what's left of the snow. He shows her a brochure from East Stroudsburg University. The pages are filled with smiling college students, so perfect they could be Barbie dolls. "Stroudsburg has a good wrestling program," he says. "I'm going to need a scholarship." He thinks about his record. One loss, no wins.

She holds his hands in hers. "I saw your mother at Foodtown. I was on her checkout line and I didn't know it was her until I was halfway through."

"She's being considered for a management position," lies Jimmy. "She probably was just filling in at the register."

"She's so sweet. She invited me over again."

"I'd like that." From the corner of his eye, Jimmy spies a black four-door Ford coming diagonally across the parking lot toward them. His heart speeds up, until he can feel it pounding in his chest. The car halts with its front tire hugging the curb. Fear races up Jimmy's legs and crawls across his back. Please, no trouble at school. Not here. Through the windshield, Jimmy recognizes the detectives. The passenger door swings open. Detective Barnes steps out. "Jim, you got a moment?"

Not here. God, make them leave me alone.

"Two plus two, it don't equal four. I'm all confused." Detective Barnes runs his hand over his shaved head. He crosses the sidewalk and puts one foot on a step. He looks massive. Roxanne's cheeks flush red. She watches Barnes, then looks at Jimmy with dread in her eyes that he's never seen before.

"Do you think we could borrow him for an hour?" Detective Barnes smiles. "Unless you want to go with us?"

"Why are you doing this to him?" she blurts. "I mean, this is school." Roxanne's fingertips are shaking in his hand.

Jimmy knows she could make things worse. He doesn't want to piss them off.

"We've had a few developments in the case," says Barnes. "You do want us to solve our case?"

"You should be talking to Mr. O'Shea," she says.

"Oh, we will," says Barnes without flinching. "Just a matter of time."

"Come on, Jim, let's go," Barnes's tone is heavy. "You don't want us out here every day."

Jimmy's stomach turns to rock.

Detective Barnes puts his hands in his pants pockets. He smiles.

Roxanne pulls Jimmy's arm gently toward the gym.

Detective Santos opens the driver's door and pops his head above the car's roof line. He removes his sunglasses. His tan face is calm. "Jim, this is routine. We developed a lead and you might be able to clarify a few things for us."

Jimmy glances toward the gym doors, just a few feet away. He imagines them slamming behind him. Would the detectives come after him?

"Then this is about you, isn't it?" whispers Roxanne.

He backs away from her. "I'll call you later." She frowns. He feels guilty for leaving her, but he keeps moving down the steps toward the detectives.

"Jimmy—" Her words are cut short with the slam of the car door.

Jimmy

JIMMY FOLLOWS DETECTIVE SANTOS INTO A MESSY SQUAD room, just like on TV. Ancient suitcase-sized computer monitors crowd desks covered with coffee cups, family photos, and papers.

"That the wrestler?" asks a woman with a stiff, whirling hairdo, like the top of a dipped ice-cream cone.

"Hulk Hogan himself," says Barnes.

Santos opens a door into a room just big enough for the table and two chairs inside. White acoustic panels on the walls are ripped off in places, exposing unpainted cement blocks.

"Sit down, relax." Santos pulls out a battered wooden chair. "You want something, a Coke, water?"

"No, I'm fine."

Jimmy scrolls through his messages:

Trevor: **wru? ru ok?**

Bones: **Greco is pissed, yo. WTF?????**

Roxanne: **call me**

Diggy: **ru in jail???**

He shoots a text to Trevor: **Tell coach b there iaf**

Detective Santos balances on the edge of the other chair, leaning forward. "I read about your match in the paper last week. Sounded tough."

Jimmy shrugs, eyes on the tabletop.

"Don't worry, I've seen you wrestle. You've got good instincts. Everybody loses sometimes."

Jimmy keeps his eyes down. He's not going to talk unless he has to.

"You're the team captain, right? How's that feel?"

"Fine."

"That's all you can say about it?"

"Yeah."

"How's your dad feel about it?"

"He likes it," answers Jimmy.

"Does he brag about you?"

"I suppose, sometimes."

"If I had a son like you, I'd never stop talking about you. I'd never put you in a compromising situation." Santos smiles. "You close to your dad?"

"I guess."

"He ever smack you, you know, when you get out of line?"

"No."

"Never?" Santos smiles again.

"No, he's not like that."

"My old man, he had hands like two-by-fours. He

smacked me if I didn't dry the dishes."

Jimmy digs his fingertips into the grooves in the table. He's not going to rat on Pops. No way. He wonders if he could end this by telling Santos he has an attorney. But wouldn't it be better if the detectives think he's cooperating?

"Our investigation, it's developing. We have a suspect."

Jimmy takes a breath and holds it.

"A night watchman."

Jimmy feels his heart again. He concentrates on keeping his breathing regular. His phone vibrates.

"You have to get that?" asks Santos.

"I'm supposed to be at practice."

"I thought you might be doing something with your girl today?"

"I can't even think. You guys just about kidnapped me."

"I appreciate you coming with us."

Jimmy shakes his head. "I wish it hadn't been in front of Roxanne. Her father finds out I'm in trouble, I never see her again."

"Are you in trouble?"

"No." Jimmy sits up. He's got to be more careful.

"That night you and your dad were stopped with that load of lumber, did you meet a night watchman?"

"No."

"You didn't? That's not what your face is telling me. When you're nervous, your mouth twitches," says Santos. "I'm a poker player. I study faces. It's called a tell."

Jimmy touches his mouth. "I told you I was sleeping."

"I forgot, you were sleeping. Are you a heavy sleeper?"

"Look, I already told you what happened."

"We didn't ask you about a night watchman. We only put things together yesterday. See, someone beat him real good."

"Are you saying my father beat him up?"

"No, I'm asking you to tell me what happened that night. The truth." Santos leans back in the chair and crosses his leg over his knee. His brown shoes have a high shine. "I'm giving you a chance to get this off your chest, once and for all."

Jimmy shakes his head.

"Do you know what cutting a deal means? The first person to come in and help us, he gets something like a Get Out of Jail Free card. Immunity from prosecution. We don't do this for everyone. I know this would be hard, especially because your father is involved, but he wouldn't have to know, not right away. This is your chance, Jim."

Jimmy can barely speak. "Why don't you ask the night watchman who beat him up?"

"We did." Santos leans across the table. "Jim, my friend, this is bigger than that single load of lumber. People are going to go to prison. They are going to do time, hard time. Do you know what hard time is? That's time that you can't do, time that you can't afford."

"You expect me to turn in my own father?"

"I'd hate for you to do hard time." Santos taps his finger on the table. "I don't want your first time having sex in a shower to be in a prison."

Jimmy holds his head. "If my coach knew I was here, he'd be—"

"What?" asks Santos. "What would he do?"

"You're talking about my father!" His voice echoes off the walls. "I can't do that. That's not me. Now please, can I leave?"

"You can go, but leaving would be a mistake. You need to think, to talk this through with me."

There's a knock on the door. The woman with the ice cream hairdo peeks in. "I have it right here." She waves a manila envelope.

"Jim, this is Detective Cruz."

She smiles. "How are you holding up, honey?" She walks inside and puts her hand over Jimmy's. Her fingers are long, and her nails have designs painted on them. "You thinking about doing the right thing?"

"He's thinking about it," says Santos.

"That's what you have to do." A tiny gold pair of handcuffs dangles from her necklace. "Don't forget who you are. You don't want to mess that up. All the hard work. You already look like a college boy. You want to be going to Penn State, not the state pen."

Jimmy's heard this expression as a joke, only she isn't kidding.

She opens the envelope. She hands Jimmy a photo of an old man, cut and beaten, one eye swollen shut. "He needed a few stitches. Forty at his hairline, nine on his cheek, to be precise. He was there that night at the development. You recognize him?"

Jimmy shakes his head.

"Take another look," says Santos.

"He's going to say he saw you," says Detective Cruz. "If you don't take Detective Santos's offer, he's going to be there first. Then, it's off the table."

"Saw me?" asks Jimmy.

"The funny thing about that old man is, he has perfect vision." She smiles. "So, if you were there, he saw you. And we all know you were there, right?"

Jimmy forces himself to look at the photo. Is the man really the guard?

"I'm handling his assault," she says. "What do you think? Is it related to the case you're involved in?" She taps her fingernails on the table.

Jimmy steadies his breathing.

"I was taking his information and it was like a lightbulb going off over my head. He works at Horseman's Estates. The midnight shift. Isn't that a coincidence?"

Jimmy continues to study the photo. The old man's thick gray hair looks familiar. He is the guard.

"He's claiming his mugging was a robbery, but I think someone felt some heat and opened a can of whoop-ass on him." She leans toward Jimmy. He smells her musky perfume. "Still don't recognize him?"

Stop, please stop.

"Someone tuned him up, and I'm going to answer who, what, where, and why," she says.

Jimmy's phone vibrates. "I'm going to have to go," he says, almost begging. "You said an hour."

Santos checks his watch. "It hasn't been an hour."

Detective Barnes comes in. His long-sleeved T-shirt bulges as if he had just knocked out a set on a bench press. "So, is my man Jimmy on board?"

"He's still playing hard ball, but I think he's starting to see the big picture." Santos hands Barnes the photo.

Barnes glances at it and tosses it on the table. "Whoever did this is looking at ten years."

He doesn't have to tell the detectives where he lives. They make the turns as if they drive the route every day. "So Jim, I wouldn't tell your father about our offer," says Barnes. "Sleep on it."

"He might not like it," says Santos.

At his house, Jimmy pulls the rear door handle. It's locked and there's no button to open it. Santos turns around in the seat. "You should definitely think hard. This thing is a slow-moving train, but eventually it's gonna be right on your ass."

His father's truck is in the driveway. His uncle Johnny's

black Ford pickup with the license plate FREBYRD is parked across the street. The shed door is open.

"You know your mother can be arrested, if she knows what's going on," says Barnes, "and I'm sure she does."

"My mother?"

"It's called conspiracy."

The door locks snap up.

Jimmy steps into the shed. Inside it's colder than the yard. A single 60-watt bulb hangs from the ceiling. Pops and his uncle are stacking something covered with layers of clear bubble wrap. "Hey," he says.

They both turn suddenly, their faces frozen with surprise. "You shouldn't sneak up on us like that, partner," says Pops.

Uncle Johnny laughs. "Talk about giving someone a heart attack." He gives Jimmy a hug. "Check out the size of this kid," he says. "What are they feeding you?" Despite everything, Jimmy smiles. "I hear you're ripping them up."

"Sometimes," says Jimmy.

Uncle Johnny's muscled arms are tattooed with skulls and dragons, sleeve style, to his wrists. He wears his hair in a mullet, short on the sides, long in the back. He's three years younger than Pops and has crystal-blue eyes. He always makes Jimmy nervous. Everything about him is cocky and big-headed, from his tan to his pre-faded designer jeans. "What are you guys doing?" asks Jimmy.

"Shooting the bull," says Pops.

"What's in the bubble wrap?"

His father smiles. "How was practice?"

"I didn't go to practice."

"You sick?"

"No." He feels the heat of the hanging bulb on his scalp. He grabs a bubble-wrapped package.

"It's moldings," says Pops, and takes it out of his hands.

"Where did you get it?"

"For your information, some of it was owed to me. The rest was bought and paid for by your uncle Johnny."

"That's right," says his uncle. "Yours truly." He bows. They both laugh.

"What about that and that and that?" Jimmy's words are razor-sharp. He points to stacks of boxes and plastic tubs of 25-pound drywall screws. "You think everyone's stupid! The detectives, they know. They have a woman on the case now. She's calling me honey and showing me photos. They all know!"

"What!" His father raises his hands, palms facing Jimmy.

"I guess you know the night watchman from Horseman's Estates got beat up?" says Jimmy.

Pops looks like someone slapped him. "Who told you that?"

"The detectives brought me to the police station and showed me his photo."

"When?"

"Today. They just dropped me off."

"Son of a bitch!" Uncle Johnny cocks his jaw to one side, then the other. "You tell them anything?"

"No."

"Didn't you hear what Frankie Scales said?" yells Pops.

"They came to the school," says Jimmy. "They called me out in front of Roxanne. In front of everyone."

"You didn't tell Roxanne, did you?" asks Pops.

"Pops, no, I didn't tell anyone." Tears well up in his eyes. "Did you hurt that guard?"

"That had nothing to do with your father," says his uncle.

"How did you know about it?" asks Jimmy.

"Knock off the interrogation and drop it," says Pops, already annoyed. "You worry about winning your next match. We'll worry about everything else."

Jimmy looks at his father's hands. His knuckles are clean and smooth. He could have worn gloves or used a baseball bat. Jimmy shivers. The O'Shea brothers are nothing more than thugs. Pops doesn't care enough about his family to stop stealing. "Pops, you know who did it, don't you?"

"No one knows nothing."

"You're lying!"

"Jimmy, I don't know, and I don't want to know, and I have company right now." Pops looks at his brother.

"And you don't need to know," warns Uncle Johnny.

Jimmy studies his father's face. He doesn't have a tell. His face is like stone. "They want to cut a deal and give me immunity," says Jimmy.

"Against me? Your own father? I don't think that's legal."

Uncle Johnny laughs into his hand. "Stupid dicks."

"Pops, I'd never do that, I'd never hurt you."

"Good boy." His father reaches to stroke his head.

Jimmy pulls back. From the open shed, he spots his mother sorting laundry in the pantry. She lifts a pair of jeans and cuts them in half with a chop, then folds them onto a pile of wash. Barnes's words swim in Jimmy's head: "It's called conspiracy."

In the yard, white vapor blows out the dryer vent under the window, making the air smell like a drawer full of clean T-shirts. Jimmy bursts through the back door. His mother jumps. "What do you think they're doing in the shed?" he shouts.

"Don't worry, I'm going to talk to your father."

"Talk to him? Ma, it's way beyond talking to him. He's filling the shed again."

"He told me all that stuff is—"

"Are you kidding me? You can't be that stupid. He's ripping that stuff off."

"Your uncle Johnny is taking that stuff home with him."

"You're as bad as him! I'm going to jail! You could be going to jail! Mom, this is for real!"

Trevor

TREVOR CHECKS THE ROOM'S THERMOSTAT. SEVENTY, BUT HE'S still cold. The curtains flutter in front of the drafty windows. He kicks the wooden trunk at the foot of his bed. He should use a screwdriver and open the trunk, but the lion-faced lock could be worth something. London has had a locksmith at the motel, but Trevor didn't remember to ask about the lock.

He checks his phone for any missed calls. It rang after midnight last night, but again no one was there. "Private number" came up on the phone.

He pulls his door open to the courtyard parking lot and leans in his doorway. Frost covers the car windshields. In a few hours, the motel will be filling up for the night.

Trevor doesn't want to stop searching for Whizzer. Bones, with his big mouth, said the dog's "dead in a ditch on the side of the highway. You might as well get over it." Trevor looks toward the road and thinks about the puppy dying, terrified and alone.

Across the courtyard, the blonde hooker darts from

room 4A, in the same red dress she usually wears at night. When Trevor told the guys about her, they laughed and Diggy asked, "Are you choking the chicken while she's doing it in the next room?" Trevor must have blushed, because Diggy was exactly right.

The girl walks between parked cars with her high heels in her hand, barefoot in the cold, then fixes her eyes on Trevor. "You didn't see a cab, did you?"

"No," he says, trying to think of something clever. It would be cool to talk to her. "You need one?"

"Aw, duh." She smiles. She doesn't have a coat and it must be freezing with just stockings on her legs. She puts the strap of her pocketbook between her teeth and places her high heels on the hood of a car. Reaching with both arms, she twists a rubber band around her hair, so that it's close to her head in a ponytail. She looks like a college girl, maybe a bit older. "I'm having the worst night," she says. "What I could use is some coffee."

"There's Gus's Diner a half-mile west on this road," he says. "It's open all night." He thinks of what she must have just done and feels like a gawky kid.

"You don't have a car, do you?"

"Just a license."

"I either lost my cell phone, or some jerk stole it." She folds her arms across her chest. "Didn't I see you here last week?" The girl squints at him. "Do you live here or something?"

"It's temporary," he says.

She hugs herself across her breasts and appears to think this over.

"Do you want to come in? It's warm and you could use my cell phone."

"You look like someone I once knew," she says. "What are you in, Molly Pitcher High?" She follows him into his room. She sidesteps around the room, looking at his wrestling posters, then stops at his two third-place medals that hang from their blue and gold ribbons. "You're a wrestler? The wrestlers in my school were always hunks." She turns and smiles at him. "You look strong."

In the room's overhead light, he sees that she's a bit round-shouldered, with large breasts. Patches of acne across her cheeks are covered with makeup. She places her hands on Trevor's shoulders as if they are about to dance, then runs them along his sides. "You're all muscle. I like that." Her breasts are almost touching his chest. He can't speak, doesn't dare to move. "Let me ask you something," she says near his ear. "How much money do you have?"

"I don't know." He's breathing hard. "Not a lot." He's heard stories about hookers getting guys naked, then stealing their wallets.

"What's not a lot?" She releases him. "I could do something for you, for say, fifty bucks." She sits on the edge of the bed and supports herself with her arms behind her.

Her legs are long and shapely. "You *do* know what I'm talking about?"

Trevor nods.

"Would you like that?" She crosses and uncrosses her legs.

"I suppose."

"Let's see the moolah."

He rifles through his dresser and finds the blue felt Crown Royal bag where he keeps his money. Thirty-five dollars.

"Let me see." She extends her fingers and wiggles them. She wears a silver ring on each finger, including her thumb.

He hands her the bills. She pulls them apart, straightens them, turns them over so they all face the same way, then folds them. "Come over here." She pats the bed. "Are you a virgin?" she asks, smiling. "Or are you the mack daddy of this motel?"

Trevor remembers his school's STD poster of a bee strolling along with a hooker on his arm. *It's up to you to BEE on guard!* Crabs, gonorrhea, syphilis, AIDS go through his mind like a ticker tape. *Crow has the crabs! Crow has the clap, stand by for an update.* "Do you have condoms?" he asks.

"What do you think?" she winks.

He peeks out the side of the curtain at the motel's office window. His mother is behind the check-in desk.

"You were expecting someone?"

"No, no, I just don't want my mother coming in here."

"Your mother?"

"She works here."

"Camille? The lady at the desk?" She crinkles her eyes and stands. "You're her son?"

"It doesn't make any difference."

"I don't know. I come here a lot." She opens the door, looks around, then shuts the door. "How old are you, anyway?"

"Almost eighteen."

"See that, you're too honest. You could have said you were nineteen, and I would have believed you."

"I'm going to be eighteen next month," he says.

She hooks the back of his neck and kisses him on the mouth. Her other hand goes down his back and squeezes his ass. "You're a cutie," she says. She unfolds a twenty from his money roll and gives the bill to him. "I'm charging fifteen for the kiss."

Trevor shoves the bill in his pocket. He's breathing easier, but still has a raging hard-on.

She opens the door and looks out. "Now, how about your phone?"

He hands it to her.

She dials quickly. "It's me," she says. "Asshole, I didn't know!" She hands him his cell. "Like I'm supposed to know they're already here."

From the doorway, Trevor watches a black town car

drive around the horseshoe and stop. "By the way, my name is Molly, like in Molly Pitcher," she says. "See you around." She hands him the rest of his money, then crosses the lot to the car and gets into the back seat.

Trevor's phone vibrates in his pocket. It reads "private number." He answers it.

"Diggy found your dog," says someone in a whisper.

"Who is this?" Trevor steps back inside his room.

"He'll be in his yard tonight. Just open the gate and take him."

"Gino?" asks Trevor, trying to recognize the voice. "Gino is that you? Is this a joke?"

The call disconnects.

Trevor

THE TOOLS IN THE BACK OF LONDON'S TRUCK RATTLE AND pound on the truck bed. Trevor speeds through the streets of Puny Town with Jimmy riding shotgun. Could Diggy have found Whizzer! How? Where? If he did, why didn't he call me? None of it makes sense, it's insane. Maybe what makes sense is Diggy found Whizzer and has been holding him. But if Diggy has any part in it, Trevor's going to show him how it feels, how he's felt. Trevor may have no house to live in and no father, but no one can steal his dog and get away with it. A teammate, his own lousy teammate!

"Slow down," yells Jimmy. "How am I going to find it if we're going seventy miles per hour?"

Trevor completes a sweeping turn around a cul-de-sac and guns the truck along a dark road past sprawling mansions.

Jimmy peers into the night. "Why would Diggy have your dog? It doesn't make sense. Diggy's solid. Give him a fair shot."

"Jimmy, don't be so stupid. Nothing's fair! Do you

think my father thought his ride home on the turnpike would be his last day on this earth? And now, I'm living in a slam-bam-thank-you-ma'am motel? Is that fair?"

"But the team is different."

Trevor swallows. "It's not."

At the bottom of another cul-de-sac, Diggy's Mustang is parked in a driveway. Trevor circles, then stops up the block. He kills the engine.

"What are you going to do?" asks Jimmy.

"I'm going to look in the yard."

They walk the wide driveway toward the white-brick façade and a giant foyer window. Inside, a crystal chandelier twinkles in front of a winding staircase.

"Man," says Jimmy. "Diggy's father could have bought him a pedigree."

A Minute Men Wresting sticker is peeling off the bumper of the Mustang. Trevor cups his hands against the rear window. An antler from the deer in his front yard sits on the space behind the back seat under the rear window. "Look at this," says Trevor, pointing at it. "Remember, someone ripped the head off that deer in my yard?"

Jimmy cups his hands on the window. "What is that?"

"An antler."

Trevor, heart thumping, passes the garage doors. Jimmy tails him, looking back and forth like they're escaping from prison. They cut the corner of the house and follow a path to a white gate. "Stay here," says Trevor. "Let me look around." His armpits are soaked. He unlatches the gate, then enters the backyard. A redwood deck steps down to a large patio, then a pool with a twisted tree branch rising from the water. Light shines from the rear windows of the house. He has to think. He has to be ready. He may have to fight. He feels the rush of blood go through his body.

Calm down. Breathe. He imagines Whizzer racing across the yard, but it's empty; there's only the cold, damp night. A shadow crosses the patch of light on the deck. Trevor stays close to the house. He doesn't want to be spotted from the windows. He inches toward the deck as if he's in a minefield. Jimmy waits next to the gate with his hands jammed in his pockets, still looking back and forth.

The rear slider door opens. Diggy walks onto the deck. Trevor's breathing stops. Any minute Diggy will turn and spot him—then what? Trevor hasn't thought it through.

Diggy clomps down the deck steps and jogs across the patio to the pool house. He pushes the door open. A dog yelps. "Hey, Mr. Burly, what are you doing? Are you hungry?" asks Diggy.

Trevor crouches, watching in amazement, still holding his breath.

A moment later, Diggy runs past the pool to the patio with Whizzer trotting ahead of him. Whizzer leaps up on the deck, his black eyes anxiously waiting to go into the house.

Trevor's throat, then his lungs, release. "Whizzer!"

He storms across the deck, stopping inches from Diggy. "You're pathetic!" Trevor shoves Diggy in the shoulder.

Diggy's eyes grow round as marbles and his face pales. "Trevor, I found him."

"No, you didn't!"

"I swear, I found him," Diggy pleads.

"Don't lie about it!" shouts Trevor, shoving him again.

Jimmy comes up. "How long have you had him?" he asks.

"Jimmy, I know what you're thinking, but I found him." Diggy lifts his hands like it's a stickup. "I swear on my grandmother's grave."

"Found him when, where?" Jimmy glances at Trevor.

"He's lying," says Trevor.

"Did you take him?" Jimmy waits for an answer.

Diggy grabs the door handle. His eyes narrow into angry slits. "I can make you wish you never came into my yard," he sneers. "And Jimmy, don't play the angel with me. Didn't the cops pay you a visit at school? So get the dog and get off my property. You're both trespassing."

Jimmy rips Diggy's hand off the door. "You either took him or you didn't take him!"

"Jimmy, come on," says Diggy, annoyed. "Trevor had the dog chained in the cold."

Trevor barely hears the words, everything's gone white. He rushes Diggy, howling, his cry filling the yard. Trevor clocks Diggy in the chin, the head, the chest, again and again. Diggy tries to block his fists, but it's a blizzard of punches. Trevor feels only rage, white-hot rage. Diggy's legs cave and he crashes into the deck rail. His head thuds on the boards and Trevor's on him like a wild animal.

Trevor feels Jimmy pulling at his shoulder, but with his knee on Diggy's chest and his hand on Diggy's throat, Trevor continues punching, his arm firing like a piston. Trevor beats the words into Diggy's face, "You. Stole. My. Dog. You. Stole. Him!" Bam, bam, once, twice, again, then again into Diggy's jaw. Trevor wants to stop but can't. "You've always been riding me, calling me names, trying to make me feel like I'm shit!" he yells. "You were pissing on my dad! And then you stole my dog!"

Jimmy bear-hugs Trevor around the chest and drags him off the deck. "Stop it, stop, you're going to kill him."

Diggy curls into a ball, holding his head with both hands.

Tears streak Trevor's cheeks. He's breathing hard and struggling. "Jimmy, damn it, let go of me."

Jimmy releases him.

Trevor wants it to be over. He wants to go home. He bends, trying to lift Whizzer, but the puppy is spooked and backs up.

The kitchen slider opens. Nick looks confused, then casts his eyes on Diggy.

"Crow came for his dog," croaks Diggy.

"You did this?" Nick comes down the deck stairs with

his eyes nailed on Trevor.

"He asked for it!" Trevor's panting, trying to catch his breath.

"He stole Trevor's dog," says Jimmy.

"You could have just taken your dog back." Nick's voice drips with disappointment. "You didn't have to attack him."

Trevor recognizes the voice from the phone call. "You called me, didn't you?"

"Just get your dog and leave," says Nick.

Diggy pushes up to his feet. He wipes his face on the sleeve of his sweatshirt, smearing blood across his chin.

Nick places his hand on Trevor's shoulder. "It's over for tonight."

Trevor shrugs him off. "You think I'm letting him get away with this?"

"Nick's right, let's go," says Jimmy.

"I don't understand how you could do this." Trevor points at Diggy. "Didn't you see the signs all over the school with my dog's picture on them?"

"For the same reason you had to ruin my season!" Diggy charges off the deck and thumps Trevor in the chest with a two-handed shove. Trevor stumbles and falls backward, holding Diggy's shirt. The moon flashes by as his feet kick into the air. Trevor flails with Diggy on top of him. A rush of broken ice and wet decomposing leaves sweep across Trevor's face, closing like a fist. It's freezing and he's paralyzed for a moment, wondering where he is, how this is happening. Then he remembers the pool.

Trevor's fighting, pushing Diggy away, when the pool cover collapses. With a whoosh, Trevor goes deep into the water. He tells himself it's only a pool. He struggles his way up, gasping for breath. It's freezing and there's something blocking him. It moves like hard jelly. He's under the cover in total darkness. He punches at the rubber ceiling over his head, then tries to swim sideways. His coat, shoes, and pants drag him down. The pool's bottom is slick and smooth. Pressure squeezes in his ears. He tries to swim up and bangs his head on the side of the pool. Which way is up? He's drowning, twisting and squirming his way through the cold, but not rising. The surface of the water is lifting, moving away into the darkness, and he feels like he's sinking. Everything goes black. Fantastic bursts of light flash before his eyes, faces appear, his mother calling him, his father waiting for his dinner, Diggy, Jimmy, Greco.

He releases his breath and sees the bubbles escaping the pool. Maybe he can follow them. Yes, they can lead him to the surface. Yet, he doesn't move. He's looking down at himself from a distance. He blinks his eyes, wondering if this is real. Seconds tick in his ears. His brain feels like it is growing too large for his head. *I'm going to drown,* he thinks. *I'm going to die in this pool. It's going to end like this. I'm not going to finish high school or go to college.* He tries to lift his arms, but he's exhausted.

He never expected this, but at least it doesn't hurt. It's so quiet. Trevor sees his father at the old house. He's painting the cement deer in the garden. The head is fixed. *Did we move back here?* asks Trevor. His dad brushes the paint on the deer. *Trevor, you don't have to fight anymore,* he says. *You can stop now. You were always my champion. It's time to stop.*

Diggy

DIGGY EMERGES THROUGH A TEAR IN THE COVER. HIS HEAD aches from Trevor's fists and the cold. Nick grabs his hand and hoists him from the water. Diggy lies on the patio bricks, exhausted, coughing, and catching his breath.

"Where's Trevor!" yells Jimmy.

Nick falls to his knees and tries to peel the cover off the edge of the pool. "Untie the lines," he screams, looking into the dark water. "We've got to get the cover off."

Diggy watches, waiting for Trevor's head to surface. Jimmy and Nick pull at cables attached to lag nuts turned into the cement.

"This is impossible!" shouts Jimmy.

Diggy charges onto the sinking cover, then plunges into the water. If he saves Trevor, he'll be the rescuer, right? Some kind of hero. Nick will forgive him. Jimmy might understand that he didn't want this to happen. He takes a deep breath and swims under the cover into the inky blackness. He knows the pool. He's been in it a hundred times.

He hits a wall of cold and can barely move. He reaches into the darkness for Trevor. He can't let him die, not over something he did. Not in front of his brother and Jimmy. Diggy comes up for air and is blocked by the pool cover. His heart is hammering. He needs air. The cold is tearing the skin off his body. He wants to scream, but he's underwater. He dives again with his arms reaching for one last try.

Diggy brushes something. A coat sleeve, an arm? He seizes it and pulls toward the surface. He follows the pool's cover to the tear where the patio lights dance in a crazy collage. Gasping, he emerges. Jimmy and Nick stand on the sides of the pool. Their faces shine in the dark.

Diggy tows Trevor through the filthy water. He's lifeless and blue-faced. Nick and Jimmy heave Trevor to the pool's side and roll him onto the cement.

Diggy's mother scurries from the house in a terry robe and furry slippers. "Yes, yes," she says into her cell. "Someone fell in my pool." She waves her free hand. "I don't know when he fell in. Nine-one-one says to start CPR," she cries.

Jimmy grabs Trevor and sits him up. Trevor's head lolls to one side, his mouth bubbles and foams. Jimmy squeezes Trevor's chest. A spurt of water shoots from Trevor's mouth.

Jimmy squeezes harder. Again water spurts from his mouth. He presses Trevor's chest, over and over, with the same result.

"He's blue, and he's not moving," yells Beverly to the operator.

Diggy wishes he were saving Trevor's life. He could cover Trevor's mouth with his and breathe life into him. Then everyone would have to forgive him.

Jimmy tilts Trevor's head to create an airway.

"Do you know what you're doing?" asks Nick, shaking Jimmy's shoulder.

"Yes," yells Jimmy. "C-A-B. Compressions-Airway-Breathing."

Trevor's face is so blue, it looks to be made of rubber. Jimmy puts his ear to Trevor's lips and nose. "I don't hear anything. He's not breathing!" Trevor's jaw droops open, his top two teeth visible between his lips. Jimmy places his hands on Trevor's chest and gives thirty compressions and then blows two breaths into his lungs.

"Come on. Come on." Jimmy blows again into his mouth. Trevor's not responding. Jimmy begins pounding his chest.

"He's still not breathing," cries Beverly into the phone. She listens. "The operator says to keep going."

Diggy crawls over to Trevor's side. "Let me take over," he says.

"Diggy, back off!" roars Jimmy.

Nick grabs Diggy by the shirt collar and yanks him away. "You did enough already," snaps Nick. Diggy falls to the cement and realizes nothing is going to be the same again.

PART THREE

Diggy

THE AMBULANCE'S REVOLVING LIGHTS STREAK THE HOUSE AND trees with red. The EMTs bend over Trevor, who is lying on a stretcher covered with a metallic blanket. He's moaning, pushing an oxygen mask off his face. They shake his shoulder. "What's your name? Say it."

Trevor doesn't answer. He leans over and throws up. Watery puke splatters on the pavers. The EMTs collapse the stretcher, lift, and roll Trevor into the ambulance.

Beverly's back and shoulders are trembling. She turns to Diggy, Nick, and Jimmy. They are all dripping wet. "Why was Trevor Crow in our yard? Why were you fighting?" Fright covers her crumpled face.

"Mom, not now." Diggy's teeth are chattering. He wants to get dry clothes on, to get warm.

"I want to know what happened. I've got to call his mother. What am I going to tell her?" Her eyes are filling with tears.

"It was an accident," says Diggy, trying to explain. His wet pants and shirt cling to him. "Can't we just leave it at that right now?"

"You went too far." Jimmy points his finger at Diggy's chest. "Mrs. Masters, Diggy stole Trevor's dog. Trevor and I came to get him back."

Beverly's lips pull in with pain. "His dog?"

"Mom, Diggy did something dumb," Nick says, cutting the air with his hands. "Very dumb." He locks eyes with Diggy. "Trevor fell in the pool and—"

"Diggy pushed him in," says Jimmy.

"And I saved his ass," yells Diggy. "Right?" His head is thumping. It's like Trevor's fists are banging inside his skull. "Mom, it was an accident," says Diggy.

"No, it wasn't," says Jimmy.

Beverly folds her arms. Her face is sick with anger and confusion.

"Ma'am, you better get in," says the EMT. "This one is going to need some explaining." He nods towards Diggy's bruised face.

Jimmy climbs into the front seat of the ambulance. Beverly gets in back. The other EMT comes around the rear of the ambulance and hops in next to her. "Ma'am, you'll have to buckle up," he says.

"Meet me at the hospital," says Beverly as the doors close.

Diggy tears off his wet clothes in his room. His lip is bleeding and his eye is swollen shut. He puts on a pair of sweats and a heavy wool sweater but can't stop shivering. Downstairs he finds Nick sitting on the marble tile with a towel over his shoulders. He's barefoot. The cuffs of his jeans have puddles under them. "This shouldn't have happened," he says. "The way you attacked Trevor, pushing him into the pool, you were really scary."

Diggy wants to tell his brother that he's still the same. Everything else changed. All he wanted was a winning senior-year season at 152—like that was too much to ask. And then the dog. Why did he take the dog? Why didn't he give him back sooner? He did want to hurt Trevor. He can admit that, at least to himself, and now Trevor could be brain damaged or something. Diggy meets Nick's eyes. "I wish I could go back and win the wrestle-off," he says. "If I had won, none of this would have happened."

Nick jumps to his feet, grabs Diggy's sweater, and presses him against the wall. "Don't you see, that's what I'm talking about!" A vein in Nick's forehead bulges. His fists press into Diggy's chin. "I called Trevor. I did, because what you did was wrong. You were wrong!"

Diggy doesn't struggle. Nick bangs him against the wall, once, twice, then releases him. "You called him?"

"Yes. I wanted it over. I wasn't going to go sneaking around with you trying to give the dog back."

Tears fill Diggy's eyes.

Nick grabs him. "I have to get you away from Randy. That's the only thing I can think of."

They hear the front door open and look toward the foyer. Randy comes in, followed by a balding man with glasses and beady eyes. They take off their overcoats and place them on the rack next to the door.

"Charlie, meet my wrestlers," says Randy, stepping from the foyer. "Boys, this is Mr. Charlie Frederick. He owns Imperial Rental Car and he's thinking about updating his fleet with a few of my luxury vehicles." Randy's eyes are heavy from his long day and one too many scotches.

"Randy," says Nick, "someone almost drowned in our pool."

"The pool?" He looks as if he hasn't heard correctly, then he laughs. "Charlie, will you excuse me? Make yourself at home." He smiles and points to the fireplace and leather couch.

Nick leads them to the bar at the back of the house. Diggy follows like he's being pulled along, his arms limp at his sides. There's no stopping anything now.

"What the hell is going on?" asks Randy. "What happened to Diggy's face?"

"One of the guys from the wrestling team fell in the pool," says Nick.

"I thought the pool was covered," he says.

"Don't you remember? The cover was torn from the sycamore," says Diggy.

Randy's face turns somber. "I know the cover was torn, but . . ." He shuts his eyes. "Where's your mother?"

"She went to the hospital in the ambulance with Trevor Crow," says Nick. "He snuck in the yard."

"What?" asks Randy. "Why would he do that?"

Nick's eyes turn to Diggy.

"What'd you do?" Randy smacks Diggy's head. "What'd you do?" he hisses.

"Randy, stop it," says Nick. "You're drunk. This is a big mess and Diggy needs your help."

"Stay out of it," says Randy. "You waltz home whenever it's convenient for you, and you think you're running the show. Diggy, start explaining." He tugs Diggy's sweater, stretching it.

Diggy only wishes he had a father he could talk to, but the man gripping his shirt, spitting into his face isn't someone who can help him with this mess.

"Randy, let him go." In one easy motion, Nick twists his father's arm. Randy shrieks, but Nick hangs on and rams the arm behind Randy's back.

"Goddamn you," Randy grunts. "You can go back to school and stay there." Nick forces his father's arm higher.

"How do you like it?" asks Nick.

Charlie Frederick comes into the room. Randy cranes his neck, with terror flashing in his eyes. "Charlie, go wait where I told you, please."

"Let him go. Nick, let him go," says Diggy.

"He's the reason we're both so messed up." Nick shoves Randy forward.

249

Randy's forehead bongs on the brass bar rail. He raises his head. "I want you gone. Out of my house," he says to Nick. "You're not welcome here anymore!"

"My God, boys, this is your father," says Charlie Frederick. "Randy, are you all right?" Charlie puts his hand under Randy's arm.

"Charlie, let me handle this," growls Randy. "I've had it. I'm making a living, paying for this party, and I have to come home to this insanity. My son assaults me, embarrasses me in front of a client." His forehead already has a cherry on it. Randy walks to the foyer, stumbles, and catches himself on the wall. Charlie Frederick tries to help him, but Randy pulls away.

At the door, Randy stops and looks back. "You two better get your act together," he roars.

Nick charges upstairs and enters his room. Diggy goes after him. Nick pulls on dry clothes. "I should have stopped Randy a long time ago. Mom should have done something." Nick slips a sweatshirt over his head. "When I got hurt and couldn't wrestle, you don't know what I thought. Nobody knows." Nick stuffs his duffel bag with his clothes. "I would think about killing myself. I told my professor I was a lousy son, and do you know what he said?" Nick gasps for breath and tears start in his eyes. "He said there's no such thing as a bad son, there's only bad fathers."

"Stay, don't leave me now," pleads Diggy. "At least stay for the night."

"I can't. You heard Randy. If you won't take me to the train station, I'll call a car service." Nick yanks the drawstring on the duffel bag and drags it into the hall. He tosses it down the oak staircase, then carries it from the house.

Diggy shouldn't be driving. His face is swelling. He can barely see the lines on the road, but he's got to convince Nick not to leave. Nick speed-dials their mother. Each time, the call goes to voicemail. "They must have made her turn off her cell," he says.

They pass the Secret Keepers Motel. Nick's eyes follow the sign. "That's where he lives?"

Diggy nods.

"You went there and just drove off with the dog?" asks Nick.

"Gino helped me." Diggy chokes on the lie.

"But it was you, wasn't it, Diggy? It was all you?"

"Yes."

They drive in silence for a few miles. South central Jersey, the exit ramps, malls, and giant box stores flash by. Diggy wants Nick to somehow understand. Diggy exhales carefully, not knowing how to ask this. "You thought about killing yourself?"

Nick stares ahead. "What was the great Nick Masters without wrestling? And Diggy, I missed it; the mats, the sweat, the moves, winning, being a wrestler. I missed it bad. I thought it was all I had."

Diggy merges onto the parkway. Northbound traffic is light. Nick turns on the radio, finds a song, then turns it off. "College wrestling is a meat grinder. You've got to be dedicated to the max. You've got to be tough, wrestle with injuries, sit in the cafeteria eating chicken breasts and salad." Nick keeps his face at his window. "When I got hurt, no one gave a crap, even the great Coach Randy stopped calling. Mom called, but she didn't know what to say. It wasn't that a part of my life had ended; it was like I had died. My coach scratched my name, and the next week he had another wrestler in for me. For a while, I went to practice and rode the team bus to matches, but being there was pointless. A cracked vertebra never really heals. At least not enough for the mat."

"You were still the best."

"In high school, I was a freak of nature. Nobody wins like I won. Maybe I won from sheer determination. Maybe luck. I don't know. The more I won, the harder that first loss would have been. I knew Randy couldn't bear to see me lose."

"I prayed you'd win," says Diggy. "I kept saying, 'Our Father who art in heaven, let Nick win.'"

"Do you know what it was like going undefeated in high school? Every time I won, they wrote me up in the newspaper. You'd have thought I was the only guy wrestling in Monmouth County."

Diggy pictures a headline from the local sport pages—*Masters Records Perfect High School Record*—framed and laminated in Randy's office at the dealership.

"In college," says Nick, "do you think the professors care if I won the Jersey Wrestling States? They never heard of it."

"It made you who you are," says Diggy.

"Maybe I should have lost one. Maybe that would have helped me when I hurt my back." Nick presses his fingertips into his temples. "Diggy, don't get me wrong, I got a lot from wrestling. When I hear guys in my dorm moaning about a test, I almost have to laugh. I don't have that kind of anxiety. I'm never unprepared for anything. I'm never late. And I'm not afraid of anyone, ever. I don't care how big he is, or how bad he thinks he is."

"I wanted to feel like that." Diggy stays in the right lane. "I wanted a little of what you have." Cars whiz by. He doesn't want to arrive at the train station. He doesn't want to be without Nick.

"Dude, don't be so hard on yourself," says Nick. "You know, if you never wrestle again, you'll always be a wrestler." Nick clasps Diggy's free right hand in his left.

"What if Trevor Crow's not all right?"

"He'll be okay. You saw him, he came around." Nick puts his hand on Diggy's leg and squeezes. "If the police get involved in this, tell them the truth."

Diggy follows the red taillights ahead of him. "I was going to say I found the dog on the golf course. You didn't have to call Trevor. We could have—"

"No, we couldn't have!" shouts Nick. "Maybe I should have done it differently, but I didn't. You shouldn't have done it in the first place."

"I'm sorry."

"And you're not going to say you found the dog. That's what Randy will want you to say," says Nick. "You should be straight up on this one. You lost the wrestle-off, saw the dog in the cold, and you took him home. That's it. You were going to give him back. You start lying about things, it's going to get worse."

"Greco will throw me off the team for sure."

"Dig, I saw you on the mat struggling. That guy, he was nothing. Last year, you would have beaten him at any weight. Wrestling is about giving one hundred percent. When you don't give a hundred percent, everyone knows it. You wrestle with anything less, you're going to get hurt." He turns in the seat. "Your last match, you were sleepwalking."

"I stepped on the mat thinking I was going to get my ass kicked."

"You're my little bro, wrestling or no wrestling. I can't forget all those nights in the basement with Randy blowing the whistle. I have nightmares about our matches. Diggy, I wake sweating like I was actually wrestling you. In one dream, I hurt you. You're lying there on that red mat and Randy's blowing his dumbass whistle."

Diggy swallows hard. "I hated those practices. I could

never beat you. Never." The words get caught in his throat. "I just wanted my name on the Wall, next to yours."

"I know that," says Nick. "And now look what you've done."

Diggy tries to laugh. "Randy thinks I'm getting a scholarship."

"It's not about wrestling anymore, or a scholarship! You went too far. You still don't get it, do you?"

"Nick, I know, I shouldn't have taken Trevor Crow's dog. I'm a screwup, like Randy says." Tears stream down Diggy's cheeks.

"It's not okay, little bro, but I'm still here for you. We'll get through this." Nick leans over and puts his arm around Diggy. "Turn around. I'll go to the hospital with you and leave in the morning."

Diggy

DIGGY WAKES ON A COUCH IN A DIM ROOM TO THE SOUND OF A baby crying. He focuses on the television and the empty fish tank under the window and remembers where he is. His head feels like there's a jackhammer behind his eyes. Sleeping at Jane's accomplished one thing: he avoided Randy. Diggy couldn't face him without Nick.

Jane, barefoot, wearing SpongeBob pajamas, snatches a yardstick next to the end table and whacks it on the wall. The crying stops. It's quiet. "I don't know why that works," she says. "Did you get any sleep?"

"It doesn't matter." He moves his jaw right, then left. It hurts. "I feel like I got hit by a truck."

"You look like you just rolled out of a sore asshole," she says without smiling. She puts her finger to her lips and they tiptoe through the kitchen. Two glasses and an empty bottle of gin are on the counter. The cat, curled on the stovetop between the burners, raises his head and meows.

They continue along the hall. Jane's mother's door is ajar. Two bodies lay under blankets.

Diggy follows Jane into her bedroom. She shuts the door. Diggy feels tired all the way to his bones. She scoots into her narrow bed and lifts the covers. Diggy gets in.

"Put your feet against mine," she says.

"I've got to look for Whizzer," he says.

"I know. I'll help you." She pushes her feet over his. Her warmth moves through him. After they left the hospital, Diggy, Nick, and Jane searched most of the night for Whizzer. They walked the golf course, one end to the other, soaking their sneakers and socks in the wet grass.

Before dawn, Diggy and Jane dropped Nick off at the train station. Nick lugged his duffel bag across his back and he and Diggy rode up the escalator while Jane waited in the car. When the train's headlight was visible in the distance, Diggy hugged Nick. The train doors slid open at the platform. A few people stepped off the train.

"I'm sorry about everything," whispered Diggy.

Diggy runs his hand through Jane's hair and lets it fall to her neck. Her birthmark is almost invisible in the early light. "My head didn't stop all night. I kept thinking about Whizzer, somewhere out there. Then I thought about Trevor challenging Jimmy, me challenging Jimmy, me beating one of them, and I just kept coming back to the same place—Trevor comes on the team and he's challenging me."

"You're trying to defend your own retarded insanity."

Her words sting. "I know." He rolls on his back. "What if we can't find Whizzer?"

"Do you know what I was thinking about?" She reaches over him and pulls a red and white pack of cigarettes from her jacket pocket on the floor. She lights one with her tiny lighter and inhales. "You should have told me about taking the dog."

"I couldn't."

"Why? You don't think I've had crap like this on my plate before? Go look in my mother's room. I'm dealing with it every minute of my life. You should have trusted me."

"I do trust you. That's why I called you last night." Diggy pulls her toward him.

"I'm not sure how I feel about everything yet," she says.

"I messed up, bad, but I don't want to lose you."

She rests her head on his arm. "We better go before the traffic starts."

He turns on his cell in the Mustang. Three messages, all from home. He presses delete. They drive to Gateway Hills. Jane sits with her knees pulled to her chest. A car passes that looks like Randy's.

"What's the matter?" asks Jane.

"I think that was Randy. He's looking for me." The skin on his back is crawling. He shivers and presses the gas pedal. After completing a circle around the golf course, he merges into the traffic on Route 33. In a few miles, he'll pass Trevor's motel.

"Stop the car," yells Jane.

Diggy pulls to the shoulder and stomps the brake pedal.

"I just saw a little dog over there." She's kneeling on the seat, pointing across the road.

"Where?"

"Near that strip mall."

Diggy takes the first jug handle and parks at a Quick Chek.

"Right there!"

Whizzer stands next to a Dumpster at the edge of the parking lot.

Diggy bursts from the car. "Here boy," he calls. "Come here, boy."

"Whizzer," calls Jane.

Diggy claps his hands. The puppy stiffens, then sprints into the road. A truck passes over him at full speed. Whizzer rolls on the pavement. Diggy runs into the road, waving his arms. The traffic screeches around him.

Jane's on the shoulder with her hands over her mouth.

Diggy carries Whizzer to the sidewalk in front of the store. Whizzer's chest is shuddering. Diggy rubs his tan coat and massages his neck.

"Is he alive?" asks Jane. "Is he?"

Jimmy

GRECO ENDED PRACTICE EARLY SO THE TEAM COULD VISIT Trevor at the hospital, but Jimmy can't go, not today, knowing the detectives could come and get him at any minute. He slumps in the passenger seat of Roxanne's Volvo. She accelerates away from the school and asks him for the third time, "Are you sure you want to go home?"

"I want to sleep." Another afternoon, another day of waiting for the police. He'd rather be practicing, running laps, doing takedown drills until his arms fall off.

"But Trevor's going to expect you to visit him with the rest of the team."

"I'll go tomorrow." He closes his eyes and sees Trevor's cold blue face in his hands.

Greco held a team meeting in the wrestling room. He talked about Diggy stealing Trevor's dog and how sorry Diggy was about everything. Jimmy looked into his lap, remembering Diggy crawling on the wet cement. "This is a setback for the entire team," said Greco. "But we're going to be stronger from it. Trevor is recovering and will be able to rejoin us." It was all just empty words. Then Greco went right into his "The Minute Men are still a team" speech. Jimmy groaned loudly and Greco shot him a look. *You call this a team?* Jimmy wanted to yell. The word no longer applies. Trevor's in the hospital. Gino's a little lying bastard. Diggy's a two-faced, thieving dirtbag. "Varsity Dad" Pops, with all the answers—he can go to hell. Jimmy doesn't want to be captain anymore. His captain title is a joke.

Plus, Roxanne is pissing him off. Suddenly she's become aware of Trevor's existence? Twelve and a half years of school and she never made eye contact, and now she's insisting on visiting him. Totally bogus.

"I don't think that's very fair to Trevor," says Roxanne.

"Stop saying that," he says. "What do you know about being fair? Huh? Your car is worth as much as my house. You call that fair?"

"What does that have to do with anything?"

"It doesn't," he says.

"This car was a gift for getting my license. I didn't ask for it."

"My family may not have earned everything they have, but I earned my wins on the mat, every one of them." Jimmy knows he sounds like an idiot.

"All I did was ask you to go to the hospital with me. You don't have to be a jerk about it." She gives him a side glance, keeping her hands on the steering wheel.

"I don't want twenty guys pounding me on the back for allegedly saving Trevor's life."

"What do you mean by 'allegedly'?"

"I don't know. I just don't like to think that if I hadn't been there, Trevor would have . . ." He doesn't want to say *died*. "Trevor would have been saved no matter what, that's all I'm saying."

"That's not what everyone at school thinks."

"Obviously." The entire day was full of congratulations and hand shaking, even from the teachers. Just wait until they learn that he's about to be arrested, that his father is a thief and he's his accomplice.

"It's just a good thing Trevor is getting better," she says.

"What is it with you," he snorts. "Are you going to make Trevor your next pet project?"

"What's that supposed to mean?"

He takes a quivering breath through his teeth. "Nothing. I just want to go home."

"Then I'll go see Trevor by myself."

"Stop being such a poser. You hardly know him. I bet you've never spoken to him." His voice is icy, but he can't stop.

"I've talked to him. He's in some of my classes."

"Did you know he lives in a motel room?"

"I heard the rumors."

"They're not rumors. He lives in a motel. A place you'll never have to go!" He's surprised at how he's lashing out at her.

"Jimmy, why are you being like this?"

Where should he start? The perfect picture she had of him has already been trashed. One thing is for sure—she never made a midnight trip with her father to steal building supplies. And, the truth is, Jimmy did know, he knew his father was stealing them. He covers his face with his hands.

"I think I know what's bothering you," she says in a matter-of-fact way. "You're in big trouble, aren't you?"

They stop at a red light in front of the Starbucks that replaced an Italian deli. "You want to get a mocha, my treat?" asks Roxanne. Jimmy doesn't answer. The light changes and the car behind beeps. She takes off.

"Do you remember when I told you I was going to be a gym teacher? You laughed and just about told me I was wasting my time."

"I wasn't trying to be mean."

"Why are you going premed, to make money or to help people?"

"Fine, become a teacher," she snaps. "Maybe you could write a book on volleyball." Her words are thick with sarcasm and they cut into him.

"I want to go to school and actually learn something, be something. I'm not going to college because my daddy is making me!"

"I wouldn't call a gym teacher being something. Besides, you're going to college to escape Molly Pitcher.

You told me that yourself."

"Why are you dating me?" asks Jimmy.

"I thought we'd have a good senior year. I thought we'd be going to the prom together."

"That's pretty weak," he says.

"Why are you dating me, if I'm so horrible?" She faces him.

"I thought you had everything I wanted."

"But not anymore, right? Is that what you're saying?"

"Something like that."

Hurt fills her face, but he doesn't take the words back. "My parents don't want me to date you. Just last night they asked me not to see you anymore."

"What did you say?"

"I told them we'd cool it for a little while."

"So you agreed with them?"

"My father talked to Detective Barnes." Her mouth twists with this fact like she's eaten something bitter. "You shouldn't have lied to me about it. Maybe if you trusted me, I could understand this."

"I don't understand it!" he shouts.

"I think you do!" She turns into Puny Town and brakes. An overturned recycling barrel has strewn plastic milk containers and bottles over the road like bowling pins in an alley. "Just tell me the truth!" A tear rolls from the corner of her eye.

"You never had your father in your room at midnight

asking for a favor. You never had to do anything for your parents. They do everything for you."

Roxanne shakes her head like it's swarming with insects. "I defended you. I called my father a liar!" She's crying now, with tears coming down her cheeks; she pulls to the curb. "I'm not mad at you, I'm worried about you."

Jimmy looks at the garbage scattered across the street. "I'll get out here. I wouldn't want you to hurt your precious Volvo," he says. "You might get dirt on your tires, or worse, get a flat and have to actually get out of the car in this bad neighborhood."

"Why are you being like this!" she yells.

"Because, deep down you think your father's right about me." He pops the door lock and opens the door. "And you're just like him."

Diggy

DIGGY'S BLOWN OFF TWO PRACTICES AND CUT MOST OF HIS classes today. He's passing the gym when Greco calls him into his office. Greco shuts the door and looks at him as if he's examining a dead bug. "Sit."

Diggy lowers himself to a chair and puts his hands between his knees, waiting to get blasted.

"Do you have anything to say?" Greco's eyes are fixed on him, drilling into him.

His mouth goes dry. How can he say anything, or try to explain?

Greco leans in closer. His breath comes across his small, straight bottom teeth. "Because this isn't over for you. You're not going to do this and just walk away from it like it never happened! Do you understand me?" Veins in Greco's neck pulse.

"Yes, sir." The hairs on the back of Diggy's neck begin to prickle.

"All of a sudden you're 'yes sirring' me?" Greco backs

off, shaking his head. "Diggy Masters, you are some piece of work."

Diggy peers through the blinds at the empty gym, wishing someone would come in and save him. "Am I off the team?" he asks.

"Did I say you were off the team?"

"No."

"Then you're still on the team!" shouts Greco. "Got that?"

"Yes."

"Yes, what?"

"Yes, Coach."

Greco huffs. "Now, let's discuss a few things you're going to do for the team, which you are still a member of." He raises his finger at Diggy. "I want you in the wrestling room on Monday. You're going to apologize. I don't want a two-second 'I'm sorry.' I want you to write it, rehearse it, mean it!"

"To the whole team?"

"If it doesn't suit me, then you'll do it again on Tuesday, and every day after until you get it right. Principal Anderson has asked me for my input on this incident. So don't disappoint me." Greco pokes Diggy's chest. "Understand?"

Diggy

DIGGY LEANS CLOSE TO HIS BATHROOM MIRROR, EXAMINING HIS eye. The lid is blue and purple. He looks over; Randy is in the doorway. "Can we talk like two human beings for a minute?"

Diggy smells alcohol on his breath under a layer of cologne. Randy lowers the toilet seat cover and sits on it. "I should have locked the door," says Diggy.

"Could you lose the attitude for ten minutes?"

Diggy sucks in a breath, holds it, and when he knows he can release it without cursing, lets it go. No good can come from talking with Randy because he doesn't have conversations. Randy talks. All his life, Diggy has been ordered to listen. But he doesn't feel like listening anymore.

"Why didn't you come to me?" asks Randy in his car salesman voice, so reasonable and convincing that Diggy blinks in disbelief. "Your mother told me about the dog at the motel, chained in the cold. I don't approve of that sort of treatment of animals either. I could have contacted the ASPCA and had the dog taken away from the boy. It would have been a lot cleaner."

Diggy studies his father's face in the bright bathroom. "The ASPCA?"

"Oh, and you're grounded," says Randy.

"I didn't get caught smoking or cutting a class," mumbles Diggy.

"Grounded until I say otherwise. Got it?"

"Trevor could have died! I almost killed his dog." These are undeniable truths and no one seems to get it. He and Jane brought Whizzer to a veterinary office. Somehow, Whizzer didn't have any broken bones. The vet listened to his heart with a stethoscope, then felt his body and said, "He's lucky he didn't break his neck."

"Your mother told me Coach Greco wants you to apologize to the team."

"Go away," groans Diggy.

"Apologizing is admitting you're guilty. You shouldn't admit anything. This is already being handled by my insurance company." Randy's voice is hard and flat. "You know I have contacts in the police department. Perhaps we'll have some cruelty-to-animal charges against Mr. and Mrs. Crow."

Diggy stomps across the bathroom, chest heaving, nostrils flaring. "Mr. Crow is dead and the dog was run over! I took Trevor's dog. I did it! I don't want your help. I'm sick of the way you think."

"Let me tell you something, mister, the police could

have pressed charges against you. I'm the one who made the phone calls!" His booming voice echoes off the tile walls.

"Leave me alone!" Diggy pushes him in the chest. "Like, now!" Diggy punches the wall, crunching the sheet-rock.

"You spoiled punk-ass little—" yells Randy.

Diggy hurls his mother's electric curler set. The curlers bounce off Randy and clatter to the floor. Diggy races down the stairs, heading for the front door.

"Grounded!" yells Randy. "Grounded!"

Diggy

DIGGY PARKS AT JANE'S APARTMENT WITH HIS HEART STILL drumming from the argument with Randy. She's dressed funky, wearing his varsity jacket and a denim skirt with knee-high socks and black lace-up sneakers. Her face is funny, sort of gloomy. She gets in and pulls her skirt over her thighs. "What's with the getup?" he asks.

"It's a look, not a getup." Her eyes are raw. "I just had some major drama with my mother," she says. "She's on her third mojito and she's drinking them from a milk glass." Her gaze falls into her lap.

"Randy, the moron," says Diggy, "he tells me I'm grounded, like I'm twelve and that's going to prove something."

"What did you expect him to do?"

"I don't know. I just wanted him to understand. . . ." Diggy can't finish the sentence. Because what is there to understand?

"Are you sorry?"

He nods.

"Really?" She blows her nose in a tissue and balls it in her hand.

"Yeah, I am." They sit in silence, looking at her green apartment door and the dead poinsettia. The bow is gone from the pot. "Can we go in your room?" he asks.

"I don't think right now is a good time. Gloria told my mother about you, what happened, the dog, everything. That's what we were fighting about."

"What'd she say?"

"Say? You mean, what'd she scream? Nothing wonderful." Jane shakes her head. "She called you a spoiled rich brat."

"That's it?

"And a parasite."

He rests his forehead on the steering wheel. "What'd you say?"

"I stuck up for you." She shrugs. "At least, as much as I could. This whole thing is ugly. The little puppy almost died right in front of our eyes. That's the first time I've ever seen an animal get run over like that."

Diggy pictures the dog rolling under the truck.

"All you guys and your precious manhood. Why do you think my brother's in jail and my other brothers can't keep jobs? All this manliness junk. You all have something to prove. Ya ever see what happens when you put two of those little fighting fish in the same bowl? They rip each other apart." She rests her head on his shoulder.

"And they both die."

"Maybe I was never supposed to wrestle," he says softly in her ear. "Maybe that's what this whole mess is about."

"Maybe your father's an asshole and he had you believing his bullshit."

She's right, but I did it, he thinks. No one told me to take the dog.

She guides in a CD she made him, lots of bands he never heard of, and cranks it.

"I have to do something. I just can't leave it like this." He rubs his eyes. Snow begins to blow across the windshield.

Trevor

HE SITS ON THE EDGE OF THE BED, A PILE OF LAUNDRY AT HIS feet, stroking Whizzer's neck. The weather station shows a radar blob of snow over Molly Pitcher. He lies back on his pillow and shuts his eyes. Highway traffic and the dead, late-afternoon nothingness of the day rings in his head.

He could have gone to school today. Yesterday the family doctor listened to his chest and said his lungs were sounding better. "Anytime you feel ready," he said. Out his window, snow falls under thick clouds. He shivers, remembering the ice-cold pool water, the panic, the fear, kicking, punching, and then that feeling of warmth. In the deep end of the pool, he finally gave up. He let go of the world, and it wasn't terrible. Dying felt as natural as that moment when sleep comes. Trevor hopes his father felt something like this.

He lifts Whizzer to his chest. "I'm going to have to leave you tomorrow," he says. "You have to stay in here and be a good boy." Whizzer licks his face. Trevor wants to get back to the mat, the mindless drills, the body heat, diet, and sweating. He misses it, and he's going to show his father that he would have been a Varsity Dad.

Trevor knocks on the connecting door to his mother's room, then pushes it open. The bed is unmade. London's Green Bay Packers hat lies on the night table. His leather sneakers are under the bed. London is spending most nights with his mother. There is a sudden tightening in Trevor's gut. He closes the door and goes back to his bed.

He feels as if he's traveled a long distance and finally arrived here. Everything is already familiar, as if he knew the shape of the motel and the dimness of this old room for a long time. The feeling that all this is a nightmare that he might wake from, that feeling is gone. It's as if he knew the refrigerator would be a light green, and the kitchen floor would be curled at the corners, and there would be traffic on the road in front, then a cornfield under a sky, dark with snow.

Someone's knocking on his door. Whizzer barks. Trevor moves the edge of the curtain from the window. Diggy Masters. What the hell does he want? A chill crawls along his spine. Trevor whips his belt from his jeans and wraps it around his fist. There's another knock. He doesn't want Diggy seeing the motel room, the exact place where he lives.

Another knock, then, "Trevor?"

Trevor leaves the security chain on the door and opens it a few inches. Diggy's eye is still black and swollen. He shoves his hands in the pockets of his jeans and clears his throat. "Can I talk to you?"

"About what?"

"About the team." Diggy looks back at something or someone.

Trevor tightens the belt around his hand. He unhooks the chain and lets the door swing open.

Diggy steps in. "This your room?" He takes in the wrestling posters tacked to the walls and Trevor's medals hanging from a nail. Whizzer jumps up on Diggy. Trevor grabs the dog's collar and walks him into his mother's room, then shuts the door.

"Whizzer looks okay," says Diggy.

"What are you doing here?" Trevor watches him closely, sort of not believing he's really in his room. And it's the same Diggy, chin raised in the same cocky way, like he's ready for a fight.

"You really gave me a few shots." Diggy rubs his cheek. "I still can't open my mouth all the way." He moves his jaw side to side.

Trevor knows the unyielding feel of his fist on Diggy's chin. He never wants to hit anyone that hard again.

"I wanted to say it was a mistake—"

Trevor cuts him off. "Really?"

"I saw him in the parking lot tied up," says Diggy. "It was too cold for a puppy."

"How many dogs have you saved in your life?" asks

Trevor. "This the first one? Just happened to be my dog? By coincidence? You never expected me to take one-fifty-two. Admit it."

"It wasn't just that."

"Diggy, you sat next to me at lunch talking about finding him. Then my mother gets a call from a veterinarian?"

"I'm sorry. I'm really sorry. That's all I came here to say."

"You've got a brother who went undefeated. But it wasn't enough." Trevor steps in front of Diggy.

"Trevor, be cool."

"I heard the way you talk to your father. Like he's nothing. I never spoke to my father like that." Trevor inches closer. Diggy stumbles backward. Trevor wants Diggy to know it wasn't okay and it's never going to be. "So tell me again—why did you take my dog, Dig-gy? You think you're going to walk in here and make it all better?"

"My father comes to practices because he thinks it's his job. All he ever cared about was winning. That's all he ever wanted from me. My father's an asshole."

Trevor forces a tight smile. "You've got it all wrong. You're the asshole. You took my dog." Trevor pokes him hard in the chest.

Diggy turns toward the door. "I didn't plan it," he says in a choked voice. "I saw him and took him. I never thought it would turn out like it did. It was a prank."

"You think I'm some piece of garbage. I mean, look at

this place, right? I'm a piece of garbage, right?"

"I don't think anything."

"You do," says Trevor. "Don't lie to me."

"Could we shake hands, or something?" Diggy extends his hand.

Trevor remembers him yanking his hand when Trevor tried to shake it. "Get out of my face."

Diggy opens the door and Jane is standing there.

"What's all the yelling about?" she asks. "Trevor, Diggy came to apologize."

"Jane, Diggy could have given Whizzer back. He had him for a week while I was driving around tacking flyers on telephone poles looking for him!"

"Let's go." Diggy pushes past Jane, then crosses the lot to his car.

Jane grabs Trevor's arm. "He's screwed up in the head," she says. "Like everyone." She trots to the car with her hands in the pockets of the varsity jacket.

Trevor

Trevor watches the Mustang spray gravel and surge into the road. Snowflakes swirl behind the car. "Dad, what the hell is this?" he yells. "You weren't supposed to let this happen!" He lifts the edge of his makeshift desk and topples his books, pens, and papers. He kicks his metal trash can into the old trunk. He smashes his heel on the lion-faced lock again and again, until it's in pieces on the floor. He's crying and he knows he has no right.

Trevor opens the connecting room door and scoops Whizzer into his arms. He stands in the middle of the mess with the puppy, shaking. Trevor touches the hard scab on Whizzer's back. The vet called it "road rash." He said it would heal but leave a scar. Trevor holds him tightly, breathing into his soft coat. "I'm sorry," he says. "Don't be scared."

He gathers his calculus text and pieces of the lock. He drops them on the bed.

He forces the trunk's wooden lid open. The hinges

creak. The smell of an old attic floats into the room. Whizzer backs away and sneezes.

The trunk's empty, except for a flat leather folder stuck into a crevice where the planks meet. He tugs it from the trunk and brings it to his desk. He peels back the tough leather flap, revealing a stack of photos. The top one is of a boy with long hair parted in the middle. He's shirtless and wears a shell necklace. On the back of the photo are the words "Joe Crow, age 9." Trevor takes a deep breath. It's the first time he's ever seen his father as a boy.

He lays the photos on the desk. Some show men on horses, or men and women standing next to streams or lined up for group shots. The people are dark-skinned, with coal-black hair. He holds the photos up to the light, examines the faces, the woods, and the horses. He finds another one of his father. A sixteen- or seventeen-year-old Joe has his foot on the bumper of a truck. He's wearing cuffed dungarees and work boots. His hair is past his shoulders. He's smiling. Tears come to Trevor's eyes.

He turns the photos over, checking for dates, names, anything. One says "Quaddy." He knows this is short for Passamaquoddy. He mouths the words "Micmac, Maliseet, Penobscot, Passamaquoddy, the Wabanaki Confederacy," as if they are magic.

Trevor lifts his desk off the floor and sets it back on the sawhorses. He slides the family photo album from under his bed and sets it on the desk. He finds a picture of himself taken two years ago in their backyard at the old house. He positions his father's photo next to his. Trevor's eyes go back and forth between the two faces. The resemblance sends chills through his body.

Diggy

DIGGY'S THE FIRST ONE AT THE CLASSROOM DOOR AND INTO THE hallway. Free period. Library or handball. He bangs open the band hall exit and hurries out. There's a chilling mist in the air. A lousy day for handball, but he has to get some fresh air and clear his head.

Little Gino smacks a pink ball against the handball court. He's wearing dark blue Levis, black Nikes, and a red T-shirt that says "Your Pain, My Gain, Wrestling." His jacket hangs on the fence. "You finished your 'I'm so sorry' speech?" he asks.

Diggy walks onto the court and slaps the ball. "And how come you don't have to apologize?"

"Because it wasn't my car, or my idea." Gino hits the ball. "You yanked the dog into the car. Admit it."

"Ah, so what," says Diggy. "You're supposed to be my friend. You could have taken the rap with me." He grabs the ball and serves it.

"My old man beat my ass anyway. I don't need the whole school giving me dirty looks. No thanks." He smacks the ball.

Diggy delivers a killer, an inch off the pavement.

Gino serves.

Diggy hits the ball. "I don't know what I'm going to say today. I feel like saying I don't want to watch my weight anymore, or sweat my balls off in that gym."

"Or get pinned in front of half the school." Gino laughs. "Or maybe you just want to get pinned by Jane."

"I'm trying to tell you something." Diggy's throat tightens. "Do you have to act like a little douchebag twenty-four-seven?"

Gino grabs the ball and faces him. "Chill out, I'm listening."

"My brother was the real deal. Right?" asks Diggy. "So what am I doing? What?"

Gino exhales loudly. "Don't you think I feel like quitting sometimes? I'm a senior and I weigh a hundred and seven pounds with my clothes on. But it's what we are. We're wrestlers."

"I wrestled because my father made me, and the last thing I want to do is wrestle in college."

Gino grabs his heart. "You're killing me." He wobbles around faking a heart attack. "And don't worry, you'll never be good enough for college wrestling."

Diggy snatches the ball and throws it at him. It whacks his thigh. Gino races after it, picks it up, and wings it back, stinging him in the neck. Diggy charges, fists swinging. He clips Gino on the side of the head. Gino strikes him with a rock-hard punch to the gut. Gasping, Diggy throws himself on Gino. They roll on the wet cement, grunting and pulling at their clothes, neither of them throwing any more punches.

"You thought you were so much better than everyone. Well, not anymore. No one wants to hang with you!" yells Gino.

Diggy pins him on his back and holds his fist a few inches from Gino's face.

"You're not your brother. You couldn't hold a candle to him." Gino spits and misses Diggy's face.

It's true, he's not Nick. Diggy's name is never going to be on the Wall of Champions.

Diggy

PRACTICE HAS BEEN SUSPENDED. THE WRESTLERS SLOUCH ON the bleachers or lay on the wrestling mats. Half of them wear iPods. As usual, Bones plucks his unplugged bass, nodding his head to a silent beat. Diggy and Jane sit at the top row of the bleachers, their backs against the wall. He's sweating. The entire morning he felt feverish, hands icy, and now he's clammy, forehead practically dripping. The guys whisper and shake their heads.

Greco opens the gym doors and comes in, with Trevor following. Trevor wears a red bandana low over his eyes. The guys fall quiet. Greco claps his hands. "Let's go slugs! Huddle up!"

The wrestlers make their way to the center of the mat. Diggy climbs down the bleachers, wishing he could just leave the gym and keep walking. What could Greco do?

Someone's cell phone sounds with a rap song. "Shut it off," snaps Greco. "Let's welcome Trevor back." Greco starts clapping.

Everyone follows.

Diggy, hands in his pockets, notebook tucked under his arm, glances toward Trevor, whose eyes are fierce and dark. The clapping dies.

"By now you all know that I shut down our wrestling program for a week," says Greco.

A few guys groan.

"Saturday's meet will be a forfeit." Greco hooks his hands behind his neck. "So, where do we go from here?" He searches their faces. "We started the season as a team, and I want us to finish as a team. Changed, but still a team. I talk a lot about sportsmanship and teamwork. I do this because without it we will always be defeated. If not by other teams, then by ourselves."

Why doesn't Greco just say it, thinks Diggy. *I'm an instigator, a punk, a creep. I screwed the team, almost killed a dog, and put Trevor in the hospital. Say it and I'll walk. No need for an apology.*

"So everyone here knows what happened," continues Greco, "and from this day on, I want it behind us. Next week, you all better come prepared to wrestle. If you learned nothing else this season, you learned that we all pay for each other's actions. This forfeit is a loss against our team. It could be the loss that keeps us from winning the division. So let's compensate with wins. If you guys have anything else to say or you want to talk about what happened, my door is going to be open for a week." Greco scans the faces, daring someone to speak. "Your captain is going to say a few words—Jim?" Greco walks to the back of the group.

Jimmy stands and shoves his hands in his pockets. "I don't have much to say that the coach didn't already say." He shrugs. "A few weeks ago, we were ready to start a new season. For a lot of us, this is our last season in this school. I want to come back here next year to visit and know I did my best. And, I want to see your names on the Wall." Some guys turn to look at the names. Diggy doesn't have to look.

"I want us to come together," says Jimmy. "That should be our team goal."

Everyone claps. Diggy doesn't join in.

"Masters," says Greco. "You're up."

Diggy walks to the front of the wrestlers and faces them. He looks at his notebook. All of his notes and jottings are nonsense.

Greco puts his hands on his hips and bounces on the toes of his black shoes, waiting. *Why give me a second chance,* thinks Diggy. *Why don't you make an example of me and kick me off the team?*

"Come on, Diggy," someone calls. "We got school tomorrow."

Everyone laughs.

Diggy coughs. "I could make up a lot of reasons and excuses, but I'm not. I did something stupid, without thinking."

"More than stupid," says Pancakes.

"Let Diggy speak," says Greco.

Diggy's mouth goes dry. He finds Trevor in the circle of wrestlers, sitting with his arms wrapped around his knees, his face dark. "Trevor, I'm sorry."

Quiet. Faces turn to Greco. His jaw is grinding.

"And, I'm leaving the team. I don't deserve to be here. Pancakes is right, it was more than stupid. I shouldn't have taken Trevor's dog." All eyes are on him. A chill shakes his shoulders. "My brother was the wrestler in the family. Trevor, I'm sorry. I didn't think . . ."

Trevor lowers his head.

Greco's eyes narrow, zeroing in. "You're quitting?"

"Look," Diggy says, hoping the tears in his eyes don't fall, "I'm sorry about the whole thing. Coach, I'm sorry."

"That's not what I asked you. Are you quitting?"

"I have to," says Diggy. "You know I have to."

"Then get out of my gym."

A few guys say, "Whoa."

Diggy hesitates, surprised.

"Get out!" says Greco.

Trevor

TREVOR IS SANDWICHED INTO HIS USUAL SPOT IN HIS ROOM, next to the window, with the blinds open, watching the courtyard and parking lot. On his desk is an oval bottle of brandy, two glasses, and two condoms in black wrappers. The brandy was his father's, a bottle that Trevor remembered seeing above the refrigerator all his life. Three condoms were passed to him on the bus today. He wasted one when he tried it on. He can't imagine wearing it and actually having sex, but he's determined to lose his virginity. "You actually had a hooker in your room?" demanded Jimmy.

"Yeah, but nothing happened."

"Nothing!" shouted Bones.

"She kissed me."

"Oh, God! How did you mess that up?"

"I told her I was seventeen."

"Lame, yo, lame," cried Bones with laughter.

Trevor pours a bit of brandy and tastes it. It burns his throat, then warms his stomach. He drops to the floor, does twenty quick pushups, then poses in the mirror. He's jacked. He sniffs under his arms. He shaved the few whiskers on his chin and showered, but the room is hot and he's already sweaty. He applies more deodorant and slaps his cheeks with blue aftershave in a clear bottle. Also his father's.

He goes back to the window, pours another drop of brandy, and waits. Molly is usually in and out of the motel three or four times on Friday nights. Trevor knows what each trip means. But he's decided to see her anyway. Five twenty-dollar bills are folded in his front pocket. That should be enough. He figures he'll just say, "Hey, do you want to have a drink with me?"

He listens to the whoosh of trucks, the television in the next room; then a car door slams. Molly's on her cell in front of a raised shrub garden London put in. She's wearing heels and a long black coat with the collar flipped like a spy in a movie. Trevor charges to the door, tripping over Whizzer, fumbling with the lock.

"Hey!" he calls, crossing the lot.

She holds up one finger, signaling him to hold on. "Okay, okay, okay," she says into the phone. "Just calm your pits." She closes the phone and smiles. "Some people should be on medication. Do you know what I mean?"

His heart starts like drums in a jungle. "Can you come in?"

She looks down the walk, then follows him inside. "Listen, about that last time, I didn't know you actually lived here, lived here!" she says. "You know?"

"Would you like a drink?" he asks.

"Do you have a beer? I'm dying for a beer. You ever get like that when only a beer will do it?"

"I have brandy."

"Brandy," she laughs. "My grandfather drank brandy."

"I have water."

"If you're drinking brandy, I'll have one," she says.

She pets Whizzer's neck as he sniffs up her legs. "This is the missing dog?"

"He wasn't missing, he was stolen." He hands her an inch of the gold liquid in a milk glass and considers telling her the story.

"I lost a cat once named Kurt. I used to be into Nirvana. You ever hear of them?"

He nods. He can smell her. What is it? Sex?

She sits at his desk chair and sets the brandy inches from the condoms. He should have put them away. He swallows.

"So, you're in high school and you wrestle," she says, remembering. "And your name is . . ."

"Trevor," he says. "And you're Molly."

"That's just a name I use. My real name is Elizabeth. My friends call me Bethy." She opens the buttons on her coat, revealing a tight red dress with black tropical flowers. She crosses her bare legs. Her high heel hangs off her foot. "Did you always, like, live in motels?"

"No."

"You never know where you're going till you get there. That's my motto." She smiles, showing two dimples. "I heard that in an old cartoon. I think that cat Sylvester sang it, or something, but think about it—it's true right?" She smiles. She swings around in the chair. Her sleeve sends the condoms to the floor. Whizzer picks one up and carries it into the bathroom.

"I'll be right back." Trevor pulls the condom from the puppy's mouth in the bathroom. There's a tooth puncture right in the middle.

"Is this what you're learning in school?" She's paging through a book on Indians of the Northeast. A gift from London. A peace offering. It's thick and expensive looking. He pushes the busted condom into his pocket and snatches the other one off the floor.

"No, just something . . ."

She closes the book. "I didn't like high school. Too many cliques. Too many people smiling in your face, if you know what I mean." She spins back, facing him. "I was six weeks from graduation, passing everything except computer science. I didn't have a computer, so I took the stupid class thinking I'm going to learn about them, but everyone was like these techno nerds. But that's, like, in another time zone now."

"One class wouldn't stop you from graduating."

"I got involved with a guy who had a major malfunction

in the brain department. I just finished three years' probation because of him, which was the biggest pain in my ass."

She tucks her hair behind her ears, then picks absently at a pimple, or a boil, on her neck. Trevor sees something in her eyes, some disappointment.

"I have some money," he says.

"You do," she laughs. "Is that what this is about?" She sits next to him on the bed. "I thought you were going to be my new friend, not my new boyfriend." She stares into his eyes.

He clears his throat, wishing he could kiss her right now. Kiss her and hold her and have her hold him. He tries to slide toward her, but the mattress seems to be gripping him.

"You got that tough guy thing going on," she whispers near his ear.

Trevor is unable to breathe. "You're pretty too." He leans in to kiss her. Their lips touch, then she tightens and pulls away.

"I don't know. You're a sweet kid. All the guys I'm with are like major losers." She makes an L with her thumb and forefinger and places it on her forehead. He bends forward, trying to hide his erection that's completely aching hard. "You're not a virgin, are you?"

He can't tell her yes.

"You are, aren't you?"

He nods.

"Tre-vor," she exhales, then groans. "I don't know." She continues picking her neck. It begins to bleed. "You might think I'd be doing you a favor, but your first time, it's supposed to be something." She wags her head, thinking. "I hate the word 'special,' but it's supposed to be special. My first time was with my cousin. He lived with us and was going into the Marines the next day. I was his going-away present."

"He raped you?"

"I didn't call the police or anything." Blood drips down her neck onto her shoulder. "My mother wouldn't let me."

"What about your father?"

"He was never around. He drives a rig, cross-country."

"You're bleeding," he says.

She smears the run of blood with her fingers, then looks at them. "It bleeds all the time. You have a Band-Aid?"

He finds a washcloth and a Band-Aid and turns on the overhead light. She holds her hair to the side. He dabs at the blood. There's a miniature volcano in her neck, about the width of a pencil eraser. He dabs at the hole, but it's not really bleeding anymore.

"I'm going to the doctor," she says. "Real soon."

Her arms are bruised from her wrist to the crook of her elbow. He's seen black-and-blues like these during a slide show in his high school D.A.R.E. class.

He tears opens the Band-Aid and places the bandage

on her neck. He tries to think of something reassuring to say, but nothing comes. He moves from the bed to the desk chair.

Molly, or Elizabeth, stares at the floor where the condom had been. The silence in the room is awful.

"Come 'ere," she says, extending her hand.

He takes it. With her other hand, she unbuttons her dress, revealing a red bra. She opens a front clasp on the bra and her breasts seem to pop. They are round, full, and whiter than the rest of her, with small, tight rose-colored nipples. Completely beautiful. "Touch them. They're real," she says. "Go ahead, I've been told they're my best feature."

He doesn't move. Can't. He's glued to the desk chair. "You don't have to do this," he says.

"You don't have to tell me what I don't have to do." She gives a little snort and shakes her chest at him. She guides his fingertips across her nipple.

He pulls away. "I'm sorry," he says.

"For what? You didn't do anything." She buttons her dress.

"Do I owe you anything?" he asks.

"No, dummy, you're my new friend." She puts on her coat. She gives him a mischievous smile and opens the door. "I have people to see."

Jimmy

JIMMY WAKES TO AN EXPLOSION THAT SHAKES THE HOUSE. HIS mother screams and he springs from bed. Men in black, wearing vests with POLICE in bright yellow letters, yell, "Police, police with a search warrant!" They point their guns at him. "Get down," they yell, "down!" Jimmy is frozen. "Down! Down!"

His mother is sprawled on the floor. A policeman kneels and cuffs her wrists behind her back. Jimmy is grabbed and spun around. A gun barrel presses into the side of his temple. "Nothing funny, wrestler boy," one of them says. Jimmy feels warmth running along his legs. He's pissing himself. He's pushed to his knees, then stomach. Handcuffs click around his wrists. He rolls on his side, squirms, and pulls his wrists apart, trying to free himself. Pain tears up his arms as the cuffs cut into him.

Trish turns her face to his. "Just do what they say." Her eyes are full of tears. A cop kneels next to him. He presses his closed fist against Jimmy's cheek and whispers, "Calm down, or I'll calm you down."

Jimmy huffs and cranes his neck to see the man's face. It's Detective Barnes. "You didn't have to do this," says Jimmy.

"Didn't I give you every chance in the world?" he asks.

Jimmy hates him, because it didn't have to be done this way. There had to be a better way.

A policeman yells, "Clear," then, "Clear back here," from the kitchen.

Detective Barnes and a policeman lift Trish by her elbows and walk her backwards toward the couch. Then Jimmy's placed next to his mother. The wet pajama pants stick to him. His guts are churning. No matter how hard he breathes, he can't get enough air. What cannot happen is happening.

Ricky emerges from his alcove and a policeman scoops him up in his arms and whisks him out the front door. Trish lowers her face and makes tiny sounds like a baby getting ready to cry.

The front door is flat on the floor. Hinges hang from the doorframe. The brass doorknob has rolled into the kitchen. Hard chunks of the wall are splattered on the brown rug. The Springsteen T-shirt is on the floor, the glass cracked in two places. It's over, thinks Jimmy. Wrestling, his chance of going to college, his life the way he knew it, over.

His mother whimpers again.

And it's Pops's fault.

Policemen drag Pops from his bedroom. Blood runs

from his nose across his lips. He's leaning forward, cuffed from behind. He looks weak in his T-shirt and plaid boxer shorts, legs white and hairless.

Jimmy doesn't feel anything for him. Why couldn't he understand that no one owes him?

They plop Pops on the couch, so that Jimmy is between his parents. Pops hangs his head. He brought this on us, thinks Jimmy. *You brought this into the house like a disease.*

"Did they hurt you?" asks Trish.

"They banged my face on the goddamn nightstand," he moans.

"Pops, you got Ma and me in cuffs," says Jimmy, seething. "In cuffs."

"No talking," snaps a policeman.

"You didn't have to break the door down," says Pops, showing his bloody teeth. "You could have knocked. We would have let you in."

Detective Barnes steps over the door and comes close to Jimmy's father. Barnes's windbreaker reads "POL" on one side of the snaps and "ICE" on the other. "You made us do it the hard way. Now there's no going back. Artie, you're under arrest."

"Just him?" asks Trish.

"That's your husband's decision," he says.

"Please God, leave my son alone!" she pleads.

"He had nothing to do with any of it," says Pops.

"No more lies," says Barnes. "Okay? If you're going to

lie, just keep your mouth shut." He raises his brows and smiles sarcastically. "Okay?"

Jimmy bites his bottom lip. He's afraid. Afraid to confirm what Barnes already knows. The O'Sheas are all liars.

Barnes reads from a laminated yellow card. ". . . the right to remain silent. Anything you say can and will be used against you in a court of law. You have the right to speak to an attorney. . . ."

Jimmy watches Barnes's lips move. The words blur together.

"Do you understand?" asks Barnes.

"Yeah," says Pops. "I got it."

"What about you, Jim?"

Jimmy understands. The right to remain silent is all he can do now, all he has done to this point.

Detective Santos comes in. He lifts the framed T-shirt and stands it against the door. A shard of glass falls to the floor.

"Look at this," yells one of the policemen coming out of Jimmy's parents' bedroom. He's carrying a gym bag. Jimmy's never seen it before. "Got to be twenty thousand in here."

Pops's mouth opens as if he's about to say something, but nothing comes out.

Barnes looks into the bag. "That's a lot of money to have around the house. This kind of money people keep in a bank."

"Unless you can't put it in a bank," says Santos.

The amount surprises Jimmy. He knew his father was stealing for a long time, knew this all along, knew it couldn't have been all for the mortgage, but a bag full of money?

A policeman tears the Egyptian rug off Ricky's alcove. He looks back at the other policeman. "This can't be up to code," he smirks. They shake their heads at the mattress on the floor, the overturned crates painted as if they're actually furniture, the stacks of kids' books and mess of clothes everywhere.

Jimmy sees his mother's face stiffen with shame. He's never felt more helpless.

Santos and Barnes hoist Pops off the couch. They lead him into the kitchen and sit him in a chair. "Artie, before you call anyone, we want to make you an offer. You start talking and Jim will sleep in his own bed tonight," says Barnes. "We want names, who's involved, what they did, and when they did it."

Trish raises her head. "Artie, you goddamn better tell them." Then she looks at Detective Barnes. "And you better keep your word."

PART FOUR

Trevor

POLICE CARS, AMBULANCES, AND FIRE ENGINES, EMERGENCY lights revolving, block two lanes of the turnpike. Cars are forced into a single lane. Camille squeezes the pickup truck over. The smell of fuel wafts into the window. An eighteen-wheeler, on its side like a giant bleeding motorized centipede, leaks black oil onto the road. A white car is crushed under the truck's rear tire. Glass and silver parts are spread across the road as if a bomb went off. A kid's baseball mitt lies in a puddle of oil. Trevor feels a wave of nausea move through him.

Camille presses her hand against her mouth and makes a gasping sound, so high and quick, Trevor's heart stops beating. Her entire body begins to shake.

Whizzer awakes and stands on the front seat. Trevor pulls him to his lap. His father's accident must have been the same way; police cars and ambulances at odd angles, shattered glass in the road, the turnpike clogged with impatient drivers gawking at the wreckage.

They crawl past an open suitcase. Clothes are scattered

in the road: a child's shirt, a tiny white shoe, a ski hat.

Camille swerves off the turnpike and rides the shoulder into a rest area, winding around the crowded lot to a stand of trees along a stretch of open concrete. She turns the car off, leans back, and shuts her eyes. Trevor puts his hand on her shoulder.

"I've tried not to think about what it must have been like," she says.

It scares him to think that his dad was alive when they brought him to the hospital. Blood loss was the official finding on the death certificate. How much pain was he in?

They leave the car under the late March sun. Whizzer pulls and bites his leather leash. The only sound is the turnpike whooshing like surf on a beach. Trevor stretches his arms. He's tight from the long drive back from Maine. The three-day trip left him exhausted—between the drive, the lumpy hotel room bed, his mother's snoring, and the student ambassador who led them around the campus, half the time arguing with her boyfriend on her cell phone, his mind is shot.

He sits next to his mother on a stockade fence.

Whizzer sniffs the ground, then tugs toward a white birch.

"I'm glad we're putting a plan together for September," she says.

Yes, there is a plan. Trevor sent three applications. He

marked the spot "Native American" under "Origin" on them, then completed a short lineage of his Indian roots. "Father: Joseph Crow—Penobscot Indian; Grandfather: Zachariah Crow; Grandmother: Spring Sky Crow—Penobscot Indians." If Trevor gets in, and his guidance counselor guarantees it, his tuition will be waived. Native Americans attend for free. "You didn't know that?" asked the counselor.

They visited the University of Maine. Beautiful, lots of open space, trees, and sky. He met the assistant wrestling coach, who only asked him about his varsity record. After hearing 12 wins and 9 losses, he shrugged and said, "Try out, who knows."

In Maine, Trevor expected to feel something like magic, something that told him he had finally found his home, but all he felt was far from New Jersey. Today, on the ride back, they stopped at a New Jersey state college for the open house. He was surprised that the college was tucked in the mountains, yet still in Jersey. The college didn't have a wrestling team, and Trevor realized he didn't care. He made a stand at 152 and has a winning record. Trevor's sure his father would be proud of him. He may not get past the second round of the Districts, but he's satisfied. He feels like a wrestler, a teammate that can be counted on to give his best. He feels it in every muscle. Greco calls him a brawler because Trevor doesn't mind mixing it up, taking punishment. He's grown used to ordinary pain. He's not afraid on the mat. He looks forward to hearing his name pounded on the bleachers, "Tre-vor, Tre-vor." A group of girls he hardly knows made a mural of a crow wearing a wresting singlet. It's all good.

"We'll have to get you a college wardrobe," says Camille. "You can't walk around wearing wrestling shirts for the rest of your life. If you'd come to the mall with me, we could hit a sale."

Trevor exhales a long breath. He hates shopping with his mother. A truck rumbles across the lot and the fence picks up the vibrations.

"I want you to have everything you need." She smiles and laugh lines wrinkle from her eyes.

"Just take good care of Whizzer." Trevor pets the puppy's back.

"I know I made a mess of things," she says. "That motel is no place for you. At college you can have a fresh start."

"What about you? What are you going to do? You can't stay at that motel with London."

"I want to show you something," she says. "I was waiting for the right time, and I thought you would notice." She holds out her hand. A small diamond ring sparkles on her finger. "Harry gave it to me. He's calling it a pre-engagement ring."

The tiny diamond. It's nothing compared to her real engagement ring.

"It's only a quarter karat, but the clarity is—"

"What did you do with the ring Dad gave you?"

"I have it."

"Are you saying you're going to marry London?"

"I told him I'd think about it."

"You like him that much?"

"I think so. He's got a good heart." She gazes at the ring.

He wants to tell her to be careful. She's moving too fast. She just lost her husband, his father. London could be taking advantage of her, but he's not certain of anything anymore. He will leave her in September. Maybe she shouldn't be alone.

She smiles watching his face. "Say something."

"I guess congratulations."

She kisses his cheek. "Thank you. I'm going to get a coffee. Do you want anything?"

"Get me one too." He smiles. "Please."

She crosses the lot to the pavilion. Her stride is confident. Her dark hair bounces on her shoulders. He watches her until she joins a stream of people entering the building.

He walks Whizzer into the trees, stepping farther from the parking area, until there is a clearing and miles of dark, still water. The feeling of being submerged in the pool comes to him, water pressing above and below him, the numbing cold leaving his body and that sensation of letting go, accepting. Trevor remembers Molly's motto about not knowing where you're going until you get there. It's mostly true, but he hopes that where he's going is where he's supposed to be.

Jimmy

THE SUPERMARKET LOADING AREA IS CRAMMED WITH MINIVANS and mothers. Jimmy leans on the brick wall that encloses the shopping carts. It's chilly, but he takes off his green and white clerk's jacket. His nametag reads "Welcome to Foodtown. Hi, I'm James." He sees his mother through the window, still talking to the butcher. She's holding a ham so large, she has her arms wrapped around it.

Tonight is the wrestling dinner. Tomorrow is Easter. His mother will hide some plastic eggs filled with quarters and dollar bills around the house for Ricky. She'll fill their Easter baskets with chocolate bunnies, jellybeans, and marshmallow Peeps. It's the first holiday since his father went to jail. Eighteen days marked off on the calendar.

At home, nothing is right. It always seems as if the front door will open and his father will come through, flinging his cap into the pantry. But it doesn't open. Jimmy hasn't visited his father. Why should he visit? It's easier not hearing Pops trying to explain that he did what any father would have done—*Jimmy, I did it for you, your mother, and*

Ricky. I did it for you. No, Jimmy's not ready for this. His mother was on the phone last night with Pops. She waved the cell at Jimmy, saying, "Here come on. Take it. It's your father, you've got to talk to him." Jimmy left the house.

Trish emerges from the supermarket lugging the ham in a plastic bag. She recently dyed her hair, a color called "brazenly blonde." He takes the bag and heaves it over his shoulder.

"You forgot your first paycheck!" She removes the check from her pocketbook and waves it. Getting the job was his idea. The napkin holder on the kitchen table was stuffed with unpaid bills. Half the calls at the house were from collection agencies.

"Thanks, Ma." He glances at the amount, then hands it back to her. "Pay the cable bill."

"Half is going toward your college expense fund," she says.

Jimmy's scholarship letter is fastened to the refrigerator next to the visiting hours at the jail. *"In recognition of your outstanding performance in wrestling, a sport that is vital to our overall athletic program, we have awarded you the East Stroudsburg College Athletic Scholarship."*

He toured the East Stroudsburg campus with the other incoming wrestler on scholarship, ate turkey sandwiches in the rathskeller, visited the swimming pool, saw the huge wrestling room, sat in the massive library filling out forms, and the entire time, Jimmy felt like he had a hard candy stuck in his throat. Leaving Ricky, leaving his mother, without Pops at home, is going to be tough. But there isn't a backup plan. Getting out of Molly Pitcher is the only thing that keeps him moving forward.

He dumps the ham in the back of their minivan and gets in the driver's seat. "Do me a favor," he says, buckling his seat belt. "Stay away from the butcher. All he wants to do is get in your pants."

She punches him in the arm. Her fist feels like a kid's.

"He's a creep," he says.

"What do you mean? There's hardly an ounce of fat on that ham, and he took the bone out and charged me for bone-in."

"Ma, that's the same stuff Pops did."

"It's a little discount. It beats lutefisk, right?"

Jimmy's not laughing. "You and Pops are like this joke my English teacher told us. A guy gets arrested and tells the police he's not a thief, he's into steel and iron. He steals and his wife irons."

"That's not nice."

"Except you stopped ironing."

"It's a five-dollar discount, for heaven's sake," she says. "And I would appreciate it if you didn't announce this to your brother. I don't need him on my back too."

"What if you get caught? You could get arrested."

"They would never arrest me for a discounted ham."

"What if you lose your job? That would be bad enough, wouldn't it?" He wants to grab her by the shoulders and shake her. Doesn't she know that something has been taken from him, not just his father, but part of him? Today, in the supermarket men's room mirror, two Jimmy O'Sheas stared at him—one wrestling Jimmy, who must win, will win, and will leave Molly Pitcher, and this other boy who once suspected his father might be a crook and now knows the truth. "It's not just Pops, it's everything," he says.

"Repeat after me: This is tem-po-rary. Temporary."

"It's not only this job." He pulls the minivan from the lot.

"When your father is released we'll see . . ."

"When is the big question, isn't it?" His father has twenty-five months left, and is trying for a sentence reduction with a new lawyer. Each court action costs two weeks of his mother's salary. She's taken a second mortgage. His mother thinks Pops is going to emerge from jail with a brand-new set of rules to live by, but can time wipe away who you are or what you've done?

She takes his hand. "Doesn't everyone deserve a second chance? You got one."

Maybe she's right. His father could learn from his mistakes, but it's too soon to think about it.

"Tonight's the wrestling dinner," she says. "We should put our problems on hold and have a good time."

"And how do I do that?"

"Things could be worse. I heard Diggy—"

"Is that the way I look to you?" he asks. "In the same league as Diggy?"

"No," she says. "I didn't mean it that way."

"For the record"—his voice explodes in the car—"I didn't steal anyone's dog. Except for the single time when Pops convinced me to help him, I never stole anything in my life. Diggy quit. I would never quit. So don't include me with Diggy." He makes a sharp right onto Molly Pitcher Road. He's doing sixty in a forty-mile-an-hour zone.

"Okay, I'm sorry," she says in a small voice.

Jimmy

THE SPARTA CATERING HALL IS BEHIND A NEW SHOPPING CEN-
ter. The neon sign, with half its letters dark, twinkles next
to a highway overpass. From the backseat, Ricky sounds
out the sign: "Co—tail Lounge, -appy -our every Hour."
He leans into the front. "What's that mean?"

"It means you shouldn't act like a comedian tonight,"
snaps Jimmy.

"Oh, your brother's cute." Trish examines her face in
a folding makeup mirror. She touches her fingertip to her
tongue and rubs it over her eyebrows. "Let's try to be civil
to each other."

"Remember last year?" Ricky laughs. "Pops took us for
haircuts in the afternoon and he got his sideburns cut off
and there were white patches on his face."

"And he wouldn't let me put a little makeup on him,"
says Trish.

"I bet he doesn't get his hair cut the whole time he's in
there," says Ricky.

Trish snaps the makeup case closed. "Your father will be

home before you know it." She turns to Jimmy and lifts her eyebrows, daring him to disagree.

Home before you know it is her mantra. Jimmy will be a sophomore in college when his father's up for parole. That's not "before you know it."

They pull next to Greco's Jeep. Jimmy jams the car into park and shuts off the engine. "Let's take a break from talking about Pops."

"We weren't talking about him," says Trish, like she's explaining to a two-year-old. "I was saying . . ."

Jimmy gets out, considers waiting for them, then strides across the parking lot toward the hall, knowing it's going to piss her off. He wants to save a table near the dais. For three years, he's attended the dinners and listened to the coach make speeches and the seniors announce their college plans. Now it's his turn.

"Hey, wait up!"

Ricky chases after him. Jimmy's hand-me-down soccer shirt flaps above Ricky's knees. "Jimmy, wait for Ma."

"Can't we walk in like a family?" yells Trish, crossing the parking lot in high heels, a black skirt, and a puffy vinyl jacket.

Jimmy stops and Ricky catches up to him.

"I want to take pictures for your father," she says.

"Here?" asks Ricky.

"Yes, in front of the fountain. We took pictures there last year."

Trish asks a waitress on her way into the hall to take their picture. Jimmy buttons his sport jacket in front of a six-foot-tall concrete Poseidon with one arm raised at the dark sky. The jacket is an Italian wool blend. A closeout, but a name brand, and he feels good in it.

"Closer," says the waitress holding the camera.

Jimmy puts his arm around his mother and brother.

"Say cheese," calls the waitress.

"Butt cheese," says Ricky.

Everyone smiles. The waitress snaps the photo.

The Olympian Room is classy: gold drapes, red carpeting, white tablecloths with red napkins, and fresh-cut flowers. A warm feeling floods Jimmy's fingers and face. He crosses the dance floor to the gleaming gold trophies and row of silver and bronze medals. Ricky dashes off toward the pitchers of soda on the bar. Jimmy won last year's "Most Valuable Wrestler" trophy, and he doesn't care if he wins it again. He's already earned a scholarship and is the only wrestler in his district who qualified for the State Tournament in Atlantic City. The other two trophies are for "Best Sportsman" and "Most Improved Wrestler." Jimmy's sure Trevor will receive "Most Improved." The medals are for "Most Exciting Match" and "Most Promising Wrestler." Thick red-and-white varsity letters are placed in front of the trophies.

Greco folds white cards for the nameplates on the dais.

"Here he is," he says, "first one to arrive."

Jimmy smiles broadly.

"You look snazzy." Greco squeezes Jimmy's shoulder.

"Is that a compliment?"

"It used to be." He swats him with a nameplate.

"So this is the big night," says Trish.

"The end of a wrestling dynasty." Greco winks at Jimmy. "All Jimmy has to do now is take a little ride down the Garden State to Atlantic City and win."

"That's all," says Jimmy, playing along.

Little Gino comes across the hall in a tight blue suit that looks like he wore it to his First Communion. He tugs Jimmy's arm. "I've got to tell you something."

Jimmy rolls his eyes at Greco and heads away.

"I heard Diggy's in the parking lot." Gino's eyes are wide with fear.

Diggy

FROM INSIDE HIS MUSTANG, DIGGY WATCHES THE WRESTLERS enter the hall with their parents. Trevor passes in a stiff new suit. "Chief Big Shit," says Diggy.

Jane dials in her lipstick and snaps on the top. "Leave him alone, he's harmless."

"More like my kryptonite," says Diggy.

"I'll call you when it's over," she says. "You sure you'll be all right?"

Diggy isn't sure. He's sweating and his hands are moist on the steering wheel. It's not missing the dinner that bothers him. It's everything else. Greco passes him in the hall like he doesn't exist. Gino and Bones don't return his texts. Trevor Crow has a fan club. And Diggy didn't get into Springfield. Randy said Diggy had no one to blame but himself. His class rank is in the lower bottom third. "Let me put it this way," said Randy, "if the school was a skyscraper, you'd be just above the trees." The guidance counselor told him not to worry and recommended a refrigeration trade school or community college. His mother enrolled him in a college entrance refresher course, hoping he could raise his SAT scores, but Diggy didn't have the energy to even copy from the blackboard. Ninth-grade algebra and tenth-grade geometry theorems, stuff he once knew—gone.

"I don't have to go." Jane studies his face.

Diggy's sure if he tells her not to go, she'll stay with him. "You're the team's manager," he says. "You earned it. The guys always chip in for flowers, and you know Greco got you a plaque."

"I know." She sighs.

"Just see if you can bring the guys out for a toast, or something." He pats a brown paper bag on the floor in the backseat of the car. "I've been to plenty of those dinners. Do you think I need another plate of limp broccoli and rubber chicken?"

"What if they won't come?" asks Jane.

"I didn't do anything to Jimmy or Bones. But if they don't want to"—he shrugs—"I'll have a party by myself."

"So you're going to wait here the whole time?"

"Don't worry about me. Randy gave me the night off. I'll have a couple of beers and you can drive me home." Saying this makes him feel like he's not Diggy Masters anymore, but some poser. Why should Randy have any control over his life? Randy, who barely talks to him, Randy, who told him "you're dead to me" after he quit the team, has him interning at the dealership. Stretched across the leather sofa, Diggy listened to Randy's speech about responsibility and earning a living in "the real world." Diggy ignored him and continued channel surfing. Randy grabbed the remote from his hand, smashed it on the fireplace bricks, and yelled, "You're not lying on the goddamn couch every afternoon!"

Diggy goes to the dealership after school on Mondays, Tuesdays, and Thursdays and stays till closing time. He wears a tie and a bright blue blazer with the Range Rover insignia on his breast pocket. His mother, trying to keep the peace, says he's got to give it a month. "You have to get used to it," she says. Diggy hasn't told Nick. And yes, it's boring as hell. The other salesmen won't let him near a customer. Diggy wanders around the shiny square cars thinking about Jane and what she might be doing. He misses the pin-or-be-pinned pressure of the wrestling season, the feeling of urgency. After a fast-food dinner in the break room, he sneaks to the back of the lot, gets in a car, and plays video games on his iPhone or talks to Jane. Randy's too busy to care. He keeps saying, "Shadow someone, keep your eyes open and your mouth zipped."

Diggy takes Jane's hand. She's wearing a silver friendship ring with a heart-shaped blue topaz on her right index finger. Diggy put the ring box in four larger boxes and wrapped each with different paper. She had no idea what was inside and kept ripping the paper on each box.

"I did tell you I love it, right?" she says maybe for the hundredth time that week.

He wants to kiss her but watches Pancakes cross in front of the Mustang. He's wearing a plaid jacket and baggy jeans. He doesn't notice Diggy and Jane in the car's dark interior.

"I think I saw him in 'Night of the Walking Couch,'" says Jane.

Diggy thinks about making a scene, just showing up at the dinner as Jane's guest. He could stroll in with her hooked on his arm, like a full-fledged couple. But no one would talk to him and he'd ruin Jane's night. Greco would ask him to leave because he didn't buy a guest ticket. Greco wouldn't make an exception.

Bones passes by with his mother trailing. He's wearing a baggy white buttondown shirt with the tails out and a tie with jeans and white unlaced Nikes. Diggy is tempted to yell, "Where's your bass?" But he's afraid Bones would look at him like he's some loser sitting in the parking lot with nothing better to do.

"You should get going," he says to Jane.

"Well, if you're sure you're going to be all right. . . ." She climbs from the car slowly, with her eyes on him. "I'll text you."

She steps in front of the car and poses like a dancer with one hand raised, her knee lifted, and her head tilted to her shoulder. She's pushing a pop star-at-the-MTV-Video-Music-Awards look in fur-topped boots, miniskirt, and blouse with a leopard collar and cuffs. She's going to blow them away.

Jimmy

Jane taps on Diggy's window. "Look who I found," she singsongs.

The door locks snap up. Jane folds the front seat forward and climbs into the back of the Mustang. Jimmy takes shotgun. Diggy smiles in the interior light. Between his legs is an open bottle of beer. "I was starting to think you guys were dissing me," he says.

Jimmy could say *I wanted to*, but says, "I can't stay long. The guys were lining up for eats."

Jane leans between the seats. "Bones was grabbing chicken like a crazed zombie." She laughs.

"Every year the food blows," says Diggy. "Catering by White Castle would be better."

"Come off it," says Jimmy. "It's not that bad."

"That's because no one on the Minute Men knows better."

Jimmy doesn't care what Diggy thinks. If he were on the team, he'd be at the buffet fighting over the last banana pudding.

Diggy tugs a bag from the backseat and slings it on Jimmy's lap. "There's beer in there with your names on them."

Jimmy removes a beer and twists off the cap. He hands the bottle to Jane. He cracks another for himself. He doesn't want to drink but doesn't want to be a buzzkill. He's only in the car because Jane asked him five times. "Some of the guys are saying you're going to crash the dinner," he says.

"Some of the guys talk more crap than the radio." Diggy's eyes flash, then his face softens. "I guess Crow's going to win Most Improved."

"He's this year's supernova," says Jane sarcastically.

"From scrub to golden boy." Diggy laughs. "You want to know what's really whacked? I was four pounds away, four pounds from one-fifty-two. Do you know what I weigh now?"

Jimmy's seen his fat face in the halls.

"One-eighty. Can you believe that?"

Jimmy has to laugh. "Dude, come on, twenty L-Bs in two months!"

"He's my cuddly bear," says Jane in a baby voice.

Diggy looks at her as if seeing her for the first time.

"Okay, sorry." She puts her hands up.

"All I know is, I could have wrestled one-fifty-two if I really wanted it," says Diggy. "Don't forget, I'm the one who quit. Greco wanted me to stay on the team. If anyone—"

"It's spent, okay? Over," says Jimmy, cutting him off.

"No one gives a rat's ass anymore."

"Yeah, well, maybe they should. All I did was pull a prank that went bad. It was nothing more than that."

Jimmy knows Diggy doesn't really believe this. How many pranks put your teammate in the hospital and get his dog run over?

"We should have a toast." Diggy inhales deeply and raises his bottle. "To the first Masters NOT getting his senior-year letter and NOT making the Wall. Let's drink to that."

Jane reaches for him. "I'm not drinking to that."

He pushes her hand away. "Why not, it's true." The hurt in Diggy's voice is naked, completely unconcealed. He still cares. Every wrestler cares. You have to earn the Wall and Diggy didn't come close. In one week, Jimmy will have his chance to make the Wall as a State Champion.

"Jimmy, I hope Greco's letting you give Jane her flowers. You're the captain."

"Chill out," says Jimmy. "You're sabotaging the surprise." He's sure Diggy would give anything to be in his place, presenting the bouquet to his girlfriend.

"It'll be the first time anyone ever gives me flowers," says Jane.

"Diggy, are you going to Springfield with Nick?" asks Jimmy.

"I was, but I'm putting in some hours at my old man's dealership." Diggy sighs. "I mean, I'm not brain dead.

325

Randy has a good thing going. What am I supposed to do, act like he doesn't own the largest dealership in the county?" Diggy finishes his beer and drops the bottle in the bag. "I heard about your scholarship. If I stayed on the team, I could be looking at a full ride too."

Jimmy smirks. Even Jane remains quiet. Man, Diggy is so full of crap.

"I'm going on cruise control for a while," he continues. "I just have to get the monkeys off my back. That's what Greco would say. You come to practice with a dozen monkeys on your back and you leave with none."

"That's a good practice," they say together.

Diggy turns to Jimmy. His eyes are intense. "Remember when you told me about you being in trouble with your old man? I never snitched to anyone. You blew that match against the Colts, and I still never ratted."

"Diggy didn't even tell me until the article was in the paper," says Jane.

Jimmy knows Diggy's waiting for him to say thank you. But should he have expected anything else?

"I'm just saying, keeping that on the down low, it should mean something."

"I only told you because I trusted you," says Jimmy with exasperation.

"How is your old man holding up?" asks Diggy.

Jimmy can't admit he hasn't visited him yet. It sounds heartless. After a pause, he says, "My father knows how to take care of himself."

"I always liked your father," says Jane. "He was the only one who bought me a soda at the matches."

Jimmy didn't know this. "Really?"

"Yeah. He was kinda cool, with the blond hair thing going on," she says. "I know one thing, he was always giving you props and—"

"I don't want to talk about my father." His words were supposed to come off as light and casual, but Diggy's eyes drift to Jane's, then back to him. "I mean, I do miss him and everything." Jimmy searches for words. "It's just that he . . ." *What? Almost put me in jail? Got our door knocked off the hinges? All of the above?*

"Forget it," says Jane. "It's like all fathers have the same disease, terminal assholeness."

Diggy puts his hand on Jimmy's shoulder. "We should hang out again, like the old days. Remember we used to do that Slip 'N Slide on the side of your house? If you went off the end, your butt got smeared with mud."

Jimmy wants to laugh. "That was like in the seventh grade."

"Yeah, but we still did it."

"I'm not saying we didn't." Jimmy looks toward the stucco hall, with its corny fountain. He wants to be free of the car and back inside.

"We could hit the raceway on monster trunk night," suggests Diggy.

"My brother knows someone at the gate," says Jane with enthusiasm. "He could sneak us in for free."

Jimmy's sure they are never going anywhere together and doesn't feel like pretending. He wants to be with the wrestlers returning from the buffet, his plate stacked with veggies, salad, and chicken.

"Here's another toast," says Diggy.

"I really have to get back inside," says Jimmy.

"How about to our graduation?" says Jane, raising her bottle.

"Sure. To graduation." They clink, then Jimmy hands back the beer. He opens the door and puts one foot on the asphalt. "Jane, you coming?"

"Nah, go ahead. I'll be in later."

Jimmy holds the door as Jane moves into the front seat. He gets this strange feeling that he's never going to see them again, like the two of them are already like that Slip 'N Slide on the side of his house. A cool but faded memory. "Stay chill," he says. "I'm outta here."

He jogs across the parking lot into the lobby, then sprints the carpeted hallway into the banquet room. Guys are already seated and digging in. He snatches a plate and gets behind Greco, who's last on the buffet line.

"You're not on line for seconds already?" asks Greco.

Jimmy releases a long, slow, calming breath. "You think they have any of those five-pound oranges left?"

Greco smiles and squeezes his arm.